2/2

The Wa

Also available from Five Leaves

King Dido

Rosie Hogarth

With Hope, Farewell

So We Live: the novels of Alexander Baron
edited by Susie Thomas, Andrew Whitehead and Ken Worpole

The War Baby

Alexander Baron

Five Leaves Publications

The War Baby
Alexander Baron

Published in 2019 by Five Leaves Publications
14a Long Row, Nottingham NG1 2DH
www.fiveleaves.co.uk
www.fiveleavesbookshop.co.uk

ISBN: 978-1-910170-64-9

Printed in Great Britain

Chapter 1

Barcelona, Spain. July 20, 1938

Deep chords sounded. Over their dying resonance the strings came in, quiet and pure, behind a soft swelling of voices. The greybeards gathered in the circle of light, stage left. The group flowed with the moving spotlight towards the temple portico. The old men sang their faith in the One God.

To Henry Croft, in the third row of the stalls, the music did no more than flow around the outer edge of his thoughts. The girl at his side let her head touch his shoulder for a moment, and she rested a sweaty paw on his right hand. At eleven o'clock at night the auditorium still held the oven heat of the day. Sweat glistened on upturned faces. Everyone was still and rapt. All the men in the rows around Croft were in uniform. His light grey civilian suit shone in the darkness as if it were phosphorescent. He was an American, a newspaper man, here in Spain to cover the Civil War.

Strong and masculine the sound rose from the orchestra pit and to answer it came a tenor voice from the wings. A spotlight sprang upon Samson. A chorus greeted him, powerful with faith and resolution.

Henry was a slender man, at forty-three still youthful in appearance, giving an impression of contained strength, but now he was sunk back in his seat upon spread haunches, his face gaunt with tiredness. He had been up since four in the morning, on a long, hard assignment; six hours roasting in a staff car, the rest of the day spent trudging with the soldiers over rocky hill paths, sweat pouring off him, his head aching from the white glare of the sun, his throat parched with the fine, white dust. Arrived back in Barcelona, there had been time for a quick, cold bath, a hasty change of clothes, a hurried walk to the Press Bureau to telephone his story to Paris, and a snatched meal before the theatre. He took his rest at last, lulled by the music, the ache and burn of his feet now a perverse pleasure.

The Philistine priestesses came out of the temple. They sang of springtime and love. There were eight priestesses, not too well rehearsed. They glanced uncertainly at one another. Emmy sniggered softly at Henry's side. Henry's eyes saw the shifting tableaux on the stage, but the pictures in his brain were of soaring mountain peaks above an upland valley, the files of soldiers moving in brown threads upon the mountainsides.

*

The second year of the war was coming to a close. The Spanish Republic had lost two-thirds of its territory to the insurgent Nationalists under General Franco. This spring the enemy had cut in two the last stronghold of the Republicans along the east coast, reaching the sea and separating Catalonia from what was now a Republican enclave in the south. The supplies and the strength of the Republic were running out. Its leaders were preparing for a last great gamble, an offensive that must break through to the southern territory, the hinterland of Valencia.

A river cut off Catalonia from the south. It was wide and deep, flowing fast through a trench in the mountains. Its steep far bank was held in strength by the enemy. A forbidding barrier: the Ebro. That was where Henry had been today, up in the mountains, looking down on the river, looking across; before he drove back twelve miles to where his own countrymen were encamped, American volunteers, the Abraham Lincoln Battalion, joined in the 15th International Brigade by British, Canadian and Spanish battalions.

Three months ago Henry had seen this brigade all but wiped out in battle, as it had been three times before, in the worst of a chain of bloody actions. Today, Henry had listened to the soldiers singing. Men never learn, he reflected. He had been (twenty-one years old) in the British Army through the climactic massacres of the year 1917, Arras and Passchendaele, he recalled how his own battalion, wasted away to ninety survivors out of a thousand men after Arras, had been built up again and marched up to Ypres in the autumn, jauntily whistling. He heard their tune inside his skull now, shrilling through Saint-Saens' majestic chords.

> Wash me in the water where you washed your dirty
> daughter,
> For I will be whiter than the whitewash on the wall.

He heard a soprano voice, strong and pure enough to prevail over his imaginings. In the cube of yellow light that confronted the auditorium stood Delilah. Now, there was a girl who knew what she wanted.

> *Je viens célébrer la victoire*
> *De celui qui règne en mon coeur.*
> *Dalila veut pour son vainqueur*
> *Encore plus d'amour que de gloire.*

Emmy whispered to Henry, "It's like a musical fuck," and giggled. A man behind hushed her. Her whisper, suppressing glee, continued, even more audibly. "This is the slow part." She beamed at disapproving hisses.

> O mon bien-aimé, suis mes pas
> Vers Soreck, la douce vallée.
> Dans cette demeure isolée
> Où Dalila t'ouvre ses bras.

From Emmy. "See? She's getting passionate."

Henry uttered a brief, "Sh—."

She overrode him with a sharper, "Sh—." And it was a blink of time before he understood, seeing her staring up towards the auditorium roof, intent; till he heard, with her, the familiar sound, the deep, deadly throb. The new sound ran like a crescendo of basses behind the three voices that contested and alternated on the stage. Now there was a hushing and murmuring throughout the crowded theatre. All the faces were looking up. The throb became a disharmony of engine noises, the Ride of the Heinkels, an orchestra of unsynchronised engines on different notes.

All the lights in the theatre went out. In the dark, the singing ended raggedly, amid the squeals of the last, slow-witted violins. A deep reverberation came rumbling through the earth; then more, one going into another. One, then another, factory sirens sounded, breaking out from point to point on the outskirts of the city until they made a ring of ululations.

The angry, manifold droning was loud now, a roof of sound above the roof of the theatre. People bobbed up and down in the dark auditorium, a crescendo of voices in different registers, but nobody made to leave. Now from the hilly inland suburbs came sharper detonations, the anti-aircraft guns. A spot of light danced on the stage. A torch lit the manager's face and tuxedo. His mouth moved. He tried again. The hubbub fell away. "Señores y Señoras—." The gunfire was an incessant far background, upon which a bomb salvo sounded deep hammer blows, upon which women's voices rose in the auditorium like gulls' cries, against the deep exclamations of men; upon which the manager's voice appealed unintelligibly. An immense hand smote the theatre. The floor and walls seemed to lurch sideways. The air tasted of dust and glass shattered somewhere amid a noise from the street close by as of a cliff falling. Women screamed.

But now, as the manager gaped wordless in the wan light of his torch, Delilah came to the front of the stage. She lifted up her small white face.

She began to sing. Her clear soprano voice came to Henry amid the raving of guns and 'planes and bombs. The darkness was full of faces gaping at her. She was singing *La Marseillaise*.

The French opera company had been performing at the Liceo for the past ten days. Everyone on the stage came forward to join hands and take up the song. Men and women in the audience rose to their feet. The song spread among them. Instruments picked it up until the orchestra was playing it. Stage hands, electricians and performers crowded on to the stage, singing. The whole theatre was full of the song. The building shook again. The air was pale with dust. The hymn rose savagely to answer the noises of destruction.

> *Contre nous de la tyrannie*
> *L'étendard sanglant est levé ...*

Ah, yes, Henry Croft had had enough of war. He had sat on a pile of mud-bathed corpses to eat his McConachie's stew. He had been present since then at all manner of horrors and disasters, twenty years of them and no sign of an end to them. He had seen history writing itself and he had written it down; not a tale calculated to encourage hope for the species. But it seemed that there was still hope in him to be awakened. Why else, holding Emmy's hot hand, did he sing now, with all his strength —?

> *Marchons, marchons, qu'un sang impur*
> *Abreuve nos sillons.*

*

Insistent hooters sounded the All Clear. The sky was empty of sound again, the streets suddenly full of it. The audience came streaming out of the Liceo, each person briefly outlined against the dim interior light before becoming a black shape among a throng of black shapes that flowed along the Ramblas. All the people who had sat unnaturally still at café tables on the centre promenade or stood in doorways were moving again and talking. There were explosions of laughter among the clamour of voices, the clack of wooden sandals, the tinkle of cups and glasses at the tables, life astir, the film running again.

Emmy hung on Croft's left arm, cuddling it. He was tall, thin. The shape of his thin face seemed sculpted by care. Emmy said, "It was wonderful, it was *wonderful*! Oh, that song!"

Henry did not speak. Emmy said, "They will never be defeated."

Henry said, "They can't win."

8

"Henry —!" But she checked herself. She knew by the feel of his body that he did not want to talk any more. They strolled on, down the Ramblas towards the sea. The café tables on the centre strip were full again. Cigarettes were innumerable dancing red dots against the darkness, which was infused with the faint leakages of light from around closed shutters, blinks of ghostly pallor from briefly-opened doors and the yellow slits of illumination in the blue headlamp masks of cars; the cars few, all official, crawling a few yards at a time only when the crowds let them. A green ambulance, its siren imploring, nosed steadily through the human surge and fire-engine bells clamoured from other parts of the city. The pink glare of buildings ablaze still waxed and waned in the sky.

They had walked a hundred yards down the street when, from the centre strip, someone called, "Henry! Hi!"

Across the other side of the street from them was a building with long red banners hanging down its front. Set between them were huge portraits: of the Prime Minister, Negrin, Lenin and of a benign Stalin. A department store building had been turned into the headquarters of the JSU, the United Socialist Youth Movement, a great power in the Republic. The display windows of the store had been bricked up. The central entrance was flanked by sandbag blast walls. A military sentry stood in the doorway. The young man who had called to Henry was standing up at a café table on the centre strip in front of the building. He was in uniform. At the table sat a girl and another man in uniform.

Emmy said, "It's Brendan." He had a room in their hotel, the Majestic. "Who is the girl?"

"I don't know," Henry said as they crossed the road. "Some camp follower."

Emmy sniggered. "Like me. Thank you."

Henry did not answer her. He said, "Hallo, Frank," to the young man.

Brendan said, "Hi! Hi, Emmy! This is Colleen Brooks, this is Juan Narvaez."

The other soldier had already risen to see Emmy into a chair. He was a major. He had a plump, innocent face and horn-rimmed spectacles. His uniform was bleached and old, a front-line uniform. The left sleeve of his tunic was folded up at the elbow. He said to Henry, in Spanish, "We know each other, eh?"

"Pinell. Last April." Henry said to the others. "It was in the retreat. We shared a crater."

"For three hours," Narvaez said, "till the shelling stopped."

Croft said, "We cleared out pretty fast."

"You were lucky," Narvaez said. "I was still running when they started to shell again." He touched the stump of his left arm. "I left the rest of this right there on that road."

"Too bad," Henry said. "Are you OK now?"

"Why not?" Narvaez gestured toward the JSU building. "I have been doing political work for the central committee. I am going back to the army this week."

Brendan said, "For the offensive."

Emmy said to Brendan, "Are you going?"

Colleen said, "Not him."

Brendan answered with the quickness of a wince, "They won't let me. I've tried often enough."

He wore a smart uniform with a Sam Browne belt. His cap on the table had a lieutenant's bar above the peak. He had come out, Henry had gathered, to do some sort of liaison work with the JSU. He appeared to have been a journalist of sorts. He had spoken of having worked on a communist weekly in London, and Henry sometimes saw him filing a story at the Press Bureau. What he was doing in uniform Henry did not know, nor much care. A lot of people had contrived to clothe themselves in smart uniforms hereabouts. Frank turned to Henry, with the painfully apparent brightness of one wanting to change the subject, and Henry noticed for the first time how young and vulnerable he looked. He said, "I hear you went down to the front today. Did you have a good day?"

"It was a hard day," Henry said. "I hiked out with the Americans. They were training."

"I bet," Brendan said. "Raring to go."

"Well," Henry said, "I've never seen soldiers quite like that but they're ready enough. They've had a lot of reinforcements."

"So have our boys," Brendan said. "The Party's sent out some big drafts. There's always plenty willing."

"I guess they were treating it all as a joke," Henry said. He uttered a little laugh. "Well, you can't take these manoeuvres seriously. It was the same in my war. They had these fellows yesterday —. Your battalion, too —," he said to Frank, "and the Canucks — all told out into squads. They had to run downhill to a dry river bed, then they all lined up as if they were hauling on ropes, and pulled imaginary boats into an imaginary river. Then they all sat on the ground like rowing crews and pulled away at imaginary oars. Then they deployed on the other side and attacked up a hill. I always used to think in France, if these manoeuvres were of no other use they were good for a laugh, before the real thing."

Brendan clapped his hands smartly, three times, for a waiter but none came. He stood up. "I'll get some drinks."

"Not for me," Henry said. "I guess I'm bushed. I think we'll make tracks, Emmy." To the others, "If you'll excuse us —."

The goodnights were said. The American and his girl went away into the crowd. Narvaez said, "A good man, that."

Frank Brendan said, "His books sell absolutely millions. He's very useful."

"I mean, the man," Narvaez said. "He's a good one. I saw him in Madrid, at the worst time. At the beginning. He went down into the Casa del Campo with the Germans. Not many came back from there. You have to hand it to these correspondents."

"There are some good ones," Frank said. "Some of them are rats. I've met them in London, in Fleet Street. They'll lick any boss's boots for the money."

"My daddy's man here is an absolute pig," Colleen said. "He never leaves the Ritz bar and he hates the Republic."

Frank flicked a hand toward her. "Her daddy is a Press lord. He's a lord. He's a millionaire. She's the Honourable Colleen in England."

Primly angry, she said, "I'm a Party member."

Narvaez smiled at her. "Surely. The best ones come to us." He asked, "Who is the girl with Croft?"

"Emmy? Emmy Bruch. She lives with him. She's an Austrian."

"One of us?"

Frank uttered a boyish laugh of derision. "Emmy? Not her. I've heard her chatter. All her brains are in her pussy."

"Then why did she leave Austria? Is she Jewish?"

Frank said, "God knows."

Narvaez was asking these questions in a business-like manner. Frank had never known quite what work the man was doing in the JSU building. It was his experience that when one didn't know what people's jobs were, they were possibly engaged in what was known as "special work" — keeping an eye on people.

Colleen said, "She's certainly not a refugee. She was out here when I came, and I've been here a year. The Nazis have only been in Austria a few months." She added, in the prim, seeking-for-approval voice she adopted when speaking to important comrades, "I work in the Red Aid.

11

For the Brigade. I have to send back the casualty lists, and look after effects and all that."

"Responsible work," Narvaez said. "She would have come here for the men. Her sort swarm here like flies." He leaned back, turning his body, and flung an arm up in greeting, shouting, "Pepe!"

A man, coming out of the JSU building, paused, saw them and came to them. He was of middle height, bulky but compact of build. His tunic, with the infantry bugle and crossed muskets on its lapels, was as immaculate as Frank's, but he was no rear-echelon dandy, for he wore breeches and high boots, the informal wear of many front-line officers. He kept his peaked cap a little back on his head, showing a spring of upstanding, glossy brown hair. Below the cap-badge were a colonel's bars. Even on this hot night he wore a greatcoat, but as a cloak, in the Spanish way, hanging in straight lines from his shoulders. Colleen, with the excitement of a schoolgirl recognising a film star, exclaimed, "It's Pepe Terres!"

Narvaez stood up and Terres hugged him. Narvaez said, "This is Colleen, an English comrade. and Brendan, from the English YCL."

Colleen looked at Terres as if she were drinking him in but his glance swept past her. He said to Frank, "I know you. You came with John Gollan to the last Congress."

"Yes," Frank said, "and I came to your brigade once, with the youth delegation. You were not there."

Terres gave him a confidential smile. It made Frank feel good to be the recipient of this sort of smile, and of Terres' confiding words, "I never am there if I can help it. I have an adjutant who looks after the delegations, especially the pretty girls who come with the flowers."

They all laughed. Frank's chest was tight with gratification. He hoped Colleen was taking all this in. He had been recognised, he was being treated as a familiar by this famous commander of shock troops. A hitherto-invisible waiter appeared at the table with a bottle and glasses. He must have seen Terres. Terres' photograph was often in the newspapers, his brigade's exploits in the headlines. Frank had been taking Colleen about with him for some weeks, but they were still only two people who walked and sat together. Frank was not altogether shy of women. He was big, nearly six feet tall, and broad of shoulder, with a mop of rough hair the colour of clay. Strong bones gave character to his young face. Since his seventeenth year he had taken up with the occasional girl for a while and enjoyed a few treats with older women, the greedy kind to be found around Party offices. But he had gone on living with his widowed mother in an eastern outskirt of London until nine months ago, when she had been taken into hospital seriously ill. Her illness had not stopped him from eagerly accepting a Party assignment to Spain. Colleen was older than him by a year. She was slim, and taller than the girls he had known, with yellow hair cut like a boy's. In a simple white dress with a narrow belt of red leather she looked to Frank unattainably beautiful, a flower of the upper class which it would give him such pride and pleasure to pick, such a feeling truly of conquest.

Terres took no notice of her. To him, this gathering was of men. His head on one side, he was inspecting Frank. He said to Narvaez, "A young one, this." To Frank, "I asked Gollan about you at the Congress. He said you were a good boy. Yes, yes — nineteen, he said you were. True?"

Frank's face went hot. He said, "I am nearly twenty."

His tone made Terres throw back his head and utter a loud, "Ha!" of laughter. "Nearly twenty! You hear him? Look at him, look at him. A baby, eh?" He leaned forward, reached out his right hand and with thumb and forefinger tweaked Frank's cheek. "A baby!"

His laugh was genial. But Frank, turned to stone, ice-cold with shame, also heard Colleen's laugh.

Terres opened the bottle and sniffed. He said, "Muck!" He took from his greatcoat pocket a leather-covered flask with a silver top. He said, "French cognac," and with one quick, waiter's movement of the flask, filled four glasses without spilling a drop. He leaned toward Frank again, head tilted, showing the confidential smile. "I was not a waiter, comrade. I studied philosophy. Philosophy makes for a steady hand."

"Evidently," Frank said, scarcely consoled by all this.

It dogged him, that word, baby. His mother had always called him her baby, and he had hated it, even that last time when he had gone to see her in hospital. It seemed to him that he could clearly remember his infancy, when the women neighbours gathered round and looked down at him and clucked over him, "How old is he?" "Go on, what a big boy!" "Nineteen-eighteen? November? He was born *before* the Armistice? You know what they call *them*. He's a war baby, that's what he is."

When he was fifteen he had joined the Young Communist League; a clever schoolboy who until then had dreamed only of becoming a writer, whose dreams of *la vie de bohème* and great loves had now come to include barricades and red flags. A chance encounter had brought him almost at once to the notice of a Party leader who saw his talents, plucked him soon out of the rank-and-file and groomed him to become a worker in the apparatus. Frank left school at seventeen with a Cambridge scholarship but his sponsor persuaded him to give it up and to work full-time for the Party. At eighteen Frank was employed by the communist youth newspaper. He had begged again and again to be sent out to the International Brigade but he was deemed too young; and the Party did not send trained organizers to be cannon-fodder. Some were assigned to Spain for particular duties, however, and at the beginning of this year Frank had at last come out to do political work for the youth movement. (His uniform was another story.) Since his entry into the movement he had been something of an infant prodigy. He was used to being pointed out as the baby of whatever group he was in. Hitherto it had gratified him. Not now.

Terres and Narvaez talked in rapid Spanish: politics, military gossip, casual exchanges of the kind of inside information which it made Frank burn with pride to share. From time to time he intervened, purposefully, for Colleen's benefit. She sat in demure silence, out of it all. Girls like her fluttered round all the headquarters of the Party like moths. They were determined to sleep only with leading comrades. They were like hunters of game, aspiring to bag the biggest. Frank, for all his youth, was an apprentice to the leadership and for weeks he had been trying to impress Colleen with that fact. Now here he was, with two leaders, Spanish, romantic, military commanders, one of them famous, and they treated him as one like themselves. Whenever they took him into their talk he felt that he was scoring points with Colleen. He was not short of inside information himself. As the threat of a great war with Germany grew in the public mind, so there had come into being and now grew a world of people who perceived common interests against the Nazis, a world in which the communists, in these days no sect apart, mingled and thrived. Frank's mentor encouraged his young apparatchiks, brought them into the midst of this great hive of speculation, rhetoric and intrigue. Frank had met, in London, leaders of all the political parties. Once he had been introduced to Churchill. He had moved among writers, artists, actors and actresses, foreign diplomats: a little pitcher with big ears. He had a story to tell about a morning spent with Malraux. He had been on a Party training course with J.B.S. Haldane, the eminent scientist as humble as a child. He had been bought a drink by Hemingway at the Majestic.

He looked at his wristwatch and said to Colleen, "We ought to be going."

She said, "Not yet. It's a lovely night."

The men's talk went on. The flask was emptied. Terres stood up. He said, "Well, *chicos*, I'm off early in the morning." He shook hands with Narvaez, then with Frank. As if, Frank thought, with a touch of resentment on her behalf, Colleen did not exist; until Terres turned to Colleen, looked at her as he had at Frank, with a quizzical smile, his head cocked on one side, and she rose at once as if she had been patiently waiting for him, wearing a demure smile of complicity. Terres turned away and she went to him, very close. They walked off, and Frank saw her looking up at Terres, talking nineteen to the dozen.

Narvaez sat down. He raised his glass to drink the last of his brandy, with an equable, "*Salud* —." He put the glass down. "— *y pesetas*."

Frank contrived to laugh. After a little while he made his excuses and went off.

Chapter 2

Henry Croft had a suite on the first floor of the Majestic. At seven o'clock the next morning he finished shaving, wiped streaks of cream from his cheeks, sluiced and towelled his face, dried his hands, cleaned the blade of his razor on a slip of paper put ready on the shelf for that purpose, closed the razor and put it in its case. He picked up the crumpled jacket and trousers of khaki cotton he had worn yesterday on his visit to the soldiers and stuffed them into the washerwoman's bag. He rinsed out the washbowl, then studied his face in the mirror, touching with his fingertips to find any bristles he might have missed. He was a meticulous man, a New Englander, a fussy old school-marm he had been called by a colleague. He had a narrow face, the cheekbones high, the nose sharp with a white mark across the bridge where the frame of his glasses rested. He did not take the sun. Curiously, it made his skin seem pale, as it made his rebellious hair look like bleached straw. He combed his hair now to a reluctant parting. His eyes softened the severity of his features. They were grey, with a look that was steady yet free from pronounced judgement, and usually a smile lurked in them.

He came from Bennington, Vermont, the son of a doctor. He went from school to work on the same local paper he had as a boy delivered, the old *Bugle*, for two years until he went to college. After his graduation in 1916 he had shipped out to England and joined the British Army. He had served in France with the Rifle Brigade; and then, when he had recovered from splinter wounds (which had rescued him from Passchendaele) he had transferred to the American Expeditionary Force, in which he had not heard a shot fired. Back in the newspaper game, he had spent most of the time since then in Europe.

He went into the bedroom and quietly closed the bathroom door. Emmy was still asleep, the sheet thrown back, naked in her bed. He had picked her up at a party a year ago. Truth to tell, she had come away from the party with him unbidden, as a puppy might have trotted at his heels. Like a stray puppy given a basket to sleep in, she had remained. He was glad of her company. He was not adventurous in these matters and he was content to have a woman about who would not be a nuisance. Perhaps she had also stirred in him a small, protective pity.

He drew back the window curtains. The rattle of the rings did not wake Emmy. Sunshine flooded past the criss-crossed strips of brown paper on the panes to gild the room. From the sunny courtyard below he heard children's voices, and from the kitchens a faint clatter of cutlery. He looked out. Two little girls ran about among the palm trees, squealing and laughing.

He opened the double doors of an immense, old-fashioned wardrobe. He took fresh underwear from a shelf and changed into it from his blue-striped pyjamas. He put on a white shirt, with a lightweight tan suit. When he had chosen a necktie to match the shirt, arranged it carefully with a small knot, and satisfied himself as to socks and shoes, he took the pyjamas to the bathroom for the laundry bag. Returned, he lifted a large, black briefcase of thick leather from the wardrobe and took it into the drawing-room.

Here, after drawing the curtains, he sat down at his work table, drew from his trouser pocket a bunch of small keys at the end of a gold cable chain, and applied a separate key to each of the two formidable locks. Stacked in the centre compartment were his diaries, ten notebooks each the size of his flat hand. They had hard covers marbled in grey and blue. There was a label on the front of each on which was typed the year, and the legend:

Notes for
ARMAGEDDON

They went back for five years. In them were many secrets he had found it impossible or inexpedient to use as yet; and a great deal of background material collected during his time in Spain and an earlier two years in Russia. He had worked for most of the big American newspapers. He now had his own news service; but the notes were for the books that he wrote about the world scene, two best-sellers so far, and a third book in his mind. He put on his glasses. They had a thin gold frame. He unscrewed a fountain pen, tried it on a scrap of paper, then opened a notebook and wrote the date: *Thursday, July 21.* Then,

The Offensive

Del Vayo is back. There is to be a War Council tonight at Negrin's villa. I asked del V. if he would talk to me afterwards. He warned that it would be a long session. It must mean, the offensive.

He was frank. The Republic is putting its bottom dollar on this one. A new Army of the Ebro has been formed under Modesto. 5th Corps under Lister, 15th under Tagueña.

(Three good soldiers.) 18th Corps in reserve. 100,000 men. 300 'planes. Maybe 80 gun batteries, including anti-aircraft. (His figures). Little material in reserve, almost nothing coming in. Enemy are superior in numbers and vastly superior in guns and 'planes. They have shown (failure of last three Republican offensives) that they can reinforce and counter-attack with speed and skill. Either the Republican army breaks through the Ebro mountains at once towards the Valencia plain or the Republic is cleaned out. *Kaput.*

Germany and Italy still pouring in men and material to Franco. A mountain of Russian war material for the Republic is stacked in French rail yards, guarded by gendarmes. Del V. has been on his knees to the French in Geneva and Paris but Daladier will not open the frontier. The French are petrified by the fear of a war with Germany.

Their fear of war is the background to this tragedy. (Must explain this in book to Americans, who did not experience the four years' inferno of 1914–18 as Europe did and cannot understand that it is still a nightmare over here. The Germans seem to have snapped out of it — the thirst for revenge is a great tonic. But the British still mourn their million dead and France has not come out of shell-shock. The British and French thought up Non-Intervention. Hope was to localise the conflict. In practice, they don't intervene, Hitler and Mussolini do. Macabre farce. Republic fights on. Tragedy.)

Henry put away his glasses and fountain pen, locked up the notebook and took the briefcase back to the bedroom. Through the open doorway of the bathroom he saw and heard Emmy washing herself, a small, skinny creature in bra and panties. After the local fashion she had turned her quite attractive dark hair into a peroxide bush. Putting the briefcase back on the wardrobe floor, Henry called, "I'm going down to breakfast."

"Tell them to send up." Her voice was always shrill and she always gave the impression of regarding her Mitteleuropa accent as cute.

"What are you doing this morning?"

"I must look for shoes. Leave me some money. What are you doing?"

"I'm going to see Charlie. He always knows what's cooking."

"Charlie! He's always good for a laugh. Give him my love."

*

The sun was up, an immense glare infusing a sky of bleached blue. Frank Brendan walked up the broad boulevard, on the way to his office. He felt as if his heels were sprung. At this time of day the burn of the sun upon his skin was genial. It made him feel good, to be alive, to be in Spain, in this city.

His life as a professional revolutionary in England was mostly dull and tiring. After midnight came the end of a long day of smoky meetings, reports to make, reports to listen to, reports or articles to be written, heaps of print to be read. It was hurry all the time from one to another, in trains and buses. In the evenings he did more work at his desk or taught dialectical materialism to groups of tired people. Early the next morning and the next a similar round began. He was sustained by belief and by a few intoxicating times that reinforced his belief. The South Wales valleys astir with marching miners. Great crowds overwhelming Fascist meetings. For Frank, the greatest time of all, Paris in June, 1936.

He was there for a week, speaking at meetings, just after the People's Front government had been elected. (In February the *Frente Popular* had come to power in Spain but Spain was still remote.) Strikes swept across France. The workers occupied their workplaces. Everyone did it. It was peaceful, merry, a national carnival. Frank danced in the street with *midinettes* on strike. Everyone in a Métro carriage or on a café *terrasse* was a friend. There must have been another Paris somewhere of people who hated all this but Frank was not aware of it. All at once came a forty-hour week, two weeks' paid holiday for all and reforms galore. There was no revolution, no socialism. The communists were in the forefront of it all and they knew better than to scare away the petty bourgeois with his government bonds and the peasant with his gold hidden away in a sock. At the Galeries Lafayette the assistants in the bedding department slept on the floor beside the beds and linen which they left untouched. No Red Bogey, everyone in France had to be roused up, and in the rest of Europe, too, against Hitler, to block his war plans. That was the great aim of the People's Front. Revolution, no, not for the present, yet a kind of revolution it was, of the spirit. Frank remembered it as a wonderful summer holiday, bathed in sunshine and exhilarating as now, this morning, Barcelona was.

Bliss was it to be alive, and now, too. He was one of those for whom the word Spain sounded in the mind like a clash of cymbals. As in France, so in Spain. We must defend liberalism here because here was the first armed clash with Hitler and his allies. Here, too, no revolution, no Red Bogey that might swing the nations away from us, away from Russia, even over to Hitler's side. All the same, Frank knew, and he felt it in his springing step, *we* were the masters here as one day we would be everywhere. For Frank there was no contradiction in these contradictory beliefs. He had been taught the dialectic! Thesis, antithesis, synthesis. How unbelievably lucky he was to have become one of those who possessed this so-simple key to the secret of all things, one of those who had learned how to steer history.

Blithe, with springing step, he had cast off the discomfiture of last night. Indeed, when at one moment he remembered it, he laughed up at the sun, loudly, striding on through these streets of future triumph. Colleen, oh, you couldn't help laughing. The cheek of these high-class tootsies. The cool nerve, the swift, calm assurance with which they took what they wanted. And all these goings-on, in another world from the grey life of Stratford, East London. Cafés, smart talk, cognac, beautiful, promiscuous girls — it was like being in a Hemingway novel. Wouldn't it be just wonderful to go to bed with that girl, a girl who only slept with celebrities. Young lust made his step even more joyful.

Big Peter was already at his typewriter when Frank came into the office. He looked up, continuing to tap at keys. "Och, here y'are. Have ye done that translation?"

Frank took some folded sheets from his pocket. "Here's the first part. I'll give you the rest today."

"Fine." Peter flattened the pages on the table and turned them over quickly. "Ay, fine." In his speech the consonants and cadences of the Gorbals were softened by years of travel and self-education. "And what have you been up to?"

"I was at the JSU yesterday. There was a mobilization meeting. People were coming in all day from the factories and the front. I really felt as if something was on the move."

"Did you now?"

Seated at his desk in a corner of the room, Frank met Peter's look, Peter's pale blue eyes always seemed at first dull, until one saw the lids narrowed at the outer corners, forever sizing-up.

Frank said, "I met some Army people I knew. All their units are in the south now."

"Is that so?" Peter returned to his typing.

The breadth of Peter's shoulders and chest made him seem less than his height, as did his usually crumpled clothes. He had a battered, simple face, a mask for an acute mind, beneath a brush of fairish hair that was tinged with steel tints although he was barely forty. He was one of those older comrades who were Frank's heroes and inspiration: born in a slum, soldier in the Great War, engineer at the Parkhead Forge, strike leader, Hunger Marcher, founding commissar of the International Brigade; and an athlete into the bargain. He was here as a civilian, the correspondent of the British communist newspaper; also as a member of the Comintern and representative of the British Party. His post as journalist was not simply a cover. He sent home first-class stories.

Frank said, "They want me to go on a speaking tour. A few of us from different countries. Factories, barracks. Some of the small towns."

"Fine. When?"

"I'm doing a meeting tomorrow, down at the port."

"Don't let yourself in for any more, not just yet."

"Why not?"

"I want you here. You can mind the office for me —." And, as Frank waited. "I'll be away for a few days."

Frank knew that he should not ask, but, "Where?" He withstood Peter's cold look. "You're going down to the battalion —." He took the plunge. "It's the offensive, isn't it?"

"I wouldn't know." Peter looked squarely at Frank. "Believe me, I don't know. They want me to go down, that's all I know. And," with emphasis, "that's enough. D'you understand?"

"Sure."

"A feller in your position —." His expression hinted at reproach. His voice was not unkind. "I shouldn't have to tell you."

"No —. I know —. Peter —."

"Ay?"

"When Bill was here —. I don't know if he told you —. I wanted to go to the battalion —."

"I suppose that's what you're all dressed up for."

Peter had been out here for a couple of months. This was the first reference he had made to Frank's uniform. Early in the year Frank had pulled strings among his JSU friends and got into one of the crash officers' courses to which the movement sent its militants in the army. He had come out a lieutenant. A purchased length of cloth and a backstreet tailor had turned him into the simulacrum of a soldier. He said, "I wanted to fight. I thought it was a step —."

"I'll bet ye did. So do a lot of comrades. Where would we be if they all went?"

"I know, but I'm the right age. I'm fit."

Peter chuckled and his jaw dropped in the grin that often transformed his face. "I'm passable fit mysel' —. Ah, come on, Frank, do you think I want to sit here typing articles for the *Daily*?"

"I know. But you do get down there."

"So will you when you're told to. There are plenty of fellers to carry a rifle and pack. We've got damn few trained to do your job. Just you get on with it." To underline the point, he let the carriage of his typewriter crash back on its track. "And I'll get on with mine. OK?"

Frank laughed, and opened a folder. "OK."

*

Charlie was an arms dealer. There were a number of arms dealers making their fortunes in Barcelona. Charlie was also a dealer in anything else that was in short supply. Everyone called him Charlie. Most did not know his surname. The hotel staff called him *Señor* Charlie. Henry knew his surname but nobody, including Henry, knew his nationality. It would not have been wise to take his Irish Free State passport seriously nor the unrevealing name in it, Peters.

Henry walked the few blocks round to the Ritz, Barcelona's grand hotel. The air raid damage at the corner of the building had been boarded up. The entrance was as resplendent as ever. Inside, he went up a wide staircase of veined marble between imposing balustrades. Charlie was at the top of the stairs talking with a stocky man who wore a hand-me-down dark grey suit. Henry waited while Charlie and the stranger shook hands. The man turned away to pick up from a chair a grey fedora hat with a solemn flat brim and a low crown that was unadventurously dented. Charlie, a hand on the man's arm, saw him to the head of the stairs, talking with him. The man left. Charlie turned, saw Henry and advanced upon him beaming, arms outstretched. "Henry! My good Henry! People! People!" He embraced Henry. "Everybody wants something from me."

"Is that a warning?"

"Henry! What's mine is yours. You know that. Come on up."

Henry followed him. Charlie, keeping a step ahead, spoke over his shoulder, loud and jovial. "Breakfast is waiting. Your timing is good. I guess it always is. Eh?"

"What did the Russian want?"

"You know him?"

"I've seem him around. At the Press Bureau. He could only be a Russian with that hat. I guess they only have one factory over there."

"His name is Kostyrev."

"I've never heard of him. Never ran across him in Moscow."

"Small fry, Henry. Not in your league." Charlie had blue eyes, porous cheeks as pink and hairless as a baby's and, although he could not have been more than fifty, flossy white hair. He laughed, as if exultant, with his mouth wide open, showing too-perfect teeth. He clapped a hand on Henry's arm. "How about starting the day right, old man?" He turned to a buffet on which an array of bottles and glasses stood next to a display of delicatessen.

"A small Scotch. Straight." Henry surveyed the buffet while Charlie poured. There were pâté, smoked fish, slices of pink beef and rolls of Parma ham, three kinds of cheese, a stick loaf, pumpernickel slices, croissants, jam and a block of creamy butter such as Henry had not seen since his last trip out to Paris. Coffee murmured in a pot on a spirit lamp. Charlie said, with an unction that hinted at revelations to come, "That Russian is going back. He doesn't know it."

"How do you know about it?"

Charlie uttered another exultant, "Ha! Ha!" He added, with relish, "He is going to be shot." And watched, patently, for effect. Charlie's English could not be faulted but his strong and jovial voice employed more emphasis and a wider tonal range than any Englishman's. He articulated with an unEnglish enjoyment, sounding his consonants like a German and his 'r's like an American. When questioned about his nationality he dropped playful and misleading hints, different on every occasion. He said, "All the same, he told me a thing or two."

Henry took a filled glass from him. "Your good health."

"Mud in your eye."

"About what?"

"What do they talk about in Moscow these days? Or rather, what don't they talk about? Who's getting shot, old boy."

"Who is getting shot that I don't know of?"

"The head of the Air Force."

"Alksnis?" Henry gave Charlie a standing-off, suspicious look. Charlie sometimes peddled outrageous rumours, either to amuse himself or to impress.

"Come. Eat." He handed a plate to Henry. They filled their plates at the buffet. A low table nearby was laid with silver and fine glasses. There was a pile of damask napkins.

"The Russian told you this?"

"He and others did."

"I'm not surprised they're going to shoot him."

"It's not for that. His number has been up for some time."

Charlie put his laden plate on the table and reached for a bottle of Meursault. Henry said, "Not for me. Just give me a cup of that coffee. The aroma's driving me crazy."

"Sit down." Charlie came to the table and poured coffee.

Henry said, "My breakfast at the Majestic was a cup of ground acorn and a Ryvita biscuit. This is Paradise."

"Feast!" Charlie watched him benevolently. "Why do they talk? Henry, I will tell you a big secret. A Russian will sell his body and soul for a case of Johnnie Walker. So!" He sat back, threw one of his heroic laughs at the ceiling and leaned forward, at once serious. "And do you know what has become of Ovseyenko, the Consul-General here? And the Ambassador?"

"Rosenberg? He was recalled. Has he been shot?"

"Both of them."

"Wait." Henry took from his inside pocket a small memorandum pad and a clip pencil. He scribbled. "Any more?"

"There'll be plenty. But give me time to hand out a few more cases of Scotch."

Henry put away the pad and pencil. "Charlie, who do you dig up all this stuff for?"

"Myself. My own amusement, old boy. The human comedy. But tell me, what about you? Why the notes? Spain is your beat."

"I was in Russia, Charlie. I still keep tabs. I kept on good terms with them when I was there. My stories mostly gave them the benefit of the doubt. After all it still seemed there was an epic experiment going on. It was bad, I hated the place. But there was a lot of striving and some real belief. For the most part I kept the bad side of it for my notebook. I aimed to write a book about it when I came out. But I'd hardly put my bag down in Paris when I had to take off for Spain. The book's on ice. But I need to keep my data up to date."

"Sure. More coffee —." He took Henry's cup and saucer. "And apart from that, was this a social visit or can I help you?"

"Maybe. I was with the 15th Brigade yesterday, They look in good shape. I'd say they were training for an assault. When do you think they'll go?"

Charlie stretched his body, looking Henry over, chuckling inside his throat. "You do ask questions, Henry. One might wonder who *you* were digging it up for."

"I'm a newspaper man. I'd like to be there when they jump off."

"And who would tell me military secrets?"

"Somebody might let a word drop. You've done them favours. A little bird at the Ministry told me you'd sold them a consignment of Bofors guns. Twelve, I think. How did you get them over the frontier?"

Charlie let an eyelid droop. "Trade secrets I don't tell. What do you think about this offensive?"

It was a moment before Henry answered. "They could just do it."

"I see you're still an optimist."

"No. Maybe I still believe in the power of prayer." He stood up.

"A game of dominoes?"

"No, thanks. I'd sooner sit down to poker with a Las Vegas cardsharp. Last time, I had my arm round my tiles but you knew every one of them."

Charlie stood up. "I can see through things, Henry. And round corners. That's why I stay ahead." He went with Henry to the door. "How's your little girl?"

"Fine. She sends her love."

"I know where they have some good handbags. Tell her to call me."

"Surely. And thanks for breakfast."

Charlie opened the door. "Thanks for the company. Come again."

*

In better days the dining-room of the Majestic must have been a splendid sight. It was of ballroom dimensions with a big glass dome. Frank, eating his dinner alone, was imagining. A communist picturing the heroic austerity he would at some future date embrace, he at the same time glimpsed himself, in visions that brushed unbidden through his mind, as being on the doorstep of a grand, glittering world, the preserve of those who were at the centre of things. The Party leader who was his mentor, a man whose life was of exemplary self-denial, had once surprised Frank by saying to him, in a confidential voice, "I am one of the five hundred most important people in the world." That was what it

26

meant to be in the apparatus. So, Frank saw in his mind's eye a throng of smart people in this room, crowded tables, snowy linen, dazzling silver and glass, chandeliers ablaze, palm trees in tubs, a profusion of flowers, a string orchestra; while from his corner table he looked at the reality, a barn feebly lit (the electricity supply in the city was poor, since the enemy had captured the main power station. There were often blackouts) and shadowy at the edges, most of the tables unoccupied and a few elderly, stooping waiters in shiny and patched tuxedos creaking about.

The menu was typed on a big card that was yellow with age, with a *belle époque* green-and-gold pattern of entwined foliage round the edges. Frank had come to look upon it as a sort of nightly joke. Tonight, the *potage paysanne* was a thin yellowy fluid in which lay six chickpeas. The *surprise de mer* was a small square of salted fish. He could only guess the spoonful of soggy green leaves to be boiled thistles. The selection of fresh fruits gave him a choice between an apple and an apricot, both shrivelled.

He counted nine other tables occupied, the talk of the diners no more than a disturbance of the dull silence. At a table to his left the photographer Capa sat with Sefton Delmer, the London *Daily Express* man. They talked with heads close together as if exchanging secrets. Near to the entrance Herb Matthews of the *New York Times* sat with his head down, forking food into his mouth with great concentration while he apparently listened to Henry Croft. Croft's Austrian girl was with them.

As Frank went by their table on his way out, Croft called to him, "Hallo, there!"

Frank went to the table. He said hallo. The girl smiled at him and Matthews gave him a not unfriendly nod. Croft said, "Have a glass of wine."

Frank sat down, gratified. He was in the company of the famous. Croft clapped for a waiter, asked for a glass and resumed his conversation with Matthews. "I thought you would have known him. We all get to the same places."

Matthews suspended his eating just long enough to say, "Never came across him."

Croft explained to Frank, "I'm talking about George Seldes. A great reporter. He gave me my first big break." To Matthews, again. "He was in the AEF press section when I transferred from the British. I'd known his brother Gilbert at Harvard. We both hung around the *Lampoon* and the *Daily Crimson*."

Matthews brought his fork to a stop, said, "I met Gilbert. A good newspaperman." He resumed shovelling.

There was a platter of ham on the table, square slices from a tin; a big wedge of gruyère; a basket of rolls and a bottle of Pommard, from which Croft poured a glass for Frank. He said, "Dig in. There's plenty. Herb sends to France for it."

Emmy emerged from a dreamy silence. "Use my bread plate."

"Thank you. I could use some grub." The bread, the cheese and the burgundy tasted like the food of gods.

Matthews was still putting away ham. He said, "What do you figure to this Czech business?"

Croft said, "It keeps on, doesn't it?"

"Maybe it's just Hitler talking," Matthews said.

"Maybe not." This was Croft. "Maybe he means to grab one country after another."

Matthews laid down his fork. "Well, Hank, I'll tell you, that's what I've been thinking. I have a feeling there's going to be a big crisis over Czechoslovakia. Maybe a war."

Emmy awoke again. "A war?"

Henry said, "It could be."

Matthews said, "We're all talking about this offensive, but maybe in two weeks Spain won't even make the front pages." He stood up, tall, thin, loose. He said goodnight to Emmy and Frank, and to Croft, "See you later, Hank."

He went out. Henry said, "Nice fellow. Best newspaperman in Spain."

Emmy said, "Except you, Henry." Then, to Frank, "Are you going to the party?"

"What party?" A familiar left-out feeling pierced Frank.

"The party at the Ritz."

Henry spoke as if to console. "It's nothing much. A bunch of Scandinavian politicians. Emmy likes that sort of thing. I shan't be going."

Emmy said, "He has work to do. Maybe all night —. Frank, you take me."

"Why don't you?" Henry said, as a spasm of electric shock shot into Frank's abdomen from his left thigh, upon which a small hand squeezed hard and was gone in a moment.

Frank glanced at her small, peaked face but she was gazing at Henry, and saying, "Maybe Charlie will be there. I can ask him about the handbag."

Charlie was not at the party but a lot of quite important people were. The *salon* was crowded. It made Frank happy to be there, among well-dressed men and elegant women, although he knew no-one except Emmy, who was away from him most of the time. Expensive clothes, all the fashion wear that went with them, and jewellery, were on display in the city even if food was short. Soap was scarcely to be had but these women shone and made clear that there was no lack of lipstick, mascara and eyebrow pencil. Emmy appeared in one group after another, overacting (so Frank thought) to one man after another, her laughter too high-pitched, her gaiety too emphatic. Frank was increasingly on edge. There were so many handsome men, so many in smart uniforms, and all older than he was. It tormented him that for a second night running a girl would go off with another man, without a backward glance; deserting him, the baby.

But when the crowd was thinning out Emmy came back to him and they left together. Now his happiness was restored. Tonight he had been invited to sit with Matthews and Croft. He had been admitted to a gathering of those at the centre of things. He had mingled with glittering people. Now he was walking to his hotel with a pretty girl on his arm, and what was more, a foreign girl, one of those unpredictable, exotic creatures. What price Stratford East? Was it all real? He wondered what he should do when they were back at the hotel but Emmy settled the matter for him. She walked with him to his room as if there were no question about it, and kept him awake till she left at five in the morning.

Chapter 3

Henry Croft wrote in his diary, *Friday, July 22*, then,

> At the villa. War Council ended at six a.m. Played poker in ante-room all night. Saurier of *Ce Soir* took us all to the cleaners. All the top military among the leaders who came out of the conference room. Del Vayo said, no statement. Atmosphere of portentous decision, i.e., they walk out in a dull, oppressive quiet, look casual, exchange small talk, throw brief greetings at us. In short, the offensive is on.
>
> I had caught del V.'s eye. When my colleagues had left he indicated Negrin, who was talking in the hall with Modesto, and said, "He will see you. A working lunch. Come back at noon. It is on condition that you do not discuss the offensive."
>
> Noon. Why is Negrin willing to give me time at such a moment as this? I have had two long, confidential exchanges with him in the past and he knows I have a book in mind. Maybe he is isolated among factions who all try to grind their axes upon him and likes to talk with someone who is out of it, an American. Maybe he wants to put himself right with history.
>
> His idea of a working lunch. *Coquille Saint Jacques. Filet de sole mignonne.* Quails on toast. A wonderful Roquefort cheese. Hothouse fruits. He talks in a rapid, concentrated way, giving me the closest attention without ceasing to eat, politely but ferociously. He helps himself to three of the birds. Crunches the small bones. He puts down the better part of our two bottles of wine. He interrupts our sharpest exchange to hold up his glass and remark that the glint of green in the yellow is the sign of a good Chablis.
>
> He can work eighteen hours a day. Keeps a harem of elegant women around him. Drives fast cars. Wears black suit, black tie, starched white shirt even in high summer, could be a civil servant. Or, puts on his horn rims and

looks like the professor of physiology he used to be. But powerful inside the formal suit. As if Woodrow Wilson had the appetites of a Danton.

Here, gist of our talk. Not verbatim but freshly remembered.

Negrin. This is not an interview.

Croft. Of course not. I saw you with Modesto this morning. Lister and Lagueña are also communists. I shall not talk about the offensive after this, but it brings me to the question most Americans would ask. It troubles me. Do the communists pull the strings in the Republic?

N. No.

C. Seven brigade commanders out of every ten in the entire Army are Party members, and most of the commissars. Your secret police is in their hands, I am referring to the SIM. They hold the navy and air force commands. These are the keys to power. Surely they could take over in twenty-four hours.

N. They have not done so.

C. It does not suit them to. Yet.

N. They have advanced in the armed forces according to their merits as fighters. You know what these are.

C. I am well aware of their bravery and discipline.

N. They are one tendency among many in a democracy to which they are loyal. I am a socialist, and of the most moderate inclination. The majority of my government are liberals and other moderates, or are simply loyal administrators. That is why we speak of a People's Front.

C. You know that the People's Front is a tactic invented by the communists. I was in Moscow at the Congress of the Communist International, 1935. Dimitrov made clear to his people that it would open the way to revolution.

N. What they hope for is their business. In any walk of life each partner has his own aims. The People's Front was needed in Europe to provide a united resistance to fascism. The communists only gave a name to it.

C. Then do you know what who-whom means? (He didn't). It is a communist catch-phrase. I think Lenin coined it. It means that in any coalition one must see who is going to use whom and who is going to destroy whom in the end.

N. The first part is obvious. I suggest that the second is your interpretation.

C. Let me come to cases. The Brunete offensive last year was a disaster forced upon you by the communists. You had to comply because you needed Russian arms. They fell out with Prieso, one of the most able men in Spain. He had to be dismissed from the government. The SIM is a law to itself. I name one of the many it has murdered because he was famous and respected, Andrés Nin. The government did not know. It had difficulty even in finding out —.

N. Slanders.

C. I have details in my notebooks.

N. You claim to know more than you have any right to know.

C. It is my job.

N. Why do you press such things? You talk like an enemy.

C. I am a friend.

After this we calm down. He offers me a peach. He reflects, speaks quietly.

N. Let me dispose of all this. If you kind people in Britain, France and America want to stop the Spanish Republic from going Red, all you have to do is to support us. Sell me arms and I will no longer be dependent upon the Russians. Enable me to deal with the communists upon my own terms and I will not have to concede theirs. You will save me a great deal of anguish. You will also then have a grateful Spain on your side in the coming general war.

C. Are you sure that war is coming?

N. Keep an eye on Czechoslovakia. The fuse is burning low.

About to leave, I ask if there is significance in his recent appeal to the Powers for a withdrawal of foreign volunteers from both sides.

N. We shall see.

C. Isn't it a pipe dream? The other side would lose two major expeditionary forces, German and Italian. You would only have to dispense with the remnants of the International Brigades.

N. Exactly.

C. Then why propose it?

N. Let me tell you this, and now I am indeed trusting you. I will send the Brigades away if there is even a whisper of a chance that this might persuade the French to open the frontier. We can do without the International Brigades. We shall perish without munitions.

*

Henry came out of the Majestic at four in the afternoon. He was in a reflective mood and set out through the back streets to take a long way round to the Press Bureau. He was not thinking about his talk with Negrin as he strolled. His mind was playing with a word, Passchendaele. For more than twenty years that name had had a trick of coming out of its cave and standing in the forefront of his mind. It had never before occurred to him to let his fancy play with the sound of it. Passchendaele. Passion. Gethsemane. Golgotha. The long, long journey on the stretcher, over the duckboards, rain falling on his face, morphine dulling the burn of fragments in his chest; himself feeling only an immense, infinite thankfulness.

From doorways and open balcony windows the sounds of work and family life came to him. People laughed. Babies cried. Crockery clashed. A saw grunted into wood. The recalcitrant starter of a truck whinnied.

Barrels rumbled over stone; all this coming out of a background of treacly radio music. Girls in flowered dresses went by arm in arm, sprightly. Older women in black nodded and conferred on street corners. From time to time he passed a block laid open by a bomb, and long queues for meat or bread. On empty shop windows he read the scrawled signs, *No Food*, *No Coffee*, *No Wine*, *No Paraffin*, no everything. Young recruits were schoolboys with soft children's cheeks and liquid, frightened eyes, in brown uniforms too big for them; every one, it seemed, with a mother clinging to one arm and a girl to the other as if to hold him back. The brave posters on the walls were torn, the banners were few, faded and listless. Yet the white glare, the electric heat, the sounds of universal everyday life, the music prevailed. It was a summer's day. This was the city upon whose frivolity strangers remarked. The enemy was pitiless and promised massacre to every town he seized. He was a morning's drive away. But, Henry was tempted to conclude, the minds of people in a threatened city excluded reality, the war was remote. Today was pleasant. Every day was today. The people in these streets knew nothing of the offensive.

It was quiet at the Press Bureau. The rush hour began when the correspondents came in at six o'clock to catch their deadlines. Henry gave his day's story to a censorship clerk and asked for a telephone line to his office in Paris. He saw Victoria, the head of the Press Department, looking at papers in her office, and went in.

"Henry!" Her glance was welcoming. "So it was an all-night session."

"Are you putting anything out?"

"We know nothing. I assume there is no reference to the War Council in your story."

He grinned. "What do you think?"

She, too, smiled. She came of one of the great families of Spain. She was slender and upright, with an aristocratic face on delicate bones. The grey streaks in her close-cut brown hair enhanced her attractiveness. Her plain grey dress was at once severe and elegant. A clerk looked in at the door and told Henry that his line to Paris was ready. Henry said to Victoria, "I'm giving them ten lines. Today's communiqué. Unless you can give me more."

She said, "I'll give you some coffee."

When he came back the coffee had come. She gave him a cup. He said, "Negrin was interesting. I tackled him about your people."

Victoria was a communist, a Party member of standing. "And?"

"He defended you, of course. But he inferred that he found your loving embrace a trifle too constricting."

"Well," she said. "He is a connoisseur of embraces."

"I admit it was just a word, and a look. The truth is, he slapped me down."

"Good for him. I should not have joked just now. The Party has spent too much blood."

"Surely. I respect that."

"Ah," she said. "That's why I love you. You are a fair-minded man."

"You mean," he could not help saying, "You like other people to be fair-minded."

She smiled. "Fair means unprejudiced, yes? Like us when we support old enemies against the fascists."

"As a rope supports a hanged man, to quote Lenin."

"Are you two at it again?" A deep voice, a Scots accent. Big Peter, the man from the London *Daily Worker*, stood in the doorway. Pale blue open-necked shirt, baggy, stained slacks, a shapeless jacket of threadbare brown tweed. He came in and stooped to touch Victoria's cheek with a kiss. "And how's my bonny lass today?"

"Busy. But happy to see you. Have you 'phoned in yet?"

"Ay." He turned a wooden chair. His fingers were big and blunt, the tips stained deeply with nicotine. He settled himself astride the chair. "But don't let me interrupt. I like a good scrap." He grinned, showing big teeth set askew, yellow and brown from smoking.

Henry said, "We only spar. Cat's-paw punching. What have you sent?"

"Precious little."

Victoria said, "Henry was at the War Council. He learned nothing."

Henry said, "Not even off the record. Not about the offensive —. Victoria, fix me a car."

"For what?"

"You know what for. For the front."

"You're crazy, Henry. There are no facilities for the Press. What do you expect at this moment?"

"I know about that. But can't you slip me into an official car? Unofficially?"

"When? Where? I wouldn't know where to send you. I know nothing, Henry, and a good thing, too. And if you even mentioned an offensive I wouldn't let a word through."

"Naturally. This is not for news. I don't want to find out anything, for God's sake. I simply want to be down there. With the men. Anywhere."

"To make a chapter for another book of yours."

"Victoria," he said, in a tired voice. "You know why."

She said, "I'm sorry, Henry. I'm on edge, too."

Peter said, "It's the waiting."

"Henry," Victoria said. "We all have to wait. And please, don't hitch any lifts down there. You've done that too often. You could get into serious trouble."

"You wouldn't be that foolish, would you, Henry?" This was from Peter. He lumbered up on to his feet. "I must be away. So, till we get good news, eh?"

"A lovely man," Victoria said, watching Peter go across the telephone room.

Henry said, "Let me buy you a drink before the mob breaks in."

"I'd love that." He waited while she made herself ready, and they went out together.

Chapter 4

Two evenings later Henry sat in the back of an open car going south on the coast road. Big Peter was with him. A soldier was at the wheel.

It was July 24th. Four hours earlier at the Press Bureau Henry had telephoned his story to Paris, a folks-back-home piece about three American seamen on a ship running the blockade, and was on his way out when he saw Peter lifting a finger to catch his eye. He went across, pushed a litter of old newspapers out of one of the old, burst armchairs that furnished the room and sat down next to Peter; who leaned back in his chair, cocked his head towards Henry and said, in a posture of idle conversation, "What are you doing tonight?"

Henry felt the old professional tingle go up into the back of his head. Peter's blue eyes were watching him sidelong, with a dull, somewhat fishy look that Henry had learned to interpret. He said, "Nothing I can't miss."

"Meet me at the Colón. Seven o'clock."

"Right." His answer was instant.

"We'll be going for a wee ride. Don't leave any messages. Tell no-one. That includes your girl."

"I understand."

Hotel Colón looked across a big square to the cathedral. Its ground floor walls were heavily sandbagged. Its high frontage was covered with the usual slogans, red banners and huge portraits. It was the communist headquarters. People and cars came and went all the time. Peter and Henry left inconspicuously in a Party car.

The coast road was narrow, snaking past red outcrops of the foothills. Two years of military traffic had broken its tarmac with potholes and long, ragged subsidences. Wild churned patches on each side were baked hard by the sun. There were few other vehicles on the road. From time to time a truck went past, or they saw a donkey cart coming north with a family trudging on each side of it, the old folk and infants perched on a pile of bundles and furniture. Twice they were stopped at road controls, each time by a group of boys in sloppy uniforms who came out in front of them with rifles pointed.

Henry said, "It's very quiet."

Peter looked up with a gesture and a comic grimace, at a sky which was at this moment empty.

Henry said, "I guess so. You know, I seem to recognise that jacket. Wouldn't it once have had brass buttons on it with the royal crown?"

Peter chuckled. He was wearing a cotton bush jacket of British Army type over an open-necked khaki shirt. Also his crumpled grey flannels and a pair of huge, dirty white sneakers. "I'm a very careful feller. You know what they say about the Scots. I've had this twenty year. Not bad, eh?"

"Come winter, I still wear an Army greatcoat."

"Ay. I was in the Palestine campaign. His Majesty's Royal Scots."

"Pontius Pilate's Bodyguard."

"Ay. Right of the Line."

"I was in France. Rifle brigade."

"Not a bad lot, the Rifles."

"Not bad at all. — Peter, I haven't thanked you for the lift."

"Glad to oblige."

"Where are we bound for exactly?"

"I have to go to the British." Peter turned that fishy look on Henry. "You know I'm kind of responsible for them."

"For the British Party."

"Ay."

"You must have a lot of pull out here."

"Oh —." Peter thrust out his underlip. "I don't know."

"The Party —. The Comintern."

Peter nodded, as if sharing Henry's speculations. "Maybe."

"Well," Henry said. "This car. The army driver. I guess you pull a lot more rank than Victoria."

Peter grinned and said, "She's a grand girl."

Henry persisted, "But she's not in the know and she can't get cars."

"It would be a fine sight for the fascist spies, wouldn't it? — to see all the correspondents scuttling south."

"Surely. I'm all the more grateful for being chosen."

Again the chuckle. "Maybe I look forward to seeing that book of yours."

Dusk was thickening when the car turned away from the coast. Darkness came the more quickly as the hills to each side of a narrow road rose higher and more steeply. Then, rapidly, a transformation scene was worked in the darkness. The throb and snort of motors broke into the silence and became persistent, voices became audible, points and small glimmers of light multiplied as Henry saw big trucks filling the entries to side tracks and waiting in lines under camouflage nets wherever the low ground made an inroad into a mountainside. Then the car had to slow, again and again, to let the convoys crawl out of concealment. Soon they were in a slowing stream of traffic that at last came to a stop.

The road ahead of them showed a long patch of grass verge on the left. Their driver pulled out, switched on his masked headlamps and accelerated. They sped alongside the traffic jam. Henry saw it-must-have-been a dozen huge low trucks with black tarpaulins covering the shapes of tanks, then a line of small trucks towing howitzers, and open trucks as far ahead as he could see, packed with troops. The car slowed sharply. A torch flashed for a moment in front of them. A voice shouted, "*Apagar la luz!*" The little blur of weak light from the slit apertures of their headlamps vanished as their driver switched off.

Now they had to keep stopping on the choked roads but each time the traffic freed itself and crawled on. Henry wondered how many other roads were choked like this one with columns moving up to the attack. There were infantry now, flitting in single file along the verge, bobbing dark shapes until they came past the car and Henry glimpsed pale faces, heard murmuring talk and sharp commands.

They eased to their right and left the road, climbing a track. Earth crunched under the wheels. Walls of knobby rock hemmed them in. They came out on to an open upland, a long slope down to a valley. The track ran on a shoulder of the slope.

Henry had been this way three days before. He fancied that he could recognise the silhouettes of ridges and peaks against the grizzled darkness. He remarked that they were approaching Marsa, the camp of the British battalion. But when at last Peter leaned forward and tapped the driver's shoulder and the car stopped, the fields above and below them on the mountain's flank were deserted. Scarred peaks showed pale above them. Patches of undergrowth were black inkstains. The *chavolas*, caves dug by the soldiers in sandstone slopes, were silent black holes. Clustered shelters of boughs and foliage gaped at them. A distant continuous traffic noise made the night tremble but here it was quiet. Peter said, "They moved out yesterday. They've left a guide." He pointed. "I know the feller. He's from Greenock."

*

A little before midnight they came to an expanse of open ground beyond which they could see the ghostly ruins of a town. Mora la Nueva. They drove slowly through what seemed like a disordered crowd of soldiers. Lines of lorries were turning off the road to one side or the other. As far as Henry could see, the open ground was covered with trucks, gun batteries, clusters of tethered mules and a scurry of men. The disorder was only apparent. A military policeman flashed them down with a blink of his torch, conferred with their driver and gave him a direction. There were more police on the road marshalling the traffic into assembly areas.

They skirted the town to the south until they stopped near to the edge of what looked like a wide ditch. A sentry unslung his rifle and came towards them. They heard his English voice. "Halt! Who goes there?"

The bed of a dried-up river ran down to the Ebro. Henry and Peter scrambled down into it and were amongst the British battalion. Their guide had preceded them and returned with another man who said, "Follow me," and then, unnecessarily, "No smoking."

They followed him toward the river bank. The men of the battalion were sprawled, mostly, against the walls of the *barranco*. A few stood, talking quietly, or sat in groups murmuring one to another. Many of these called out to Peter, who stopped each time to exchange a few words. The greater part slept. Henry saw the gleam of their cradled rifles and the packs and strapped blankets heaped at their sides. He passed a line of heavy machine-guns, Russian Maxims with fat, snouted waterjackets like Vickers guns but with shields and small trolley wheels. Most of the gunners slept but he saw two pairs of men still loading bullets into belts, heads down, intent and deliberate.

The men lying rolled in blankets, the men sitting slumped against the wall, some with ponchos round their shoulders, looked like groups of war memorial statuary; inert, insentient. Henry, seized since his arrival with a tension that was becoming intolerable, felt his heart knocking loudly, rapidly. A memory came to him and for a little while it took him away from where he walked.

He was in the first-line trench again at Arras, in 1917, a spring dawn. He had come up during the night in a draft of reinforcements; his first time in the line. And straightway he had been hustled off to a rifle company, in the last minutes before they attacked. His heart knocked loudly, rapidly. It was hard to breathe. He stared at the ladders propped in readiness against the forward wall of the trench, the piles of barbed wire, trestles, timbers, iron sheets, drums of signal cable to be carried over the top. He stared at the men waiting to attack. Some were sitting down, chins on their chests, apparently sleeping. Some lounged against the trench wall. Some were pissing. Many snatched last smokes from butt-ends held between finger-tips. All seemed indifferent, inert, insentient.

His eyes saw night again and the crowded *barranco*. Sleepers stirred. Talkers abruptly stopped. Henry saw heads lifted, alert eyes gleaming. He heard what had already aroused them. Small-arms fire, to the north. Peter said, "It's started." But the stir subsided. The muttered conversations were resumed. A few sleepers grunted before they hunched down again with the others to sleep. Henry alone (it seemed to him) was prickled by the anguish of wondering.

A group of officers conferred some yards ahead. Nearby a car waited on the rim of the *barranco*. Henry, who knew better than to intrude, said, "I'll see you later. I'd like a word sometime."

Peter said, "Sure," and went to join the conference. Henry climbed out of the ditch. He had recognised the officer who leaned against the car, and who now turned to him, a hand outstretched. "Hank! Good to see you."

As they shook hands, "Hello, George."

George Gamble was a lieutenant, an American; a Bennington boy. He was short, scrawny, with a doughy face and steel-rimmed glasses. A railroad clerk on the Vermont Central, a young man with no politics at all except support for FDR and a fair deal for everybody, he had enlisted for the Brigade and had written about his decision to Henry, a hero of his. He was a supply officer at Brigade Headquarters. He said, "I should have known you'd be here. I'm waiting for pretty boy down there. I came along to make sure the rations hadn't been hijacked. All soldiers rob each other."

"In my time, too. How's the leg?"

"Gimpy. That's for keeps. I get around, though. Lucky to have the leg, I guess, and after Belchite the job's a soft option." The Americans had stormed that town brilliantly a year ago and left half their number dead among the ruins. Gamble had been hit badly.

"George, what do you think about this?"

"I don't. Did you ever think, Hank? In your war?"

"Not that way."

"We're at full ration strength, that's all I can say. The British and the Lincolns are up to six hundred and fifty each. Take some feeding —. I'll tell you this, though, Hank. The Brigade ain't what it was. We've lost the cream. Too many battles, I guess."

"You've plenty of good fellows yet."

"Hey, you bet! But you should see what we've been made up with. What are we gonna do? I mean, they've closed down all the rear echelons and sent the guys up. Some of them are cripples. And guys from the hospitals. They've sent the goddam jailbirds back. And some of them are pretty mean, I can tell you. Not to mention the Spanish recruits. Have you seen 'em?"

"Yes, I've seen them."

"All they can do is cry for mama. By God," Gamble said, "We're in Lister's corps. You know what that means. Merry hell to pay. And with goddam babies to nurse."

"I guess you'll make out."

"We'll make out like always. Another fuck-up. Trust the IB for that. But we'll go, like a lot of damn fools."

Henry listened to the distant small-arms fire. He said, "How are you off for cigarettes?"

"I'm in supply, my friend. We even sent some up to the battalions. The last they'll get for a while. Hey, you're wanted."

Big Peter was beckoning. Henry wished Gamble good luck and went down into the *barranco*. The group was dispersing. Officers, some of whom he knew and who greeted him, went past him to their companies. Peter remained with the battalion commander, and Dunbar, the Brigade chief of staff. Henry shook hands with both of these. He gestured to the north, where the noise was now continuous and overlaid with detonations. "That is a crossing, isn't it?"

"Tagueña, on the left flank." Dunbar was a slender and dandyish young man. "Let's have a teeny look." He unfolded a map. Wild, the commander, snapped on a torch, shielding it with his free hand. The map was ragged at one edge where it had been ripped out of a guidebook. Natural features and military symbols had been finely drawn and hatched in by specialists in the battalion. They had no printed military maps. "The river makes a big curve." He made a span with a thumb and forefinger. "This is the sector of attack. We are in the centre. They've given the main objective to Lister." He put a fingertip to the map.

Henry said, "Gandesa."

Wild was a small gypsyish man with slicked black hair showing from under a beret. He spoke, with a Lancashire accent. "Bloody Gandesa."

"I know," Henry said. "I was there in April." The Brigade had been all but wiped out. Wild had broken out of an encirclement with a remnant of the British.

"It's the key," Dunbar said. "It sits on four roads."

Wild switched off the torch but Henry had already studied the map. He said, "Of course, there's the Pandols."

Dunbar said, "Goodness, yes. There is the Pandols."

They all knew the Pandols. It was a sierra, a mountain range about six miles long rising abruptly out of the plain. It was no more than four thousand feet at its highest but it climbed out of green flanks to precipitous slopes of bare rock, sheer walls, towering bluffs and jagged peaks; and it was fissured by many ravines.

"It dominates your line of advance," Henry said.

Dunbar spoke cheerfully. "Slap bang alongside."

"Like a bloody battleship." Wild was an old Royal Navy man. "And bloody fifteen miles to go, nigh on. We could smash through in a bloody hour if we were on trucks. but we 'aven't got 'em."

"Then we shall have to do it without," Dunbar said. He looked at his wristwatch. "I shall be going over with Brigade HQ. Must be off. See you over there."

25 July. Four a.m. Pewter daylight. Henry stood on a small rise above the river bank. The ground fell away to a narrow beach upon which the wide Ebro lapped, stained dark towards its edges with disturbed sand, green and glistening as briny olives as it deepened, with a surface of whirlpool swirls and running eddies. The slope before him was like an anthill. Men swarmed, manhandling pontoons off the backs of big trucks and dragging them to the water's edge. Others pushed them out into the water to other men who pulled them on towropes to extend a bridge upon which clusters of sappers toiled. The British were going across in dozens of small boats, eight men to a boat, more and more men coming down to the beach in files from the mouth of the *barranco*. At Henry's back, among the ruined yellow houses of Mora, tanks waited and truck convoys and guns. Looking round, Henry saw the raised snouts of anti-aircraft guns in place around the bridgehead. Over all was the noise; shouts and clangour from the bridge-builders, the grinding of truck engines, the gunfire now incessant and louder, from both north and south, and in the sky the beat-beat-beat of aero-engines.

There were outbreaks of small-arms fire on the far bank. Grenades coughed. Henry saw handfuls of little figures scattering up the bank and coming together in larger groups. Himself experienced, he judged it to be an efficient battalion deployment against only local opposition.

The noise in the sky was growing louder. Deeper and discordant notes quarrelled with the even beat of the Republican air patrols. All at once a column of water, crystal and foam, lifted up in the middle of the river and then four more, running like an arpeggio across the path of several little boats and then subsiding. Another salvo dropped upstream. The swarm of toil on the bridge did not slacken. The ground shook as sticks of bombs burst along the shore in a shaking of thundersheets. The British appeared and disappeared behind drifts of black smoke, running the little boats into the water, rowing across, another line of boats dotting the water on its way back for new loads. Anti-aircraft guns were banging. Overhead a tumult of combat had broken out. Looking up into a pale blue infinity gilded by the rising sun, Henry could see a whirl of shining insects. He heard machine-guns. One insect fell away and dropped plumb, leaving against the sky a line of woolly black smoke that turned to charcoal. A group of midges separated out of the swarm and went away, pursued.

Peter came back from the beach and said, "That's that."

On the far bank Peter and Henry saw a smoke-devil spring up among the scatter of little figures. The sounds of the burst and of a distant gun came almost together, and occurred again and again and once more. The shell smoke dissipated. Apparently untouched, the battalion was forming up, in column of threes. That was for speed. Henry had heard Wild give the order. Two little flags went up at the front. The column began to move, spreading a little. The battalion bobbed away, a little procession, seeming at this distance forlorn. It moved among trees and broken houses. Harmless as a seeing-off salute, a few shells burst wide, their thinning smoke left behind. Henry could only see the tail of the column now; then it went out of sight.

From his elevation he could see beyond the foreground to a wide plain dotted with vegetation and, rising against the sky behind that, a long, low, blue hump, the Pandols.

Peter said, "We'd better be going," and they started off to look for the car.

Chapter 5

Whichever way Frank looked he saw uniforms and upturned faces, as far as the high enclosing walls in which rows of windows were filled with more faces. His own voice bounced back at him, overlapping itself in the boom of amplifiers. Here he was, standing on the bonnet of an armoured car (precariously: it sloped, and he had to hook one arm round the gun-barrel, clutching a microphone with the other). But like Lenin in Petrograd. "Soldiers of the Republic —!" The other speakers clustered round the car, looking up at him. "— From all the youth of my country I bring you brotherly greetings. On behalf of the youth of Great Britain I pledge our total support to the end, to victory! Forward to victory!"

He was panting, battered by sunglare, sweating into his uniform. He listened to the shouts from the JSU comrades among the packed recruits, and from the NCOs in front, all round him, shouting *vivas* for the fraternal youth of England. Like echoes a scatter of *vivas* floated back. He had seen the recruits in clusters at the barrack gates with their weeping families, or wandering, childlike and dazed, in search of the reception hall. Pilar, a girl leader of the JSU, clambered up on to the car and took the microphone from him. She was slim, vivid, with shining raven hair. Ardent, feminine, in a filmy white blouse with red polka dots and a red skirt small at the waist, she cried, "*Adelante a la victoria! Viva! Viva!*"

More of the recruits shouted with their cheer-leaders, "*Viva! Viva!*"

Pilar's high, clear voice, through the amplifiers, "*Viva la Republica!*"

The answer surged back, "*Viva! Viva!*"

Pilar, Frank, the youth leaders and the fraternal delegates round the armoured car joined in. It was a roar, "*Viva! Viva! Viva!*"

The roar, the rhythmic beat, worked like adrenalin in his blood and filled him, still, with exhilaration when he walked away from the Pedrera barracks at midday. He felt as if he had entered into a new lifetime. Forty-eight hours ago (but how remote it was!) he had paused from his typing to listen to the loudspeakers in the streets, unable to make out what they were saying but hearing the unmistakeable voice of exultation. In moments the entire building became astir with noise. Footsteps banged in a rush down the stairs, the door flew open, Colleen burst in, crying out, "They're over!" He stood up in time to catch her in his arms. He held her close while she kissed him wetly, on cheek and cheek and cheek and cheek and then on his mouth, breathing hard, sobbing, muttering, and hugging him so tightly that he tightened his own embrace as if to crack bones. Their bodies pressed together soft and hard and blazing. The most erotic moment of his life. They hugged and hugged, until she broke away and he heard her running from room to room, crying out and no doubt kissing. He hoped for much from her but he did not see her on the Ramblas that night. Perhaps she had found a general. But he sat with Emmy, who treated him once more as a casual acquaintance, and Henry, back from the front, too tired to talk much. The crowds around them seemed no more animated than usual, but he and Henry sat in a state of quiet joy, Emmy making imitative noises. They drank four bottles of wine. Frank went to bed drunk.

From building to building across the streets through which he walked, new streamers hung, proclaiming FORWARD TO VICTORY. Hundreds of great posters shining fresh with paste looked down from the walls, of mighty, sculptured soldiers who beckoned with upraised rifles. The city was speckled with the bright colours of flags. He was sunstruck, tired, hoarse and glorified. In two days he had spoken at four factories, three schools, a street market, an orphanage and the Pedrera barracks. This afternoon he was to speak at the port and at the Voroshilov barracks. He had a favourite restaurant in the Barrio Chino, handy to both. Two sardines from a tin with a piece of grey bread, a plate of beans, a bunch of grapes and a glass of acidy red wine were fiesta fare. Bliss was it indeed to be alive.

He thought of the army's commanders: Lister, a quarryman; Modesto, a woodcutter; Tagueña, a student. They had sprung up from the crowd like dragon seed, dragon seed the thousands of communists who were officers, commissars, first to advance, last to retreat. He was of their order. He had been taught such things, invested with such knowledge that he could answer any question and perform any task. Lenin had said that every cook would learn to govern. To Frank, "we alone" knew the limitless potentialities of every human being. "We alone" had a limitless belief in Man. (Therefore "we" must be prepared to drive other people beyond all known limits, as well as ourselves.) He knew that history *must* lead to the wonderful classless age. He knew why. It was the dialectic. He was in the company of the most noble people on earth, revered leaders like Peter, girls with brave, beautiful faces like Pilar. He must prove himself no matter what ordeal awaited him. He must show himself to be brave and good and noble like them. "Noble" was a word much in his mind. That Emmy was a cool one. He wondered how many men she slept with, then looked through as if she hardly knew them. He had his speech pretty well off by heart now, for this afternoon. It seemed to go down well. He must study more. One must never cease to study theory, to equip one's self. Even the leaders still studied theory. Ooh, that Colleen! She was a tease. She had a lovely body. At the defence of Petrograd against the Whites even the wounded had gone back to the firing line. A man whose legs had been amputated crawled back because he could at least pull a trigger. Frank had seen the film. He wondered if he would be capable of doing that. The women would look at him when he came home sunburned from Spain. He wouldn't say much. He would let them imagine. To belong to a Party that *required* one to be splendid. Wasn't it wonderful? Walking down to the port, admiring his military reflection in shop windows, he heard inwardly the sound of his own voice through amplifiers and dreamed of fair women.

Boys and girls in uniform ran in front of him selling newspapers, their voices a gulls' clamour crying the headlines.

GANDESA FALLS
OUR VALIANT COMBATANTS ENTER GANDESA

*

Frank walked into the office next morning to see a stranger with Peter, sitting at the side of his table. Peter broke off from a conversation to look across at Frank and say, "This is the comrade."

Frank lingered for a step under the man's scrutiny and said, "Hallo," but the stranger had already turned back to Peter, saying something in a deep voice.

Two letters lay on Frank's table next to his typewriter. Puzzled at what had just happened, and a little apprehensive, he picked them up. Within the warm flow of Party life there were icy little currents of secrecy, matters not explained, that might unsettle; as now. The letters were from England. He opened and read them one by one, while he strained to listen to the mutter of talk behind him. Peter called, "Frank, give us a moment, will you?"

Frank went and waited, expectant, across the table from the stranger. Peter told him to get a chair and he did so. The newcomer was of, perhaps, the same height as Peter but he looked taller because he sat upright. The breadth of his shoulders was emphasized by his posture and by the square cut of his suit, which was a cheap-looking affair in electric blue with a chalk-stripe, the kind of suit worn for best by a lot of Spanish workmen. A workman, too, would have worn the, coarse looking white shirt striped with black, with a narrow, thick attached collar, set off by a flaring red tie. He did not, however, look like a workman. He said, "Peter has been telling me about you. He tells me you are an experienced comrade, although you are young."

Frank could not think of anything to say. The man said, "Let me see your *carnet militar*, please."

Frank handed over his army service book. The man flipped it open and studied it, frowning. He had close, grey hair and a large face that reminded Frank of an oblong stone slab, with bushy eyebrows, a jutting nose and severe lips. Its strong outline was broken in the right jaw, where there was a long, puckered indentation in various shades of purple, red and yellow. He spoke a little throatily, his English without fault but excessively precise in accent. "Tell me about your personal connections."

Frank could only echo, "Connections?"

"You have a wife? A woman?"

"No."

"Family?"

"None. There was only my mother." He fished into a pocket of his tunic and pulled out the letters. "I've only just heard. She's died in hospital."

Peter said, "I'm sorry, Frank. if I'd known in time I'd have sent you home."

Frank said, "She was ill for a long time. I wouldn't have gone." He waited for more questions.

The man stood up. This made him bigger and more imposing than ever. A pillar of authority, in a suit that looked more ill-fitting than ever, the trousers too short. As if he had climbed into it on the off chance. He gave Frank a brief but not unamiable smile. "Thank you, comrade —." and to Peter, "Peter, you must come and see us."

Peter said, "Give my love to Marta."

The door closed behind the stranger. Frank lingered at Peter's table, full of vague worries. He knew not to ask who people were. At home, all sorts of strange persons, patently from foreign parts, turned up, sometimes to appear unexpectedly at subsequent meetings. But he could not help it. "Who was that?"

Peter had already applied himself to some papers. Without looking up, he said, "Ah, you know these fellers."

"What's up? I mean —. Have I done something?"

Peter grunted with laughter. "Don't be daft, son. Don't worry yourself. These fellers come round."

Frank said, "Oh —. Yes."

He went back to his table. He was puzzled and still alarmed. He had heard words of reassurance addressed to others and he was not to be put off by them. He had felt himself brushed by — was it suspicion? What could he have done wrong? What nonsense! He thought of the title of a Russian book he had read, about a Komsomol, a Young Communist like himself, who had become a national hero: *How The Steel Is Tempered*. No sentiment. No softness. He took the two letters out of his pocket again. One of them, from a woman neighbour, accused him of deserting his dying mother. He was one of the people of a new type. The true, tempered steel. He tore up both letters.

*

At the Majestic that evening he had just sat down to dinner when a cherub in page-boy's uniform came and told him that he was wanted in the lobby. Peter, who was waiting there, said, "I've been called away. You'll have to run things. I've left some notes."

Peter wore a black leather zip-jacket with a woollen scarf hanging loose round the collar. A full knapsack hung by a long sling from his right shoulder. Frank saw the army car waiting outside. He said, "How long will you be gone?"

"I don't know. I'm going down to the battalion."

"In Gandesa?"

"Uh? — Na, na. Not there."

Unease stirred in Frank. "We have got Gandesa?"

Peter gave a little, blind shake of his head. "Na, na. No, no. Not yet. I must be going."

Frank watched him go, and stayed where he was until the car had gone.

Chapter 6

Henry sat under the long, gnarled branches of an olive tree on a grassy mountain slope. In a clear blue sky the sun, a blinding radiance directly overhead, poured heat down like burning liquid on his bare head and his shoulders. At a distance around him rose rock walls and sharp outlines of ridge and peak, dramatic, picturesque. Unpicturesque was the nearer scene and he sat in no peaceful silence.

Guns thumped. Shells crashed. From beyond a concealing skyline came continuous crepitations of rifle and machine-gun fire. From time to time there was a rushing in the air or a tight screech and a detonation shook the hillside, amid smoke and an eruption of earth from which rock splinters spattered. Stray bullets cracked close by or twittered as if insects were disturbing the air. Drifts of smoke left a chemical tang, a relief from a prevailing taint of sweetness that the nostrils could not ignore. Other inhabitants of this slope sat under scattered olive trees or lay in the shelter of terraces; a reserve company of the Lincolns.

The men sitting against the tree-trunks, each alone, might have been resting in a park. Each sat hunched, thoughtful, his rifle against the tree beside him or lying in his arms. None seemed to regard the noise or notice the stretcher-bearers who kept appearing over the forward ridge to lope with their burdens from one doubtfully-sheltering tre: to the next. High, high up in the heavens, the soft roar of engines never ceased, a soporific.

Henry climbed to his feet and went up the slope. When he was near the top he lowered himself and crawled, and stopped just below the ridge. He took his field-glasses from their slung case and eased himself forward.

He saw another ridge in the distance. It was hard to estimate how far it was, across the dip and rise; perhaps a half a mile for a bullet, two or three times that for the men dotted about the downward slope, widely scattered, and toiling up the steep ascent beyond. He could see no human movement on the far ridge. The only discernible activity was that of the attackers among whom shells burst randomly and incessantly. Many little heaps lay still. Climbers dropped from the ascending slope. That was small-arms fire. Some of the little heaps squirmed. He heard faint screams. He noticed a spurt of earth a yard to his left. Interested, he waited. Another bullet struck further off. He looked through his glasses to the right and fancied that he saw a twitch of movement on a high ledge. Enfilade fire. He wriggled downhill until he was able to stand up in (at least, to that particular sniper) dead ground and scuttle back to his tree.

He heard shouts. Officers made arm signals. The idlers under the trees, tired after a doze in the park, got up and ambled forward. Men trudged up from the terraces. Down the hill Henry saw lines of other men coming up, another company moving into reserve.

By now he was resigned to the expectation that the attack would fail. So might the soldiers be. Scattered, they went over the ridge and out of sight. The noise continued. This had been going on for three days. After a rapid advance the brigade had turned off into the mountains and climbed fifteen hundred feet to deal with a last obstacle before Gandesa, a height (fortified, they knew now) called, from its altitude in metres, Hill 481.

Henry, when young, had been through worse than this and so looked on death without emotion. The feeling that stirred in him now was of simple affection for his fellow-countrymen. They were always as he saw them today: casual, deliberate, thoughtful, even under stress; resourceful, tolerant and, in whatever danger, ironically humorous. Drawn to England since his boyhood — he had fought for England and married an English wife — he felt himself to be more of an American every time he came to the Lincolns.

Little clusters like gleaming grains crawled across the ceiling of the sky, remote, mercifully unable, one hopefully imagined, to notice this one spot among the tiny, walnut corrugations of the earth. As regular as a bus service the bombers went to and from their attacks on the Ebro crossings, all day long, the thump and crump of each raid audible among the other noises of war.

Henry moved again, this time working along to his right in the shelter of a terrace. He reached a tumble of rocks which heaved up through the thin soil, grey and pitted. He crouched in the lee of a boulder to peer down at the plain. There it was, almost below him. An American rifleman had said to him, you could piss on it, bud. That huddle of whitish ruins was Gandesa.

Lister's Spanish troops had broken into it on the first night. They had fought in the cemetery with enemies as furious as themselves and had been wiped out. For two more days and nights the terrible Lister had thrown in attacks but his men had been driven back. Now the town sheltered batteries that fired at close range at the Republicans on the

Pandols. Every day the number of guns in the surrounding countryside increased. Convoys and columns moved towards Gandesa on its converging roads. They had nothing to fear from the air. The Republican air force was almost spent.

Henry went to the far side of the slope, where the mountain was cleft by a deep ravine. As he approached it the sickly smell of dead became stronger. Against the noise of the gunfire he could hear a faint mooing and bleating as of cattle. He looked down. Corruption thrust a finger down his throat. Trees sprang thickly from the steep walls of the ravine and thick among the branches hung what might have been bundles of laundry hung out to dry, but for the black faces and the claws protruding from sleeves. A continuous blasting of explosions was loud between the walls of the *barranco*, the floor of which was almost hidden by upwreathings of smoke in which fires blinked. He searched with his glasses as patches of the valley floor appeared and vanished. Among scattered bodies a pond glittered like a fragment of mirror. Some of the little shapes moved in spasms toward the pond, from all sides. In the lens he picked out arms extended, reaching for water. Moans and cries filtered up to him. Gagging quietly, he contemplated this ultimate spectacle. Men went to war as to a bridal. The consummation was a different matter.

He backed away until he could stand up. He started towards his tree. Two men were going down the hill in front of him with a humped stretcher between them. Hot air and a detonation knocked him flat face down. He lay for a moment in a sulphuric reek. He raised his head and saw grass glow and shrivel. He beat at his clothes in places that scorched and, so moving, concluded that he was unhurt. He tottered to his feet. Not more than two paces behind him was a four-foot crater burned to the colour of new rust and still smouldering around the edges. A weak but clear voice called to him. He turned. The two stretcher-bearers were flung apart, both dead, unpleasantly ripped. The poles of the stretcher lay crossed on a heap of torn red cloth. But the wounded man was trying to raise himself on his hands. His face and shirt were sooty and his trouser legs were cut open from the knees down to show bandages stained brown. He said, "Give us a hand, will you?"

Henry's senses were coming back to him. He stooped and pushed his hands under the man. He said, "This'll hurt."

The man gave a great yell as Henry hoisted him and dumped him over a shoulder. Henry staggered down the hill. He was unsteady under the weight, having to bump down from one terrace to the next. His head down, he had a dream impression of men flitting past him up the hill, none taking notice of him. At last a gentle lower slope went down in front of him. At its foot he saw the road, two trucks waiting. His car was parked lower down. Men streamed uphill. Others sprawled on the ground in groups. Officers clustered round an unfolded card table on which a map was spread. Walking wounded supported one another as they came down. They were making for a roofless adobe cabin. The aid post; stretchers dried against the walls. He lurched that way. Two men came from it and took his burden from him. Once more on a stretcher, the wounded man put out a hand. He said, "Hey, thanks."

Henry shook the hand and said, "Good luck."

He had been noticed by someone among the officers. Faces turned his way. One of the officers came to meet him. Henry knew the man, an observer-officer from Brigade headquarters, a lieutenant named Kulich. Henry extended a hand again. "Joe —."

Kulich's face was set. He said, "What are you doing here?"

Taken aback, still grinning, Henry said, "Looking around, I guess."

"They tell me no-one knew you were here."

"I saw the wounded coming down. I didn't want to miss out. I went right on up."

"Without permission."

Henry said, "They know me here, Joe. Do I have to stand on ceremony?"

"The rule is, you stay with the command post."

"Right. But just this once, I thought —."

"That's the rule. You know the rules."

A deafening bass snarl enveloped them. Men were shouting, dropping to the ground. A line of earth spurts to a man's height stitched between them and a shadow swept overhead. They turned to watch cannon-shells explode until the 'plane lifted and climbed away over a crest. It did not turn to make another pass at them. Henry said, "I'm sorry. Try to see my point of view. These are American boys. I want to tell people back home —"

"What you tell is for us to decide."

"God damn it, I give everything to the censor. He decides."

"I'm not talking about newspapers. I'm talking about people snooping around during military operations. Spies, maybe."

"What are you talking about? I'm not a spy."

"Maybe. But unlikelier ones than you have turned out to be spies."

"Yes," Henry said, "like all those leaders of the Russian Revolution, you mean?"

Kulich's face screwed up red and furious like a baby's. He shouted, "That's enough."

"I'll talk to Milt." Milt was the battalion commander.

"No you won't. This is my responsibility."

"In a battalion area?"

"Anywhere in this brigade. Vigilance, you know what that means? That's my job. Now get out of here."

"Just cool down. Listen —."

"Out, or I'll have you arrested."

"You're crazy."

"For the last time."

Henry stared at Kulich for another moment, then turned to go down to the road. The wave of a hand arrested him. It was the commander, Milt. Henry fancied that the young man's smile was apologetic. He waved back and started down. Kulich went back to the group.

Soldiers were leading three mules up from the road. Gamble trudged behind them. As the mules passed, Henry looked into the drums that were slung one on each side of each animal. Water slopped from three of the drums. In two of the others were heaped food cans, and one was full of loaves. Gamble paused, grinning. He said, "I saw that. You'd better get going, old pal. That crazy guy is the law around here." He lowered an eyelid. "Know what I mean? Your driver's in the cookhouse." He went on his way.

Chapter 7

Frank had just returned to the office after a midday ham roll and coffee with Colleen when Peter came in. He looked freshly bathed but tired, in his town clothes, the tweed jacket and baggy flannels. Frank said, "When did you get back?"

Peter went to his table and took a sheaf of papers from under a book. Frank said, "It's all there. I've seen to everything."

Peter remained standing, flicking sheets over for a glance at each. Frank tried again. "What was it like down there?"

Peter had a reflective, watery gaze when he was displeased. "Has Heriot been in yet?

Heriot was in charge of reinforcements for the battalion. Frank said, "No." Unease made him stupid. "Were you expecting him?"

"What do you think?" This was almost a snarl. Then, matter-of-factly, "Ring him. Tell him to get his skates on."

"Has there been a battle?"

"Ay."

"Were you there?"

"Ay —. Listen." Peter drew folded papers from his inner pocket and tendered them. "Take this upstairs. They can start notifying the next of kin."

Frank unfolded the sheets. On each of them names were scrawled from top to bottom in pencil, in a slanting, childish script. Frank said, "I can't read some of this."

Peter spoke irritably. "Then bloody well ask me, and type it out. I can't guarantee my handwriting under shellfire."

"There's a lot here."

"There'll be a damn sight more —. Get on with it then."

Looking at the list for names he knew, Frank said, "It was pretty bad."

"Ay." Peter sat down. "Be quiet now. I'm busy. I haven't slept. I had a job getting back. The bridges were bombed."

"How did you get across?"

"I bloody swam." This was malevolent and final.

Frank rang Heriot, then took the list up to Colleen. when he returned Peter was gone. A note was stuck under the carriage of Frank's typewriter. *Meet me Colón. Canteen. 7 p.m.*

The Party headquarters seethed with activity on every floor when Frank arrived just before seven o'clock but the canteen was still quiet. The Spanish did not eat until later in the evening. Peter sat at a table with Heriot. Frank sat down and said, "Hello, Angus."

Angus Heriot was a lieutenant at the International Brigade base at Montblanch, thirty miles south of Barcelona. He had been wounded in an early battle and hobbled with a walking-stick. It was said that he had lost a couple of yards of gut and could not go far from a latrine. He nodded to Frank and continued, to Peter, "I reckon I can raise forty. Then there'll be convalescents."

"There'll be a draft out from England."

Heriot stood up. "Well, then —. It could be worse."

"Ay. Stay and eat something."

"No, thanks. I've had my bread and milk. *Salud*."

Frank said, "— *y pesetas*."

Peter said, "Ay."

Heriot left. Peter and Frank went for bowls of mutton stew. When they were seated once more, Peter said, "Well, you're to go there."

"To the battalion?"

"Ay."

"Yes," Frank said. "It sounds as if they need people."

"You'll have to stay here for a few days while I'm busy. Then you can report to Montblanch."

"I'm very glad."

"I know you are —. Frank, listen. You'll have to get rid of that rigout."

Frank could not help fingering a button of his tunic. "I realise I'll have to start at the bottom."

"Ay. You don't want the fellers to see you looking like that. You'd be their first good laugh in weeks." Frank's hurt look produced one of Peter's disarming grins, open mouth, tombstone teeth. "You know, they have a song in the IB, about the Barcelona Hussars."

"Right —. Sure. I expect I shall do political work there once I've settled down."

"I expect you will. I know you'll do a good job."

Elation and a full bladder were first among Frank's muddle of reactions. There was also resolve, the response he knew to be proper for a communist when setbacks had to be dealt with, and a general notion of himself being noble. Not so noble was a simultaneous decision to present himself tonight to Colleen, an undismissable candidate for bed. He said, "I'll be on my way."

But Peter said, "Na, na. I want you here. I've got a meeting with the leadership. You can stay and translate."

Frank was dashed only for a tenth of an instant. Admitted to an important meeting. Peter's right-hand man. A cadre. Tomorrow's leading comrade. Hallelujah.

*

Henry Croft wrote, *August 3,*

> Hill 481 was not taken. 15th Brigade pulled out. Heavy losses. (Following from my notes.)
>
> *Aug. 1., 1.p.m.* Heat intense. Am on a rise above British command post. It is in open behind piled rocks. Only commander, two runners, telephonist. Rest of HQ with companies.
>
> These gone out to attack. Today an English Bank Holiday, traditional celebrations, fairgrounds. Men shouted jests to me, all the fun of the fair, this way for the merry-go-round, etc.
>
> This is 6th day. Men in a pitiable condition. Emaciated. In rags. Footwear cut to bits. (Almost barefoot over scorching terrain studded with sharp rocks.) Not slept for nights. In six days hardly any food or water. On July 30 they attacked six times with no water at all. (This was day one company lost five commanders.) Wounded lie out in sun all day. Brought in at night great danger, difficulty and can only be taken out on mules down precipitous trails. Thirst! I am reeling after four hours in the sun, pouring sweat, shirt sticking to back, lips cracked, tongue swollen. What must they feel like?
>
> Even back here shells come in every few seconds. Screech-bang all the time. Troops are getting it badly. Enemy firing airburst shrapnel over their heads. I can see black puffs and streamers. Ground littered with rubbish of war and rocks fragmented by explosive. Thick with rotting corpses. Loathsome stench everywhere.
>
> Attackers have to get up bare slopes that become almost sheer up to ridge jutting on its own steep slopes. Sunk in this ridge are concrete bunkers from which every approach is raked with fire. British call this hill The

Pimple because it is dwarfed by surrounding heights but it is a fortress and from surrounding heights snipers fire down and observers direct accurate continuous artillery fire. 'Planes come at all times to bomb and strafe. On reverse slopes enemy infantry well dug in. Against this Republicans attack with little more than rifles and grenades.

British have reached crest many times. Stand there and throw grenades till have no more. A few men lucky to get back. Spanish Listers took hill four times. Blown off each time. 13th Internationals made several tries in vain.

Odds hopeless but they still attack. British now on final slope. Seem stuck.

Aug 2. British kept it up for 12 hours. At 10 p.m. were reorganizing for another go when they were called out. Relieved by Listers. Night march (how?) to a "quiet" ravine. (Still in mortar and shell range.)

The mad British. Unbelievable British. l thought I knew them. These Communist Party puritans, earnest young fellows trying to act like Ironsides and all the old soldiers, the grumblers, grousers, leadswingers, skivers, connivers, barrack-room lawyers, Bardolphs and Ancient Pistols. Wild gathered them round him. Had what the British call a sing-song. Apparently Wild is a bit of a bar-room tenor. His commissar Cooney (a fine young Scot) added his voice, what a sight! and the tatterdemalions all round joined in. I wonder who in the distance heard them singing in the mountains. *Walter, Walter, Lead Me To The Altar.* Couldn't believe my ears. Wept.

What is it for? Has it become futile? Heartbreaking. They carry on. Seem to know why. I don't.

Chapter 8

Everything was going up at night, the driver told Frank. He threw the wheel over and they canted with a crash of springs into a crater and righted again as three trucks came out of the darkness and passed at high speed, empty, tail-boards rattling. From the back, amid a shifting and thumping of bodies, came curses in a strange tongue. Frank said, "Are the 'planes that bad?"

"For my money, the *camiones* is worse than the *aviones*," the driver said. "But we sure can't move by day. You look out for the wrecks."

"I've seen them," Frank said. A mile back there had been a line of them, burned out, pushed over on to the verge. It was after midnight. The smart uniform was gone. At Montblanch Heriot had given him an Army-issue shirt and trousers, a canvas knapsack with a long sling, run up out of two sandbags, into which he had put his few belongings, and a coarse brown blanket rolled tight and tied at the ends with string. Heriot had hung this round Frank's body like a bandolier and told him to hold on to it whatever happened, or he'd freeze at nights in the mountains. After a few days he had put Frank into the cabin of a truck taking a dozen men back to the 13th Brigade. They were Slavs, rough, sturdy men, among whom fierce moustaches seemed to be the thing.

Frank said, "Have you been at Montblanch long?"

"That lousy dump. I'd go back to the Lincolns any day only I don't figure on getting shot again. Did you see the place?"

"It looks pretty disorganized."

"You can say that again. I've been out here a year. I sailed out of Portland, Oregon. Deck hand. Jumped ship at Bordeaux. The IB was something in those days." They were driving south at a fair speed, in a stream of vehicles. "You were never at Albacete —? That was a real base. A real military establishment. Yes, sir, it was real good then."

The base had been hastily moved to Catalonia when the enemy advance had cut the Republic in two. The driver said, "It's just a fuckin' mob at Montblanch. Every nationality mixed up. They teach these guys to load and fire, and they show them a dummy grenade. Then it's a one-way ticket to the Ebro."

A lantern waved. They slowed down and were ordered off the road. They waited. No sound came from the back. The Slavs were asleep again. Then a troop convoy went by, truck after truck like the interminable wagons of a goods train, each truck packed with troops. These wore steel helmets. The driver said, "Looks like the Basques. I seen 'em goin' into the line once. With priests."

They were rolling again. Frank was wide-awake, taking in everything, replete with pleasure. Scenes imagined. Scenes from films. But happening, to him. Troop trucks going past in the night. Packed, silent men, glimpses of white stern faces, steel helmets, rifles. The driver broke into his reverie. "What's going to happen to the IBs?" and before Frank could answer. — "You hear anything in Barcelona?"

"Everyone's very proud of the IBs —."

"Ah, shit! About goin' home."

This startled Frank. "The IB's going home?"

"I heard they were going to send us home."

"Where? Where did you hear this?"

"Scuttlebutt. Maybe it's just latrine talk."

"It's not true." Frank was vehement. "It's crazy. We've only just begun to fight."

Frank caught a sidelong glance from the driver, who said, "Is that what you think?"

"I know, I know."

"Sure, are they slowing up again in front? Sure. Sure." He steered on to the verge and stopped. Soon another convoy went by.

In time the traffic slowed to a steady crawl. It was all stops and starts. The driver said, "This is it."

Frank could not see the river but when the truck stopped in the midst of a turmoil of waiting vehicles and hurrying men he once again felt that he was witnessing and memorising a scene to be remembered. As far as he could see the ground was pocked with craters and gouged by a dense pattern of tyre and tank tracks. Men stripped to the waist swung long shovels, working with what seemed a demonic haste to fill craters. Gangs went past carrying planks and timbers, skins shining, eyes gleaming, bowed under their loads, coming from darkness and disappearing into the throng, lines of infernal slaves.

In the back of the truck there was stirring, scraping, bumping, deep, alien voices. The Slavs were jumping down from the truck. With alarm he saw them move away and disappear among the mass of parked vehicles. Frank said, "Suppose we move?"

"Fuck them. I want to get my ass out of here. It ain't healthy."

Somewhere in front of them the crash and clamour of work went on. Frank's itch was mainly on account of the absent Slavs. Because he was a Party professional, albeit only an apprentice, he always felt that he would be held accountable for any failure to take charge.

A convoy of ambulances climbed the slope and came past, away from the Ebro. It seemed endless. For the first time Frank's imagination went chill. Since he was ten years old, when *All Quiet* came out, he had read every one of the torrent of war books, all the horrors retailed, and (one of a generation whose minds were saturated with that knowledge and whose attitudes were governed by it) he could picture a whole catalogue of terrible mutilations, truncations and agonies with which those ambulances were packed, so many of them. Which he would soon have to see himself, and might himself suffer. A last ambulance came by. The driver grunted, "About time."

Movement was audible in the line of vehicles ahead. At last the truck in front jerked forward a few yards and stopped. They followed. This happened several times until a stop prolonged itself and traffic came rolling off the bridge once more towards them. Empty trucks this time. One bridge was open. The other, bombed, swarmed with sappers. On each side was visible the gleam of the river. Frank grumbled, "Those bloody fools —." He gestured at the back of the truck. "Where the hell are they?"

"They ain't your worry. You worry about daylight. It ain't so bad here in the dark even if they bomb. I don't want to get caught over there in daylight. They come down to machine-gun. The bastards damn nearly put down on the road."

Movement again. A twenty-yard crawl toward the bridge. Whooping Slavs came out from among the parked vehicles, waving bottles, and stormed the truck in a cascade of thuds and crashes as it lurched on to the bridge.

They crept across on planks that sagged and twanged like a musical saw beneath them. To Frank's right men worked on the gapped bridge. The side of the truck overhung their own bridge and from his swaying seat Frank could only see green water swirling on his left. The far bank appeared. Men impelled the truck up the bank with strong arms, urging the driver to go with shouts that were answered by a great shout from the Slavs.

They were away, out of Mora. Behind, to the east, dawn lay a white strip upon the skyline. The driver accelerated. The wheels ate up empty road. All at once there broke out over the river a tumult of bangs, spreading reverberations and a bass throbbing of aircraft. Behind them flashes split the darkness. Flares shimmered down. Coloured lights hung and vanished in the sky. The glow of a fire leaped up and died down. The raid ended as instantly as it had begun. Frank recorded it with satisfaction. The raids in Barcelona had not worried him but this one, well, this one was a front-line experience.

And when those noises had ended, his ears picked up another. It was in front. A burst of thudding, silence, another, then a spell of it, distant but plosive upon the eardrums. The darkness thinned. Frank's eyes were open for new sights. A line of parked trucks. In them, soldiers slept. A file of men with rifles trudged at the roadside. Moving up. Across the fields he could make out a long black bulk couched against the sky. He knew what that was. He said to the driver, "The Pandols."

The driver said, "You watch it. You'll see something."

It turned blue, in a paler light. In a field by the road small trucks were parked this way and that; men moved about, shoving black, exciting, snouted shapes away from the trucks. Howitzers. Poles were being put up, camouflage netting hauled into place, pits dug, shells carried by human chains. There were more vehicles now, outracing one another to get off the road before sun-up. More soldiers straggled untidily at the verge. The expected, stimulating spectacle of war. The Pandols was turning violet. Then on one section of its summit nicked off by a notch at each end, a line of small flames sprang up and ran like a lit fuse along the skyline. (Did everything happen suddenly here?) Flames shot up from the bare rock as if a forest was burning. The driver gave an I-told-you-so grunt. A rumbling rolled from the Pandols across the plain. The sky, with a touch of sapphire in its pallor, was stained by an uprolling of smoke. On the mountain top explosions flashed among the flames. The driver said, "Listers up there."

The battering of gunfire seemed to shake the air in front of the mountain and the mountain itself. A multitude of specks rose up into the sky, to dart and whirl about the mountain. Distinctly against the din Frank heard the crying of birds. From the back of the truck, low, unexcited conversation continued.

The rumbling stopped. Much thinning smoke persisted, and a few little bonfires. Frank remained thoughtful. The Pandols came nearer. Its flanks were a patchwork of different greens and indigo clumps of forest, with ochre or orange earth visible where the covering was scanty. The mountain rose in buttresses and ramparts of diseased grey rock, bluffs of red sandstone, blue basalt wells, to toothy ridges and peaks. No life could be seen on it. The sun brightened the air now and gave warmth. The mountain was now only a few fields away. Lanes led to it, bordered by straggling, thin bushes. The truck slowed, to stop at one of the lanes. An empty packing-case was wedged into undergrowth at the corner. On two sides of the box was painted: 15. Above the idling engine sound Frank heard 'planes, but elsewhere. The driver said, "Haul your ass. I'm in a hurry. Good luck."

Frank got down. The 13th Brigade men shouted to him and waved. he waved back. The truck went out of sight. He was alone. The sound of guns had stopped. Birds sang. The sun shone.

He started along the lane. It was rutted by tyre tracks. His boots padded in the dust. The fields on each side of the lane were deserted. No soldiers, no peasants. Here and there, a solitary hut. Soon he was walking between knolls, then the ground rose on both sides of him and, less steeply the road rose, too, taking him into a cleft in the mountain. As it became steeper he walked between pine woods, the road now between earth banks. He went round a bend. There was a clearing ahead. The banks now were riddled with round holes like the mouths of a giant rabbit warren. *Chavolas.* He knew about them. Gaunt, unshaven faces looked out of some. In others men slept. Above, soldiers were coming down into the clearing, at a funeral pace, bowed under their slung rifles. Soldiers gathered in the clearing. Many others slept under trees. He called to a man who sat on the bank, "*Qué battallón?*"

"Who do you want?" The voice was American, the face was smudged, haggard, heavy-eyed, covered with stubble, and hostile.

Frank looked at the torn filthy uniform and the blackened toes sticking out of split espadrilles. He remembered his elegant Barcelona boots. "The British."

The American pointed at the road. Frank went on.

*

The goat trail was a pencil-line of worn ground wandering up steep slopes and climbing among boulders at angles which made the ascent not unlike that of a ladder. In the dark, Frank hauled himself up a staircase of blistery rocks upon which his feet kept slipping. Unbalanced by a rifle and pack, he grasped at branches with one hand, his other hand pulled back by the loop of a leather thong. At the other end of the straining thong was a mule. Six boxes of ammunition were slung in pairs over the mule's back. The mule did not appear to share Frank's difficulty in climbing with a load. The animal's hooves picked lightly among the rocks. Its ascent was positively dainty. Only when they came to an easier slope did the mule object. Its head went up, its stiff legs braced apart and it leaned backward. Frank had to throw his weight back on the halter, a tug-of-war contestant; until the mule without warning changed the game and ambled on, a picture of meekness, dragging Frank until he regained his feet and took the lead.

He had found the British a mile up the road from the Americans; at least, their cookhouse and stores, and a collection of headquarters wallahs. It had all been rather bewildering; not at all the reception he had imagined. He had, to one or another, announced himself or asked where to go. No-one had bothered to tell him much except to push off. In time he had got a rifle and a tin bowl from a man in the stores and, from the cooks, coffee, a hunk of bread and some salty anchovies. Frank had been able to learn only that the battalion was up the mountain.

He felt uncomfortable in his new clothes among a crowd of ragamuffins, as he had with the Americans. He looked in at the window-hole of a crumbling adobe cabin and saw someone more military: an officer seated at a table, in a tunic, breeches and top boots which showed no sign of front-line wear and tear. He went in and said, "I'm new —." And, meeting a blank look, "Brendan." He held out a letter. "This is from Big Peter."

The officer was tubby and rubicund, with a snub nose and carroty hair *en brosse*. He took the letter, read it and looked again at Frank, not returning the letter. He appeared to deliberate, then said, "You can go on up there, tonight."

His accent was foreign: not Latin, not German. Frank asked about him at the cookhouse. A cook said that the bloke was always around but was not one of "our lot." He was from Brigade they reckoned, armament officer or technical officer or something. Czech he was, or Hungarian, somewhere like that. He always stayed with the rear details when the battalion was in action. Frank was a trifle dismayed. He had looked forward to handing his letter to the commanding officer, to be welcomed with a handshake, a valued acquisition. He told himself that this fellow would certainly pass the letter on.

A huge man with the appearance and snarl of a Guards sergeant-major had come out of a cabin, told him not to stand there like a tit in a trance and put him to work digging a rubbish pit. Occasionally from up the mountain he heard a shell thud or small-arms fire racket, and other noises of war from farther off; to him, sinister, to those around him of no interest.

Supper had put some heart back into him: hot soup spiced with peppers and full of meat. He gathered from cookhouse talk that Hill 481 had been a bugger. The march back to the line after a rest had been a bugger. So was this hill. The battalion was having a bad time up there. It had been quiet today but most of the time it was a bugger. After supper he had helped to load up the mules. When it fell dark a ration party had set out carrying big drums of food, each with a whitewashed number on it, of the company to which it was bound. The two muleteers had followed. Since then, Frank had been climbing for four hours. He was tired to the bone, jarred, aching, sweating in cold air, chafed by the slings of rifle and pack, his legs going dead with the effort of not slipping on rocks. He was lost in darkness and time. He had no idea of how long he had yet to climb; he felt as if it would be forever. He heard the bump and clang of the food drums above him, and the voices of the fatigue men.

He had become used to the stifling smell of the mule and the acrid tang of its urine. Now another smell crept into the air. He came up on to a small plateau. The smell came intensely from some rocks on his right. He moved that way. He knew what was there and he had to see, although he gagged and pressed a hand to his face. Bodies were heaped behind the rocks, all in a pile of rags, limbs and black faces. He could not tell how many. He was fascinated. This was another moment expected since childhood; his first corpses. This moment, too, was to be recorded and remembered. The mule did not like the smell. It tugged, Frank tumbled and the mule trotted. He scrambled up, grabbed at the halter and went on.

*

There was a background of pale light in the gloom when Frank and his mule wandered into an ill-omened landscape of piled, black rocks, the gleam on their slippery surfaces warning of an adamantine hardness. Here, men were scattered, toiling at various occupations, most of them hacking at the ground with shovels in what appeared to be a despairing way, some already sprawling in pits of (if they were meant for protection) pathetic shallowness. A man growling about ammunition not sent up took the halter of Frank's mule.

A group of men were gathered under an overhanging ledge. Frank recognised the stocky commander; and in the past he had seen the commissar at Party conferences. He went across to them. All were preoccupied. The commander, Wild, talked angrily into the telephone and listened to equally angry sounds coming from it. Bandages could be seen behind his unbuttoned shirt collar. Three men around the commissar were in some way expostulating and he was nodding, patiently but obviously waiting for a chance to speak. Cooney, the commissar, was an upstanding, sandy-haired man. He saw Frank hanging about. He called across, "Well?"

Frank began, "I've just come —."

The commissar said, "Not *now*," and turned back to his interlocutors.

Frank waited. A man strode in from the open. He held out, by its carrying handle, a light machine-gun with a big drum magazine. He said, "What silly fucker said this was usable?" He noticed Frank, and was no less aggressive. "What do you want?"

"I'm reporting for duty."

"All on your own?"

"Yes."

"Oh, Christ! Can you fire a rifle?"

"Yes."

"Thank God for smell mercies." Four men were piling rocks to make a wall round the command post. The man said to one of them, "Take him to Paddy. They've got fuck-all down there."

Frank followed the soldier. Shovels clinked on rock. Men passed to and fro. On a rise of ground big machine-guns peeped out of loopholed parapets. Men were hacking out an emplacement for a mortar. The air was rank. A far slope was thickly littered with bodies. The guide said, "You just out?"

It was simplest to say, "Yes."

"More fool you." The guide lifted his head and sang out, "Paddy!"

They were going down into a dip in which men, perhaps thirty of them, were digging in. Frank and his guide went towards two men at the end of the line, one standing with a shovel, his foot on the blade, the other sitting by the beginnings of a hole scribbling in a notebook. The guide said to the man with the shovel, "Present for you, Pad," and went off to talk to someone.

There was at least friendliness in Paddy's Irish smile. "Just come up?"

"Yes."

"Glad to have you with us. We could do with some help." Paddy pointed to a pile of shovels. "You'd better dig yourself a hole."

The seated man looked up. "What's your name?"

"Brendan. With an a-n."

"I've got it. You'd better get stuck in. 'Planes'll be over any minute."

Frank found an empty space and set to. Nobody showed any interest in him. It was only later, in one offhand exchange or another, that he learned which company he was in, and that the commander was named O'Hagan, the commissar, Haxey.

*

Men (except for an unfortunate few) acquire a basic education in war quite quickly. Frank spent nine days in this lofty wilderness, during which he underwent daily barrages of shellfire, was bombed and machine-gunned many times from the air, helped to stand off mass attacks by fanatical Navarrese troops in bright red berets, and took part in a strange attack in which he did no more than run up a hill, lie under a wall, out of breath, for what seemed a long time, and run down again, without seeing the enemy or any sign of their presence but noticing on the way down a lot of his company dead or being taken away wounded. He became unheeding of the day's heat, the night's cold, of thirst, hunger, lice, dirt, his own smell, that of other men, and the battlefield smell of dead bodies, fresh blood, old iron and chemicals. To live under the sky like an animal and sleep on bare rock rolled in one blanket became the natural way, an earlier life remote. He knew not to think about the men laid open or with parts missing, living or dead. His boots had gone. He wore a pair of rope-soled *alpargatas* that he had taken from a body after a search for feet of the right size. His clothes were filthy and torn. There was a brown bloodstain on his shirt like a map of Australia. He was unshaven and had sores on his cheeks and forearms where the flies had settled on cuts. For three days the risks and exertions of battle had been complicated by frequent, violent diarrhoea; and since, his insides had been baked with constipation. As to the danger, he had been stunned and terrified by heavy bombardment but kept his wits about him and now, coming out, he felt bodily relief as if tightened violin strings throughout his body were being slackened on their pegs. These things apart, he had not found fear to be a problem. What, indeed, had surprised him was the equanimity with which his comrades (for all the fierce grumbling with which they relieved themselves) bore it all. At every lull they talked about ordinary things and life became very ordinary. A sort of open-air domesticity took over. None of them, even those whom he had identified as political men, seemed to care where they were, what they were doing or how the battle (let alone the war) was going. Grumbling, they let themselves be moved to and fro about the mountain like street cleaners shifted from one task to another and wondering only when their working time would end. It was clear to him that they had not been attacking on that mountain but defending it against an enemy advance. Was the offensive over, then, so soon?

He had become like the others, He could not pretend to care, yet. The good side of the balance sheet was that they had come out. The bad side was that they would have to go back. He still had his faith, oh, yes, but it was at the bottom of his baggage. His only concerns for the moment were to sleep, eat, drink, feel cold water upon his skin, shave, shit, find out what day it was, set his watch right, get mercurochrome for his sores and a needle and thread for his clothes.

Chapter 9

There was a soft tap at the door of Henry Croft's room. After a moment's silence there were two more quick taps and two again. No-one was in the room. The door moved open. A man entered the room. He wore a blue *mono*, workman's overalls, and carried a leather tool-bag. He closed the door silently and spent a few moments looking around him as if making an assessment.

He was fortyish, bald with a black tonsure, a face brown and pockmarked with walrus folds, made genial by a walrus moustache. A decision made, he went through the bedroom, put his head into the bathroom, turned to look over the bedroom then set to work.

He started on the beds, feeling under the mattresses, leaving the beds immaculately made. He went to the chest of drawers, opening and closing drawers and flipping through their contents. He opened the wardrobe doors, went through the pockets of Croft's suits, saw Croft's briefcase and lifted it out. He tried the locks, put the case on a small table, opened his tool-bag and took out a small implement, a nest of blades. He selected one and snapped it out. He probed gently at a lock, moving the blade to and fro, annoyed when the blade scraped slightly against an edge.

The bedside telephone jangled. He went to it, listened, grunted an acknowledgement, returned to put the briefcase back in the wardrobe and shut the wardrobe doors. He went back to the drawing room and still had his hand on the door-knob when the outer door opened and Henry Croft came in.

Henry said, amiably, "Good day. What are you doing?"

The workman said, "The plumbing, *señor*."

"Why? There is nothing wrong with the plumbing."

"An inspection, *señor*. The fault is not here."

"Good. Cigarette?"

"*Muchas gracias, señor*."

The man went out. Henry looked around the drawing-room, opened drawers in the table and inspected them, went into the bedroom, considered, opened the wardrobe doors, glanced at the clothes, then stooped and lifted out his briefcase. He held it up, peering closely at it. He put it away, then, looking thoughtful, went into the bathroom to wash.

*

"The Republicans are holding on —. Are you getting me? It's a bad line." Henry sat in a telephone booth at the Press Bureau. It was soon after six. He spoke against a hubbub of typewriters, banging doors, shrilling 'phone bells and voices. He read from his typed story. "Quote. Republican machine-gunners emerge from dugouts after terrific bombardments to mow down advancing Nationalist troops."

Across a dusty floor littered with cigarette butts and all kinds of scrap paper, girls sat at tables, listening in to the calls through earphones, checking them from carbon copies, their hands ready over cut-off keys to silence any departure from the approved text. Boys hurried to and from them with censored dispatches. Henry resumed, "The Republicans are inflicting decisive casualties on the enemy. Their spirit is undimmed —. That's right, undimmed. I was informed today by an authoritative source that the offensive will be resumed when the enemy's force is spent. End. Unquote —, O.K? — Fine. How are things with you —? Listen, Saurier's on his way to Paris. Pack me some supplies, will you —? That's fine, and some cologne —. For my girl, idiot —. He'll pick them up from his office —. Thanks. *Chau!*"

He hung up. He saw Victoria standing behind one of the telephone girls, reading his dispatch. He went across. "Hallo. I'd like to talk to you. Will you be free later?"

"I'm having a drink with Buckley. I'm waiting for him now. Can I help you?"

"Maybe. Let me read you something." He took a slip of paper from his pocket. "Gallo. Commissar-General of the International Brigades. I quote. Concerning the so-called withdrawal of volunteers, all of us are anxious for the withdrawal of foreign troops from Spain, but the problem is far from being solved. Our task for the moment —." Henry looked up. "For the moment, note that —." He resumed. "— is the strengthening of our fighting capacity, the preparation to move into a new offensive and to deal a final blow at the fascists."

Victoria said, "Well?"

"Well, there's no smoke without fire, wouldn't you say? Here we are back in the land of official denials. *The so-called withdrawal. For the moment.* Have you any notion what's cooking?"

"No. I wouldn't say anything if I had, would I?"

"Negrin spoke to me about letting the Brigades go."

"I don't know anything about that."

"Is it a peace feeler?"

Her face went pinched with anger, "That's unforgiveable."

"I'm sorry, Victoria. I have to ask these questions."

"Why?"

"It's the job."

"I know about the job. But you haven't got much faith in us if you ask questions like that."

"You think so? You read my story."

"Yes. but do you believe what you write?"

"I don't see you resuming the offensive, Victoria. I was down at Mataró today, at the hospital. Yesterday I went to the big hospital at Vich. I've talked with a lot of the wounded. Things are pretty bad. You don't seem to have any air force left down there. Lister has told his men to stand or be shot as cowards. Tagueña says *vigilance, fortification, resistance.* You don't build fortifications if you're going to resume an offensive."

"We shall. The Ebro will be the Marne of peace."

"You can't win with slogans, Victoria."

She laughed. "Peace, Bread and Land. What did that slogan do? — I think Buckley has finished his call."

Henry spoke on an impulse. "Victoria, a minute —. I went into my room this afternoon. There was a fellow there —. I don't know, l had a feeling. This has happened to me a good many times. You know, I was expelled from Italy —. I had a look around. A lock on a briefcase of mine was scratched."

She laughed. "Henry!"

"I know. But is there someone around who doesn't like me? Could it be that I'm not trusted?"

"I think you're imagining things, Henry. But if anything like that does ever happen, remember, please, we have to be *vigilant.* There *are* enemies everywhere, believe me. We can't take any chances. But you've nothing to fear. Really, Henry. I must fly now." She stood on tiptoes, kissed Henry's cheek and turned away to meet the Englishman.

Chapter 10

The rest area was in a combe among the foothills. Its flanks were heavily overgrown with trees and bushes that screened the battalion's dugouts and shelters. When three 'planes dived along the combe whistles shrilled and the men dotted over the hillsides vanished into cover. Frank was bathing in a stream. He watched the 'planes come at him. It would have been futile to move, and dangerous. They streaked over and he heard bombs explode high up at the head of the combe.

It could have been worse. Carpet raids from a high altitude could strike like shell barrages. The new dive bombers were worst. They dropped like screaming black monsters on to their targets. All 'planes were enemy. Frank had only seen one brief appearance of Republican aircraft since he had come to the front.

He came out of the stream. Baked dry at once by the sun, he dressed. He had been given a new shirt and trousers. Amid a group of men nearby an accordion wheezed, played badly. A soldier came through the trees showing a hand that was like a red magnolia on the end of his right arm. He was shouting, "I'm hit! Thank God, I'm hit."

The accordion stopped for a few moments, then started again. Frank relaxed on the grass with *The Oxford Book of French Verse*. It was the only book he had brought, apart from a tiny volume bound in soft leather, which his Party mentor had given him: the new, 1936, Soviet Constitution. Frank liked to read of all the freedoms that were guaranteed by law to the Soviet people. At the moment he was reading Verlaine. Degenerate, maybe, but it was culture, and the sound of it in his head was lovely.

The accordion player was a Spanish boy, a company runner, one of the reinforcements, a waif of sixteen. Every time 'planes came over he bolted into a hole. The British soldiers were resigned to the probability that he would be no better in action, but they treated him like an adopted orphan.

Of different stuff were the battalion's Spanish company, volunteers from the JSU with a splendid commander who had been with the battalion from the beginning. The three other rifle companies, the machine-gunners and the mortarmen, were British, Even taking reinforcements into account, the battalion was only half the number that had crossed the Ebro. Frank's company had started out over a hundred strong. It now had thirty-six men.

A voice from the nearby group came to Frank, Welsh cadences and accent, a man named Morgan. "— pheasants, I ask you, boys! And a waiter bringin' round the wine! It's like the Ritz Hotel."

A Yorkshire voice, from a long, skinny, older man who was Morgan's mate. "Bloody officers!"

Morgan, "A bloody Officer's Mess! Like the bloody 'Ouse 'Old Cavalry! Fat of the land. And cold chickpeas for us. How is that right?"

The Yorkshireman, "It's a bloody disgrace."

A Londoner. This was Knibble, who came from Clerkenwell. a character from Dickens. Very tall, stooping, with a small hump. Eyes magnified by thick glasses with steel rims. Member of the Labour Party. "Your eyes are bigger than your belly, Taff. Hooky does wonders for us."

"Oh, yes," Morgan said, as Frank came over to them and squatted to listen. "Four-course dinners he gives us. Beans, beans, beans and beans."

The Yorkshireman, "Them chickpeas go through you like scouring pads."

"Hi, aye," Morgan said. "Heads down. Here comes the comic star."

Haxey, the commissar, was short with a small sharp-nosed face. He was a Party member, a former assembly-line man from the car works at Oxford. He held out a round tin of boiled sweets in wrappers. "Here, have some —. Take a few."

The tin went round. Morgan said, "What about some soap?"

"I'm trying, Taff."

"You were trying last week."

"I reckon I'll be trying next week. Anyway, you wouldn't know what to do with soap if you had it."

Morgan said, "Get away, you uneducated communist git."

Haxey went. Morgan said, "Bastard!"

Twentyman was middle-aged, with grey hair. He had a married daughter. A printer, a radical working man of no party. He said, "He's only doing his job."

"Get away!" Yorky said.

Frank took a folded pamphlet from his pocket. "Anyone want a read?"

Knibble said, I'll have it."

Frank said, "We don't seem to get much literature."

"I miss it," Twentyman said. "I like a good read."

Yorky said, "Never mind a good read. What about some soap? The bugger promised us soap."

A rough Scots voice. Burke. "Them and their promises! The feller who signed me on in Edinbrae promised me wine, women and loot. I've seen little of the first and fuck-all of the other two."

Frank said, "We ought at least to get the *Daily Worker*."

Morgan, "Get it, boy, get it. I'm fed up with wiping my arse on grass —. Come on, Yorky, get them cards out."

Frank left the group and overtook Haxey. He said, "That Morgan's a loudmouth."

"He's all right."

"All the same, I think we could do with a bit of political education." Clean, hair cropped, free of lice, Frank had time to think beyond survival. He did not want to push himself but he had a responsibility.

"Sure." Haxey stopped to give sweets and exchange chat.

When they strolled on, "I mean," Frank said, "— if I can help."

"Why not? Sure. Thanks."

"I was sent to do political work."

"Oh, yes?" They paused at another group. Afterwards, Haxey said, "I know you were a full-time comrade, but you'll have to bide your time. These fellers will only take it from someone they know well. Now, Dan Erickson, he's the comrade that'll take over if I cop it, he's a tough chap, he was a trawlerman, but he's brainy, too. He's respected. And there's this little Jewish lad, London School of Economics and all that, but he's done well. They'll have to make commissar before you do."

"I wasn't thinking of that. But we ought to tackle these backward elements. You heard Morgan. And Burke was on about women and loot. It's a disgrace."

"Burke was a hero up the hill. I've put him in for a citation. Morgan is the last of five miners who came out from Mardy. He sticks it out but he's nervy."

"Yes, sure. But we ought to get some literature going round."

"When I can get it." He stopped and turned, in a sudden, impatient way, to face Frank. He looked and sounded strained. "Look here. These fellers are OK. They're so willing, it breaks my heart sometimes. Now, don't push it, comrade. Please!"

"Sure." Frank lingered when Haxey had gone, and decided to walk down to headquarters.

*

Outside the headquarters cabin Wild was taking his ease in a seat out of the truck. The battalion secretary (in Britain he would have been called the adjutant, or in the States, executive officer) sat at a little card table riffling through papers. Wild showed a lot of bandage. He had been wounded again on the hill. Perhaps that was why he spoke nastily. "Here comes the lieutenant. What do you want, lieutenant?"

Frank grinned with embarrassment and said, "Oh, bugger that."

They had seen his military *carnet*. He wished they had not. That lieutenant nonsense was all right for Barcelona but he was no lieutenant here. He said that he was looking for Bob. The commissar was away, pursuing one of his ingenious schemes for getting food. The secretary asked if he could help.

Frank said, "I brought a letter. From Peter. I gave it to that foreign officer."

"Eddy?"

"Didn't he give it to you?"

The secretary said, "I haven't seen any letter. Perhaps Bob has it."

Wild growled, "I saw it. I don't know what it was about. Something for Eddy. Peter sent this feller up for Eddy."

"Oh, that," the secretary said. "You're on Eddy's lark, are you?"

"What lark? I'm supposed to do political work, aren't I?"

"Don't ask me," the secretary said. "We've our work cut out without him."

"The cook said he was something to do with armaments."

"That's right," Wild said. "He's down with the machine-guns now. Why don't you go and ask him?"

*

Eddy saw Frank approaching and beamed at him. "Ah! The very fellow —." He turned again to the ring of machine-gunners sitting on the ground around him. "Now, you saw what happened with the magazine. Be careful when you are loading or you will say goodbye to one of these." He held up a forefinger. To a sergeant, he said, "Carry on," and came out of the ring. "It is not a bad gun at all," he said to Frank. "The first good light automatic the Soviet comrades have designed. It is getting a good trial here. They will improve the magazine. Well, now," he said, walking Frank away, a hand on his arm. "I think these fellows are getting on well enough."

The machine-gunners were busy training their reinforcements. They put a large crew on to each of the heavy guns, to replace casualties and carry ammunition. All had to be taught to work the guns. The machine-guns were the heart and soul of the battalion and had at all costs to be kept going in action.

Frank said, "You've still got that letter."

Eddy gave him a sharp glance. "Yes. Why not?

"It was for Sam. Or Bob."

"To be passed to me." He stopped and detained Frank. "What have you been told, comrade?"

"I'm to do political work. Not this armament stuff."

"I see." Eddy leaned his head confidentially toward Frank. "Hans did not tell you? About your duties? Hans — our Prussian Guardsman?" He laid a finger along his own jawbone and Frank remembered the mutilated Hans in Peter's office.

"No."

"Well, dear boy, you are going to do a little work for the SIM."

"The SIM?" Frank could not find any more words. Eddy had taken out a packet of Gauloises and a lighter. He offered. Frank took a cigarette.

"You were to get some battle experience first. So, you have had your baptism. How did you like it?"

"I suppose I managed."

Eddy chuckled. "An English response. They give you a good report. You are a soldier, eh? Now you will become a Chekist." He snapped the lighter and held it out to Frank. Frank lit up and took a long drag of smoke. "It is a big compliment and a big responsibility. You are trusted. The British Party recommends you —. You know how great is the need for vigilance."

"Yes I do."

"Think of what happened in the Soviet Union. Traitors in the highest positions. Leaders of the Revolution. Men we had revered."

"I've studied all the trials."

"Good. Good. Stalin rooted them out, yes? He showed us how to treat a snake. You crush its head. So we must do here. Here in the Interbrigade."

"Of course."

"Here is the vital sector. In Spain. And in Spain, the Brigades are the point of greatest danger. Thousands of men from all over the world. Who, from where, how do we know? There must be agents of the enemy among them. There must be."

"It goes without saying."

"Exactly. And you see, too, what harm they can do, what harm they have perhaps already done. Our attacks sabotaged. Thousands of comrades killed. Think of that. Keep it here." He tapped his head. "Then you will show no mercy." They were coming down to the cookhouse. Eddy inhaled. "Mm. Smells good. So we root out the snakes. We crush their heads. You and I, we will work together, I am at the headquarters, you are responsible for the British companies. The Party is placing a great trust in us. Every spy we must root out, above all, every *derrorista*, every defeatist, every man who in this difficult time spreads the little complaints that weaken the spirit."

"I understand," Frank said. "But the men all grumble. It's their way. How do I —?"

"My dear boy, all the English grumble. I know. I know you people. London? I know London like the back of my arm. You know the Café Madrid, Old Compton Street? I think many people would say hallo to me if I walked in there tomorrow." He allowed himself another chuckle. "And the women. Who said they were cold? So you see, comrade, you have a great responsibility. Discriminate. Distinguish the bellyacher from the traitor. But, remember, it's better safe than sorry. Better some innocent suffers than a criminal goes free. The problem is now, that we must protect you. You must move to headquarters."

Frank said, "No, I can't do that."

"I will say what you can do."

"It would be shameful if l wasn't on the same footing as the others."

Eddy looked at him sharply but kept silent for a couple of paces. Then, "You are right. A new man snooping about. A Nosey Parker from headquarters. They will not talk. And a young comrade should have military experience. I only hope you have a good run —. We'll walk back, yes?"

They turned and started back along the path. Eddy said, "You are from the youth movement. Good. We make you the youth organizer."

"I don't know what I can do. Haxey says they gave up trying to recruit for the Party. I suppose l could pass round some literature. I've been thinking of that."

"Excellent. It can do only good. You will walk around this company, have a little coffee with that company, take with you some cognac to another one. Be friends with everybody. Help with their problems. Win confidence. Keep these open." He tapped his right ear. "And so you can pick the bad apples out from the good ones. But, please, my dear, boy, you are not to be killed. Stay with your company, good, but no hero stuff, I'm ordering you. Cadres decide everything and we need you. You will win your decorations on another front. Do you want to ask questions?"

"No. I understand the problem. Maybe later on I'll have questions to raise."

"Good. Good. So now, Frank, be proud you are a Chekist. Eh? It's an honour. Be worthy of it."

"I will." An honour it was, a new task to broaden his Party experience, a test of his steadfastness; and he would perform the task honourably.

Chapter 11

Emmy unwrapped tissue paper and lifted up a large handbag of shining brown crocodile leather. She went to confront the long looking-glass and posed herself with the bag, now letting it hang by its strap from one arm, now clasping it to her breast, turning herself one way and another, pivoting on her toes, raising her face, trying out expressions. She made little arrangements of her bright blue silk shirt blouse and shifted the waistband of her navy blue skirt. She put on white, high-heeled shoes and left the bedroom.

Charlie was sitting in the lobby. When he saw her he folded his copy of *La Vanguardia* and rose, smiling. Emmy cried, "Charlie, darling!"

She stood before him, arms outflung. He did not peck her offered cheek but took her right hand, drew it down and bowed over it. "My dear kitten. It refreshes me even to look at you."

She let herself thump down into a club chair, flinging out her arms again. "What a day, Charlie! I just jumped into that bath but it was no use, I'm dead!" When Emmy was excited her voice became operatic, rising dramatically at every point of emphasis. "It was so hot today. It was like a furnace. I had to run all over the town, just for six lousy apples, that's all I got. My God, I wish I was home in Vienna. You don't have to queue there, I can tell you."

"There is a war on here."

"The war! It's an excuse for everything. It's the Spanish. They want a boot up their backsides."

"A German boot, perhaps?"

"The Germans would show them a few things."

"Perhaps they will soon, my love."

"Here? Don't be silly."

"Franco will be here soon."

"You think so? Well, what do I care?"

"If Franco comes the Nazis will come."

She hesitated, as if on the brink of intelligent thought. But, "Charlie!" She was ecstatic again. "Look!" She thrust the handbag at him. "Look!"

He took it, opened it and examined it like a merchant. "Very nice. He has some good stuff."

An elderly waiter arrived, put three empty glasses on the table and went off. Emmy cried, "Good? My mouth watered. Silk stockings.

Oh, wait till I go back to him. Henry will give me money. Where is he?" She looked at a wristwatch. "I'm getting hungry."

Charlie was occupied with a pocket flask. He filled two glasses with clear gold liquid, screwed a silver top back and put the flask in his back trouser pocket. "Henry is a busy man. You don't mind a little time with me? I find it delightful to be with you."

Emmy lifted the glass to her lips and touched the liquid with the tip of a pink, kitten's tongue. "Mmm. It's good. Everything is the best with you, Charlie. I just mentioned your name to that man, he couldn't do enough for me. And the price! Dirt cheap. Oh, Charlie, you are a magician. What would we all do without you?

"*À votre service, mademoiselle.*"

"Do you know what I could do with, Charlie? Shoes. A lovely pair of white shoes. Look at these —." She lifted a foot. "Look at the toe. It's all worn away. I'm ashamed."

"Leave it to me, little pet. You will have a lovely new pair of shoes."

"Oh," she moaned. "Darling!" A shadow of thought flitted in her eyes. "Charlie — about Franco. You mean it?"

"He will soon ride through in his big car, yes."

"But why the Nazis?"

"He owes them. They will have their price."

"But me?" She put her hand on her breast and laughed. "On their shopping list? Little me?"

"He will take all the refugees back."

"I'm not a refugee. I was in England when the Anschluss came."

"You are a Jewish girl."

"I don't look like one. Charlie, I had a good job in England. A nanny. A funny name, trust the English, that's what they call a she-goat. I told them I was a Catholic." A high, delighted snicker. "I had so much time off. Always to go to church, I said. I had a good time there, I can tell you."

"You could go back perhaps."

"No. Twelve months I had. Then, no labour permit, out. And everywhere else I tried. No visa, no work permit. Out. So here I am." A pause "You really think Franco would send me back?"

"You must count on it."

"They could tell I am Jewish?"

"The Germans would sniff you out. Your papers. Your parents. Your grandparents. They're very efficient."

"You're telling me! — My God, the things they are doing! I had letters from my mother. In England. She doesn't know I'm here. I suppose I should have written. Charlie, you make me frightened. What can I do?" Her voice rose again. "Where can I go? I tried every country."

"I know a way."

Her face became radiant. "Oh, Charlie, I knew you would."

"Henry. He could marry you."

"Ha!" It was a little angry explosion. "Him? I'm nothing to him. You know he was married before? He doesn't talk, but I know him, once was enough for him."

"A marriage of convenience."

"I never dared to ask him. Not yet. He is trying to get me a visa. He is an important man, you would think he could. He says it takes time. This. That. He says the State Department doesn't like refugees. I'll wait and it will be too late. You'll see. Charlie, you can do anything. *You* get me a visa. I don't care where I go. Anywhere."

Charlie pondered. "Maybe, maybe."

"Charlie, darling, I could never repay you. Oh, God, Charlie, you're a handsome man, I could lick your feet, I could love you, just say the word —." She leaned across and laid a hand on his.

He squeezed her hand and gave it back to her, smiling. "That's nice, that's really nice. A beautiful little thing like you. Unfortunately, to me, you're my friend's girl. You'd be surprised, I am an honourable fellow."

"Charlie, you must get me a visa, please try."

"I'll try. Of course l will. Ah, how tired Henry looks. Poor fellow, on the go all day. Henry, I've got just what you need."

Henry sat down. Charlie filled the third glass. Henry said, "You're damn right it is. Thanks." He drank. "Sorry I kept you."

"Don't think of it. You saw Del Vayo?"

"Had an hour with him. We didn't talk about Spain. It was all Czechoslovakia. He says Europe can't be bothered with Spain. The German army's almost fully mobilized. Manoeuvring on the Czech border. New Press campaign against the Czechs. Unprecedented ferocity. The French are manning the Maginot line. The British are holding mass air tests every night — bombers, fighters, ground defences. The Russians are burning down frontier forests to clear fields of fire. After all, how can they let Hitler grab another country?"

Charlie said, "You think it's going to be war?"

"It's beginning to look like it. And who's got time for Spain when Armageddon is brewing?"

Emmy said, "Henry, I'm *hungry*."

Henry said, "Let's go in to dinner."

*

After dinner they came out to the lobby for coffee. As usual the electricity went off at ten o'clock. The lift stopped working, the lights were out and they sat amid an array of lit candles in a gloom infused by feeble, fluctuating light.

They played pontoon, the English blackjack. Emmy twisted a card and declared that she was bust. Henry bought a card and called, "Stick." Charlie, the banker, turned over his cards. He had a king and an ace.

Charlie scooped in the stakes and dealt again. Henry took three cards and nodded, leaving them face down. Emmy twisted twice, and uttered a happy shriek when she was bust. Charlie turned up his cards and dealt himself another, giving him twenty-one. Charlie said, "I pay pontoon," and took the stakes.

Emmy gurgled with pleasure. "Charlie, you've won every trick."

Charlie said, "I cheat."

Henry said, "It would look better if you lost a trick or two."

"That would be underhand, old friend. I am asking you to admire the performance."

"Wait," Henry said.

When he came hack he had a new pack sealed in waxed paper. He broke it open, cut the pack, shuffled and gave it to Charlie. "OK I'm watching."

Charlie won three more straight tricks. He sat back. "Well?"

Emmy cried, "You're wonderful. Isn't he wonderful, Henry?"

Henry was looking past her through the gloom, toward the entrance from street. He stood up. Emmy and Charlie turned to look. A newcomer was talking to the hotel porter. Henry said, "Oh, sweet Jesus!"

The porter pointed at Henry. Emmy and Charlie saw the stranger looking their way. Then, striding toward them, he called "Dad! Hey!"

A few long strides brought him face to face with a silent Henry, at whom he beamed. "Well, Dad," he said. "Here we are. Surprised?"

Henry said, "Dick —."

He dropped his hands on the boy's shoulders and held him at arm's length. "Dick, what are you doing here?"

The boy was almost as tall as Henry, broader in the shoulder, with a powerful stance; but with a child's full, soft, rosy cheeks, guiltless eyes and rebellious fair quiff. He spread his arms, showing off what he wore: army shirt and trousers. And said, "Well, look."

Henry let his hands drop. "You're in the army? Here?"

"It doesn't look like the navy, now, does it, Dad?"

Henry turned to Emmy and Charlie. "This is my son, Dick."

Dick said, "Hi!"

"This is Emmy," Henry said. "— Charlie."

Charlie said, "I am pleased to meet you, Dick."

Henry said, "You were on holiday. I had your card from Heidelberg."

"That's right. I knew you'd be surprised."

"How did you get here?"

"I biked here."

"You biked?"

"As far as the frontier. I sold the old pusher and hiked over the Pyrenees. That was great fun."

"You're with the Internationals?"

"Right."

"You're down at Montblanch?"

"That's the place. It's a proper old mix-up. I've only found a few English there. Five, to be exact. Nice chaps."

Henry said to the others, "Dick's English. My wife was English." To Dick, he said, "What about school, Dick?"

"Oh," Dick said. "I shall be back there by Christmas. Don't you reckon? This dust-up can't last much longer."

Henry said, "He's at Winchester. He's going up to Oxford next year."

To Dick again, "Why have you done this, Dick?"

Dick said, with a big, innocent grin, "You know me, Dad. I can't resist a scrap. I just decided all of a sudden."

A pause. Henry said, "Have you eaten?"

"Not since this morning. And, I say, I could do with a bath. I haven't had one for days."

"You'd better come upstairs —. Charlie, will you get them to send some food up?"

"You go on up," Charlie said.

"Come on, you," Henry said to Dick, ushering him with an arm round his shoulders. He turned to Charlie. "He's seventeen years old."

Henry and Dick went upstairs. Emmy said, "He's gorgeous. I could eat him."

"I am sure you could," Charlie said. "I must find the head waiter."

*

Dick said, "This is the life!"

He sat up in the almost brimful bathtub. A bed tray rested between the rims of the bath, with a plate of veal sandwiches and a bottle of white wine. Dick wolfed sandwiches and swigged wine, rosy with the heat, his wet body gleaming. To his father, who leaned against the doorpost, he seemed at once a young Corinthian and the image of his mother.

"How long have you got?"

Dick spoke through a mouthful. "Twenty-four hours. They dropped us at some station near the docks. The truck'll be there at six o'clock tomorrow evening."

"You'll put up with us." He paused, "Emmy lives with me. There's a couch in the other room."

"That's grand."

"Dick —. I admire your pluck —."

"But?"

"But first things first. You're still at school, for heaven's sake. You must get that behind you, and Oxford as well, before you go adventuring."

Dick turned his happy grin Henry's way. "I'm here, aren't I?"

"Hell, Dick, think again. There is time. I can put in a word."

"You mustn't do that, Dad."

"You're too young. The British have had trouble with the law, at home, and they've sent back all the young ones,"

"Oh, come on, Dad, you wouldn't blab on me, would you?"

"One look at you —."

"You'd be surprised where I've been taken for older."

"Dick, I am responsible for you —."

"Now, then, Dad. we don't see much of each other. Don't jaw me."

"For God's sake!" Henry lost control. "What put this crazy notion into your head?"

"You did, I reckon." Henry was silent. "I read all your articles. Uncle Fred takes the *Transcript* specially and sends your things on to me. I bet you didn't know that."

"He never told me," Henry said.

"If you must know, I paste them up. I've scrapbooks going back to when I was a kid. It's great stuff, honestly, Dad."

"I see."

"This is the side you're on, isn't it? I thought it would be a good side to fight on."

"Dick, you may be fighting for your own country soon enough, I'm sorry to say."

"This will come in useful, then, won't it?"

"You're not old enough and it's not your country."

"You came three thousand miles to fight for a country that wasn't yours."

"I believe in England. You don't know what this is all about."

"I believe what you write."

"Dick, I don't know if you realise what you've got into. This isn't some romantic mob that you can join and leave when you like. If you stay, you've joined the Spanish regular army and it's for the duration. Internationals have been shot for trying to quit."

Dick laugh "Oh, come off it. It's a bit early to talk about doing a bunk."

"There's another thing. The Brigades are run by the communists. You put yourself under them when you join. They have commissars, like in Russia."

"You haven't written about that."

"No —. It wouldn't do."

"Well, then, it can't be important." Dick pushed the tray away from him and stood up.

Henry unhooked a bath robe from the door and held it out, "Well," he said. "Maybe you'll sleep on what I've said, and we can talk again."

Dick, out of the bath, backed into the robe. "Dad, do you think you could get some more sandwiches?"

"I'll ring down. You'll find cigarettes in the drawing-room."

*

Henry said, "He's fast asleep." He finished a brandy. Charlie refilled the glass. "I don't know what to do. His mother was a proud girl, contrary as the devil. If I stop him, I'm afraid I'll never see him again."

"He need not know," Charlie said. "You only have to say a word to Big Peter and the British will pack him off."

"He'll only go to another battalion. The others aren't so scrupulous. I've seen sixteen-year-olds with the French. What am I to do then? Chase him? He'll soon find out."

Emmy huddled in her chair, mournful, large-eyed, all sympathy while, transparently, thinking of, for instance, silk stockings.

"I couldn't bring myself to tell him more. I wanted to tell him what I knew about the hopeless battles, the massacres. He would just have laughed."

"That should not stop you. You are his father."

"I know —. I was so feeble with him. You see, I'm afraid of losing him."

Charlie offered a cigarette. Henry shook his head. Emmy took one. Charlie said, "He cannot have seen much of you."

"His mother died when he was two. His Uncle Frederick has brought him up. I've always been shy with the boy. I always saw myself as a stranger visiting. We've never been close, at least on the surface. But I'm very fond of the boy — to put it mildly. And it seems he is of me."

Emmy spoke up. "He'll listen to you. He's such a nice boy."

"He's his mother's boy. He's one of a tough breed. They'll ride at a fence if it breaks their necks. They've always soldiered. Fred's two brothers were killed in the war. This escapade comes as natural as school to Dick. More natural. I guess Lucy was like that, and I lost her."

Charlie said, "An old tradition among those people. The wild streak."

"Well," Henry said, "Fred's the other sort. Runs his own estate. Magistrate. Pillar of England. But when they go wrong they go to the devil. I married Lucy in 1919. She was an English girl, by Gainsborough. Fair hair, clear eyes, roses and cream in her cheeks. Like the boy. But it was Paris after the Armistice. Her brothers killed, and damn near all their friends, too. Crazy. She went along with a crazy crowd. I guess she turned over a new leaf for me. Dick was part of the new start. But I was away, a newspaper man. She went back to it, Dick was packed off to the family, she went over the edge of the Grande Corniche in 1923, in a car with some lounge lizard. I was in Germany reporting the inflation. I lost her because I couldn't be with her, and maybe that'll happen with Dick, as well."

Emmy said, "Oh, darling, shall I talk to him?"

"I don't think that would help," Charlie said.

"But thanks, Emmy, all the same," said Henry. He addressed himself to Charlie, "You know, he's at one of the great English schools. Five hundred years old. It has a motto, Manners Makyth Man. That's what I love about England. The men in Lucy's family have always gone there, and then to New College at Oxford. Dick has his grandfather's set of rooms there reserved for him." He laughed shortly. "I want him so much to have all that. Maybe it's for myself. It's the kind of thing I dreamed of when I was a boy. It's why I shipped over and joined the Green Jackets, I suppose —. Manners Makyth Man. —. But, for God's sake, what shall I do?"

"You know what you will do," Charlie said. He stood up. "We are all at war. I am glad l have no child. Goodnight, my dears."

*

Henry and Dick walked down the Ramblas in the mild sunlight of late afternoon. Dick was talking about his holiday in Germany. "They love the English. Honestly, Dad. They just love us. Tom and Rupe are going on to some camp, Hitler Youth, all that nonsense. They're staying on till the end of the hols. I nearly went. The girls were smashing. But I'd been thinking about bunking off down here, and I decided, well, now's the time to do it."

There was only small talk left and this dried up. Dick had a parcel of necessities and some money. They turned into the big plaza, and Dick stopped. He said, "Look, Dad. I know the way from here. We don't want a fond farewell do we? Seeing the troops off at Victoria Station and all that?"

"No, we don't want that."

"Do you ever get down to where I'll be?"

"I do sometimes. I shall look out for you."

"I'd love that."

"But you will write?"

"Cross my throat and hope to die."

"Good."

"Well," Dick said. "That's it, then."

The briefest hesitation: Henry wanted to embrace his son but he put his hand out. Dick shook it briskly, and said, "'Bye, Dad."

He turned away, flashing a smile of great gaiety over his shoulder and soon disappeared among the crowd.

Chapter 12

Frank took his nomination as youth organizer seriously. To break the ice he decided to arrange an under-twenty-fives football match. The battalion commissar found a football for this. However, when Frank went round asking for volunteers, he found that the younger men did not take kindly to being labelled and only four, all former Young Communist League members, turned out and were soon lost among the crowd who came onto the field and punted the ball about in a disorganized kick-up.

He tried to get youngsters to come forward by offering to put them in touch with girls at home who would send out their photographs and supply regular cigarettes. The only takers for this were older men who insisted that everyone took the same risks and deserved the same comforts. One of these was the middle-aged printer, Twentyman, who (when he was not explaining the intricacies of Marxist economics) liked to tell tales of his prowess as a seducer.

Still, these activities enabled Frank to wander among the companies, soon taken for granted. He sat in at a good many discussions. He was surprised that, among men who had in the main come here for political reasons, he hardly ever heard politics discussed. The merits of football teams, the vagaries of wives, past holidays, Spiritualism, the true nature of Jesus Christ and the merits of ale from different brewers were among the topics that were aired earnestly or light-heartedly. As to seditious talk, he knew better by now than to be alarmed by the ferocious grumbling of the men. He was determined to be careful in the exercise of his new responsibility. So far, he had nothing to report.

In his own company he knew everyone to talk to and was good friends with a few. He did not try to stand out as a political activist. His respect for Haxey had grown since their talk. He was content to leave the matter of political leadership to the commissar, who concentrated on looking after the men's welfare and seemed to have won from them at least a good-natured tolerance.

At dusk one evening, after they had eaten a particularly good supper of ham and chips with bread, marmalade and plums, Haxey went round with a piece of paper which he showed to one group after another. Frank saw men reading it and giving it back to the commissar without any sign of interest. When his turn came he read a letter to all companies, informing them that at a meeting of officers and commissars at Brigade

Headquarters, the Brigade Commissar, John Gates, an American, had directed special attention to the outstanding work of the British Battalion, which had worthily won the title of the shock battalion of the 15th Brigade.

Soon after, coming back from the latrine, he saw a group assembled and heard from their midst a familiar Welsh voice. He went across to them. Morgan was standing pugnaciously face-to-face with Knibble. "They can put their bloody commendation where the monkey put the nuts."

Knibble said, "They're only saying what's right."

"What sort of a damn fool are you ? It's a carrot, that's all, and we'll go after it like donkeys, all the way to the knacker's yard."

At his shoulder, Yorky said, "Ay, that's right."

"All I'm saying is," Knibble persisted, "I came out here to do a job and I'm glad it's appreciated."

"We'll be appreciated. We'll be bloody exterminated. Flushed down the bog and pull the chain, we'll be." The men around listened in an inert silence, appearing as detached as spectators at a street accident. "It's not a commendation, it's a death sentence, that's what it is, for a lot of us. You know what we are? We are the willing horses of the 15th Brigade." These were the first words that brought a reaction; a stir and murmurs among the listeners. Morgan heard it and repeated, "The bloody willing horses." There were voices of assent. "They know who they're dealing with — the poor, silly British, the lads that always carry on, the mugs. Look at you all. I could bloody cry."

Alarm moved Frank to intervene. He said, "You shouldn't talk like that, Morgan. Mates of yours died getting that commendation."

Morgan turned to look at him. "Look who's here, boys. It's our Frank. Frank the Wank. Why don't you go up the mountain, sonny, and toss yourself off?"

There were grins at this, and chuckles. Frank kept his voice steady, "We all volunteered to fight fascism and someone has said we're doing it well. Is there anything wrong with that?"

"You don't have to tell me, sonny boy. I was out here when you were still on the titty. Look at him, you can see the mother's milk round his mouth. You had one week up the hill with us and you think you're a bloody hero, Frank. I've left four buddies buried all over Spain and two of them with wives and kids."

Frank raised his voice. "Then don't do dirt on them."

Twentyman said, "Hear, hear," and others voiced agreement with him.

It was to these others that Frank spoke. "Sure, we're having a bad time but we should have known that when we came. We didn't make conditions, did we? We can't see the results, we're too near it, but it does count. Every shot we fire counts. Not only in Spain. All over the world."

There was a response to this and it enraged Morgan. "He's giving me a lecture! Him! Wait till you've got some service in, boy. Here, Yorky, show him —." He made a gesture. Yorky pulled open the front of his shirt to show a cluster of four healed bullet wounds. "When you got some of them," Morgan said, "you'll be out of your nappies, kid."

"When Ah joined up," Yorky said, "they told us lot that we'd have leave to England if we did six months in the line. Well, Ah've done a twelvemonth and most of the others is dead or on crutches, but bugger-all leave we've seen."

"I don't know who promised you that, or when," Frank said. "It'll be time to talk about leave when things quieten down."

"He doesn't want leave," Twentyman said, "He wants to get out of it."

Morgan said, "Don't *you*?"

Tom Knibble said, "I don't blame Taffy if he does, mind you, not that I do. I think this is the happiest time of my life out here, really I do."

Morgan threw out a derisive laugh. Burke spoke, from the back of the group. "Fuck it. We might as well finish what we came for."

"When are we going home?" This caused heads to turn as if it had struck men awake. This came, quietly and reasonably, from Tingey, a young borough council clerk from Worthing in Sussex, a dependable man who never complained and was always ready to lend a hand.

Morgan said, "When pigs have wings, that's when, boy."

Knibble turned an earnest gaze, enlarged through lenses, upon Frank. "You were in Barcelona, Frank. Do you know anything?"

"What about?"

Tingey said, "All this talk about the IBs being withdrawn."

Tom Knibble said, "It is unsettling, you know."

Frank began, "I don't know where you got it from —."

Someone behind him shouted, "Then you must be fuckin' deaf."

"— but it's not true."

"Well —," this was Tingey. "I keep on hearing it."

Morgan said, "We're just pawns in a game, boys. We'll be the last to know. Next time they send you up the 'ill, just say to yourself, perhaps I shan't come down and perhaps it's all for nothing. That'll cheer you up, won't it?"

Frank felt unease around him. Men were talking to each other. Haxey was standing at his shoulder. Up the slope he saw O'Hagan talking to some men, then turning away towards others. Haxey said, "All right, lads. That's enough rabbit. Put your gear together. Clean your rifles. We're moving out."

*

It was another long trudge in the dark. In the company, not even O'Hagan and Haxey knew what was in the wind or where they were going; except that it was not up into the mountains.

After monotonous hours they entered a wood, came to a clearing where they saw soldiers and shelters under the trees, and stopped. The men settled themselves down under the bank. It was still dark. They heard steady shelling. It was out of sight, on the other side of a low hill that rose in front of them, black against the night gloom. On the road, wounded were being put into an ambulance and a truck. More walking wounded and stretcher cases kept coming down the hill.

Officers talked. The darkness thinned. The sound of shelling stopped. Frank, prospecting around, learned that they were relieving a Spanish battalion. The enemy had been attacking for five days. The Spanish battalion had been driven back but had dug in on this hill. There was a lull. Wild went up the hill with some British and Spanish officers. Most of the company were asleep. Spanish soldiers came down the hill with slung rifles, tired, silent, formidable-looking. O'Hagan came down the hill and spoke to Haxey. The two of them went along the road waking men up. The company went up the hill.

They came to a stop below a long, almost level skyline. Spanish soldiers were moving about between them and the skyline. Officers talked again. Most of the company lay down again and slept. Frank saw Wild higher up arguing, it seemed with a Spanish officer. The darkness was greying. The hill fell away to both sides, and across an extent of plain to his right which he could not yet see were the mountains, overlooking the hill. Directly in front of the hill a higher bulk of blackness showed beneath the sky: another hill.

Haxey and O'Hagan woke men up again. One by one the three sections (as they called platoons) of the company went up in file and moved behind a Spanish company. The Spaniards filed away. The British moved forward and at once filled the gloom with a loud grumbling because the vacated weapon pits were shallow and filthy.

Frank went up to the skyline, not showing himself over it. The hill fell away gently in front. It was strewn with boulders, and rocks projected. To the left he lost sight of it in the darkness. To the right, lower down, he saw the edge of a ravine. He judged there to be a mile of fields in front of the hill, then the ground rose again covered in scrub and a rock butte thrust up to a sharp ridge which dominated this hill.

Haxey came to Frank. "Sam wants you."

Wild was expostulating to his opposite number in Lancashire-Spanish. Behind the Spanish officer a couple of dozen men still lay close up to the skyline, over which two more appeared with a stretcher between them. "Here," Wild said to Frank. "I've never got a bloody interpreter when I want one. I want 'em out of here quick. Tell him. It's getting light. They'll bring down fire."

Frank spoke to the Spanish captain. After a little while he said to Wild, "He won't go till they've brought in all their wounded."

"What the hell are we here for? Tell him we'll get 'em." He turned round and yelled, "Paddy!"

More men with stretchers came in while Frank, Wild and the Spanish officer negotiated. O'Hagan waited; Wild said, "There's some wounded out there, Paddy."

"I know," said O'Hagan. "I want the lads dug in properly before it's light, but I'll get someone out."

Frank explained to the Spaniard, who left, followed by his men. He said, "I don't need to dig. I'll go."

"Right you are," O'Hagan said. "Find who's idle. I'll get some stretchers up."

"And be quick about it," Wild said, "or you'll be out there in daylight like a bee on a bald fucking head." He went off.

Most of the company were busy improving the position. Twentyman had no work to do, Tingey also volunteered and a medical orderly, Scott, came up. They left their rifles behind and went over the top of the hill. They worked to and fro across the face of slope, and brought ten wounded in. A mist came up towards daylight. By the time the sun was up, the mist covered the face of the hill and concealed the plain. Frank and Twentyman came back over the top and handed over their stretcher. The other two had already come in. Frank said "I think that's the lot. We can't see, anyway."

Scott went off with the wounded. Tingey returned to his foxhole. Twentyman set, thoughtfully, at the top of the hill. He said, "You know, there's a ravine lower down. Did you see? There might be some in there."

Frank said, "The mist is clearing."

Suddenly it had begun to roll away over the plain, milky and billowing, pouring away between the hills. Twentyman said, "We did promise those fellers."

"Righto," Frank said, and the two of them walked over the top.

They went downhill. There was all at once no mist around them. They were in brightening sunshine. They veered to their right, toward the ravine. Frank could not help looking across the fields towards the far ridge. On its crest nothing broke the skyline. They went on in silence. They came to the edge of the ravine and looked down. It was a shallow cleft, full of tall canes. Some bodies spread upon the canes. They eased themselves down and examined the bodies as well as they could. Frank found a man breathing. A lot of broken ribs showed among the red tatters of the man's shirt. It was probably a waste of time to move him but they could not bring themselves to leave him. He made no sound while they raised him in small, fearful movements, out of the ravine. While they did so they heard a soft mewing. They went down again and found another man who was hit low down in the body. Twentyman had to take his own shirt off, fold it and tie it tightly round the man's belly before they could move him. When they had brought him up they had each to hoist one of the wounded men in a fireman's lift. They went up the hill with their burdens. The sunlight was beginning to glare. Frank toiled uphill. He was clenched for the impact of a bullet in his back but the far ridge remained silent.

When they appeared at the top, O'Hagan only said, "All right, come down off that skyline." And then, "The Spanish lads have all gone. You'd better take these two down on the stretchers. Are you fit?"

They said that they were. Yorky heaved himself up from a nearby foxhole and said, "I'll give y'a hand." Of course, Morgan came with him.

They came down to the road. A lot of Spanish were still on the bank to one side, mostly asleep. Some of their wounded lay at the roadside, waiting for the ambulance to come back. On the other side of the road, British headquarters men were busy in the clearing and the reserve company were lying among trees. A car waited, with a driver at the wheel. Near it some officers were assembled. Wild saw Frank and called, "Here, you, come over here."

Frank crossed the road; and recognised the Spanish officer who was talking to Wild, the broad-shouldered man in leather jacket and breeches, his cap jauntily back on a thick, silky spring of chestnut hair. Frank nodded and, though he did not dare to imagine that he would be remembered, said, "Comrade Terres."

Pepe Terres, whose brigade they must have been relieving, looked at Frank. Wild was saying, to Frank's consternation, "This is the lad — *este soldado, voluntario portar tus heridos.* Terres was beaming. He uttered an exultant laugh of recognition, put out his arms and clasped Frank's shoulders "See who it is!"— he said, and turned his head as if to address all present, "My baby! My Barcelona baby!"

Laughing, he pinched Frank's cheek between a finger and thumb, pulled him close and kissed him, first one cheek, then the other, And, raising his voice, called to his men at the roadside, "*Chicos! Chicos!*" — and told them that Frank had brought their wounded out.

Spanish soldiers clapped decorously. From the British side of the road came loud, happy catcalls. Frank was in a daze of shame.

Yorky and Tingey waited, each with a rolled stretcher on his shoulder. Morgan came across to Frank, pinched his cheek between thumb and forefinger, and said, "Baby!"

Frank raised a clenched fist and muttered, "I'll kill you!"

Morgan went away, laughing.

*

Later, lying in his pit in the furnace heat, letting his mind drift, he felt better. He had been given an accolade by the famous Pepe Terres, in front of two battalions. It would be something to joke about one day: one of those comic, self-deprecating yarns that reflected well upon a chap. He had a recurrent vision of the time when all this was over. He saw Victoria Station, in London. It was packed by crowds. Crowds lined the streets. The battalion marched out of the station between cheering crowds, behind bands. He was among them, just one among many in the ranks, modest but in glory. He saw the great reception afterwards, the sea of faces in the hall, the standing ovation. He saw the girls listening to his reminiscences, their faces intent, adoring. Ah, the girls! Once more he enjoyed his vision.

Chapter 13

There was no shelling and there were no more attacks. Behind the mountains they heard frequent outbreaks of merry hell but their sector was quiet. They buried the Spanish who lay on the face of the hill, and made it more agreeable. Wild was packed off to have his wounds treated. A few reinforcements came. The company did a stint on the hill, came down for a rest in the woods and went into forward positions again. This time they were on the far flank of the hill. It ran down to a dirt track which was commanded on the far side by hills occupied by Republican troops.

A continuous trench, well dug into the soft valley earth, zig-zagged over knolls to the track. It had a parapet of sandbags, an emplacement for a light machine-gun and shelves cut into the parapet on which grenades could be laid out. Behind the trench a wood offered shelter for men not on duty.

The sections took turns in the trench. At night they put out sentries. Scouts went a mile down the track without finding the enemy. The quiet days flitted by. Even the aeroplanes left them alone.

*

An evening. Frank sat on an ammunition box, under a tree, six men sprawling around him. One of them, Twentyman, was telling them about his job and his memories. This was a notion of Frank's. He had enlisted three volunteers from among them, each to talk for five minutes on any subject. At least this would rouse their minds. Haxey knew about this initiative and was pleased by it. The commissar was taken up with hunting out necessities for the men and in writing letters on behalf of dependants who were in need. He was sitting, now, under his own tree, scribbling in his notebook.

Twentyman had his listeners laughing. According to him, the most valuable lessons of his apprenticeship had been given to him by the master printer's wife.

"Where did you manage that?" — asked Harris, a dockyard man from Plymouth.

"On the printer's stone, with me underneath. I had a cold bum but I didn't notice."

Tom Knibble said, "Whenever I read about the Chartists and them, it always mentions printers. And bookbinders. Why do you think that is?"

"They have to do with the written word," Twentyman said, "don't they? Print is man's greatest discovery. Food for the human mind."

This led others to talk about their earliest visits to the public library and, all of them, to name books that had meant a lot to them. Frank was delighted. He stood up and thanked Twentyman. He reminded Tom Knibble that he was the next to speak. He said, "Later on, if you like, we could talk about something a bit deeper. Something political. So that we don't get rusty. I've got a book. It's about the Soviet Constitution. It's amazing. People don't know, it's the most advanced democracy in the world —."

He stopped because the others were grinning. He glanced over his shoulder and caught a glimpse of Morgan, standing behind him, gesticulating, grimacing and miming silently. He said, "Oh, it's you, is it?"

"Go on, go on, I'm enjoying it."

"Why don't you just clear off?"

"Oh, Frank, I want to be educated. I want to be stimulated. I want to be enlightened, like all these serious chaps."

"Standing there and imitating me, you mean?"

"I'm practising, see? Learning the art of the speaker. Politically valuable, that is."

"Shove off or I'll clout you."

"You shouldn't talk like that to a man that's cut coal. You might get your bottom spanked. That's what bad babies get."

Morgan had become a torment to Frank. He had broadcast the Terres incident among the company and never saw Frank without calling him baby or throwing a kiss to him. When Frank was talking he would ape him, or walk past singing a hymn or shouting, "Hallelujah!"

"Just leave me alone," Frank said.

"It's all in fun. What's the matter, boy? Can't you take a joke?"

Knibble said, but gently, "Put a sock in it, Taff."

"It's only a laugh. Where would we be without a laugh now and then? God knows we could do with one."

"Look," Frank said. "What harm have I done you? We're only having a bit of intelligent talk."

"Oh, and very nice, too. I'm sure we appreciate it, don't we, boys? Us poor prolies that never went to grammar school."

Twentyman said, "Leave it off, will you? He's a decent kid." The last word upset Frank even more.

104

Barnard, who was a shop assistant from Coventry, said, "Push off or sit down and listen, Taff."

"I'm listening now." Morgan cupped a hand at his ear and bent his head toward Frank. "I want to stand here and catch every word of wisdom from his lips. Go on, Franky, I'm waiting."

Frank said, "I declare the meeting closed."

Morgan raised his hands as the men stood up, and intoned, "Amen. And may the Lord bless you all till next Sunday."

Frank said, "You make me sick."

"Ay, well, perhaps you've that effect on me," Morgan said. "The little boy with all the answers."

Bailey, the section sergeant, passing by, had paused to listen. He took Morgan's arm. He said, "Come on, Taff. Let's find your mate and look for a sup of coffee."

*

Frank was dozing in the trench that night.

"Halt! who goes there?" The cry cut into his waking sleep. He scrambled to his feet, clutching his rifle, as other men stirred. But the sentry only said, "It's that daft Taffy again."

Morgan and Yorky were ambling down the track toward the trench, rifles slung. Bailey was on his feet, looking out over the parapet. He called, "What do you two think you're playing at? Get back up that road. You've got another hour's turn yet."

The two men were road sentries, their post at a bend about eight hundred yards away. Morgan came right up to the trench, "No we 'aven't. Two bloody hours we done, I'll swear to it. And the bloody reliefs fast asleep. As usual."

"I'll bring the reliefs out," Bailey said. "And I'll bring 'em out on time."

Morgan said, "We been out more than an hour. Two, more like it."

Mournful, Yorky said, "More like ten, I'd say."

Bailey showed his forearm, tapping his wristwatch. "Don't argue. Get back on your post."

Yorky started to turn away but Morgan still glowered down. "Takin' advantage, you are."

Segal, the LSE student, was at Bailey's side. He said, "Let 'em come in, Jack. I'll go. Will you come, Harris?"

"All right," Bailey said. "Come in, you buggers. You're no more use out there than my mammy's china pigs."

The two men climbed down into the trench. Segal and Harris went out. The rest of the men settled down. Frank considered for some time, then went to sleep.

*

The company came off the hill. Frank went to see Eddy. Walking through the wood with him, Eddy said, "Well, and what is the voice of the masses saying these days?"

"Nothing much."

"Come, every little bit is a help. It is not only vigilance. We must be tuned in to hear what the people want. You are an ear to the ground —. At least don't you hear dirty jokes?"

They both laughed. Frank said, "Oh, lots. The trouble is, I can never remember them. I shan't bother you with the usual grumble. There's leave, of course."

"Naturally. I can do a bit of grousing myself about leave. So. Nothing worse?"

"— Not really —."

"You are sure —? A little hesitation do I see —? You are uneasy, you smell something? Trust your instinct, comrade. It can guide you to uncover treachery."

"Well," Frank said, "there is one man —. I may be wrong. I'd like your opinion. Morgan, in my company. He doesn't just grumble. It's vicious."

"And vicious means what?"

"He deserted his sentry post one night. He persuaded another man to come with him. If it was just an incident —. But he jeers at the Party, he said he would wipe his arse on our literature. And then, I thought this was especially dangerous, when the battalion was commended he held a regular mass meeting —."

"So. This is it —."

"He told the men they were just being led on and they were all donkeys going to the slaughterhouse —."

"My God!" Eddy said, "That is enough, isn't it?"

"But, wait, you know how uneasy the men are about this rumour, that the IB might be withdrawn, well, he really pours petrol on that one. He tells them that they'll get killed for nothing. And the trouble is, he gets a hearing. I've seen good comrades nodding as if they agreed, and they ask questions."

"In other words, he opens the front to the enemy, he preaches desertion and defeatism, and he conducts fascist propaganda."

"If you put it all together, yes. And I suspect that he's running a campaign to discredit me, because he knows I represent the Party."

"Then I must say this, Frank. I cannot understand why you hesitated."

"Well, they say he's nervy."

"Nervy? What does nervy mean? Who is not nervy at the front? I am nervy and I am not up there with you fellows. I suppose he uses it to get sympathy."

"He could do. But, then, I sometimes think, he did volunteer, and they say he's upset because his four mates were killed. They were all miners."

"We have all lost comrades. Perhaps he was a spy all the time, even in the coal mine. Then he would be told to enlist with the others. Thus he could worm his way into the ranks here. Tell me, why is he alive? Do you know —? Maybe he took good care not to be killed and it is all crocodile tears."

"It's possible."

"Possible is enough. No chances, eh, Frank? This one we must think about. We watch him, watch him —. Tell me," he said as they walked on, "do you like these Spanish cigars? Anti-tanks, as you fellows call them. Ha ha —! Go on, keep the packet."

Chapter 14

Two days later there was a slight disturbance of their peace. Frank saw it, a black howitzer shell that hovered in the blue and fell behind them. After that, it happened several times each day. The shells dropped well beyond headquarters, apparently a routine attention to the road, not aimed at the battalion.

He had just been dismissed one blazing afternoon, at the end of a sweaty trudge around the hills, a round-up of deserters which was conducted without enthusiasm and which ended when the patrol ushered four miserable Spanish boys back to headquarters much as they would have brought four errant schoolchildren back to a playground.

He was standing idly at the head of a long slope, looking down the road when he saw, toiling uphill between high banks, three men. He saw their Brigade berets and their improvised packs. He knew that Battalion HQ was waiting anxiously for a promised batch of replacements.

The trio came on. Then one of them left the others, scrambled up the bank and disappeared among the trees. This surely could not be the awaited draft. Only three?

The two came on at a dead-beat crawl. Then Frank heard a familiar disturbance of the air above his head. He glimpsed the fat black shell, one of those dubbed flying pigs by the British soldiers of 1914–1918. It fell and exploded on the road. Two manikins went up in the air, sailing apart and shedding their clothes before they fell.

Frank started down the road at a run. He had almost reached the crater when someone called, "Hallo, there," from the top of the bank. He looked up to see the third man. "One of them's up a tree," the soldier called. He had a clear youthful voice. He pointed. "The other one's here. What's left of him. Both starkers."

Frank climbed the bank. The newcomer said, "Lucky I went off for a pee. Never mind." He smiled gaily as if the naked body at his feet, the trunk split open like that of a calf on a butcher's bench, did not exist. "There's me. All present and correct." The other body was folded over a high branch, entrails hanging between its legs.

"There were just the three of you?"

"Yes." The replacement was as big as Frank but his face was more boyish. He had an easy, broad-shouldered stance. His army trousers were tied round the ankles. He wore good boots. "That was a turn-up for the book. I've come to the right place, I trust."

Frank said, "Come with me."

The secretary was at his work in the open air. He looked up when Frank and the stranger approached. Frank said, "There were two others. They copped it just now."

"Two? Where are the rest?"

The replacement said, "The rest were Americans. They dropped us off down the road."

"God damn it!" the secretary said. "Then you're the fucking draft. Were there no more British down there?"

"I saw a few around."

"God give me patience," the secretary said, opening a notebook. "What's your name?"

"Croft. Richard. Dick."

"And the other two? Names?"

"Haven't the faintest."

To Frank, "No papers on them?"

Frank shook his head.

"Two more unknown," the secretary said. "That'll please London." To the boy. "Your *carnet*? Didn't they give you a service-book at Montblanch?"

"Not a thing. And they took my passport away."

"Bloody chaos," the secretary said. "Any training?"

"No thanks to our so-called training camp. I can do rifle, l.m.g., grenades and two-inch mortar."

"Eh?" The secretary looked up sharply. "What were you in Blighty, a boy soldier?"

"I got an OTC certificate at school."

"Yes —." The secretary gave him a longer look. "One of the posh schools."

"Any objection?"

"No, son. We've had some good ones like you. Only don't go up there —." He flipped a hand towards the company lines. "— thinking you know everything, or you might come down feet first."

"Don't worry about me."

"I'm not —. Is that all you've brought?" The secretary meant the canvas bag slung from Croft's shoulder.

"That's all they gave me."

"Bloody hell," the secretary said. He looked at Croft, whose face was bright pink with the heat but not sweating, then said to Frank, "Get him a blanket or he'll get his bollocks frozen off at night." He looked at the boy again. "Now tell me, how old are you?"

Croft gave him a big smile. "Guess."

"No lip."

"No need to get shirty. Twenty-one."

"And again. Come on, I'm not as green as I'm cabbage-looking. I can ask Montblanch about your passport."

"Nearly eighteen. It's all right, though. My dad will give permission."

"Who's he when he's at home?"

"Henry Croft."

Frank looked at the boy and said, "Henry Croft, newspaperman. The American."

"I know who Henry Croft is, thank you. —. All right, Dick. I'll say, welcome, for the time being. I wish there were more with you. Fit him out with a bundook and a blanket and what else you can find, get him some grub and take him to Paddy —." As they turned away, "— and, Frank, keep him out of trouble. His dad could cut up rough."

As he walked away with the boy, Frank said, " My name's Brendan. You'll be in my company. I knew your dad. I was in the same hotel."

"Oh, super. He's a grand chap."

"You can say that again. Was this his idea?"

"No fear!" Croft began to tell his story.

*

Paddy said, "Glad to have you with us." To Frank, "Has he got everything?"

Dick (the two of them were using first names now) was carrying a rifle and a blanket. A mess tin and mug were attached to the strings of his pack. Frank said, "We've been to the stores. Haxey's got his details. I'll look after him." He pointed to a pile of spades and said to Dick, "You'll want one of those."

They walked down the company lines, among men engaged in chores or making use of their leisure. They were ignored except for some curious glances at Dick.

Dick said, "Not many, are you?"

"We expected at least two dozen today. It's been pretty rough."

They reached Frank's slit trench. A few yards further on Frank kicked at the ground with his heel. "You can dig here."

"Right. D'you get much shelling?"

"Aircraft. Mark your pit out first."

"Oh, I know about that," Dick said, and went about his work. He looked up. "Where's the enemy?"

"That way." Frank pointed along the track.

"How far?"

"Don't you worry. I'll take you round the chaps later."

"Thanks. I expect you have patrolled."

"What do you take us for?"

"How far?"

"A mile."

"Not enough."

"Look," Frank said, "I know all about the OTC but you pipe down or you won't be popular here."

"Sorry," Dick said merrily and went on with his digging.

Frank stretched out on the ground, opened his book of French verse, turned his back on Dick and was soon absorbed in "*La Mort du Loup*", a poem which so impressed him that he was learning it off by heart. Soon he dozed off.

He opened his eyes. He could not hear the sound of Dick's spade. He turned and saw that Dick's pit was dug. But the sound of Dick's voice came to him from another direction. Some distance away Dick was sitting on the ground with a group of men around him. He had not had to wait to be introduced. In his clear voice Frank heard both the ring of authority and the tones of good humour. The men listened intently. A burst of laughter went up from them, Morgan's the loudest. The boy evidently had a gift that he lacked, the natural ability to be at once accepted.

Later, when Dick returned Frank said to him, "I'll take you round the battalion positions."

"Oh," Dick said, "I've had a look-see already. Thanks all the same. Do you play poker?"

"Not much. Why?"

"We're getting up a school. Me and those fellows."

The poker school went on for hours. It was still in progress when Frank went to sleep in his pit.

*

The cold dawn woke him. As he turned over, something slipped off his body. He groped for it and brought up a forage cap, blue with red piping. He sat up, looked round and saw Croft sitting on the edge of his hole rinsing his face with water out of a new aluminium bowl. Frank held up the cap. "Do you know anything about this?"

112

"Oh, that? I thought you might be interested."

"It's a bloody Falangist cap."

"Is that what it is?" Croft grinned. "Jolly good."

"Where did you get it? Off a stiff?"

"He was dead all right."

"The Fascists haven't got any Falangist troops up here."

"They have, you know."

"What are you talking about?"

"They're down there. Where you'd patrolled. But they're nearly two miles off. I paced it out. OTC stuff. Two thousand paces to the mile. Your patrol really wasn't good enough. They could have come down on you at any time, couldn't they?"

"You've been down there?"

"So it seems. I've got this." He held up the bowl. "And clock this." He reached behind him and brought to view a black leather belt with an open holster on it from which the butt of an automatic pistol protruded. "It's a standing patrol, I should say. Dug in by the road. There'll be more behind them." Frank was silent. "This —," he held up the pistol, "— was the officer's."

"I see," Frank said at last. "They had sentries, didn't they?"

"One." Dick undid the string from his right ankle and pulled up the trouser leg. "I've got this, you see." A leather sheath was strapped to his ankle. He took a knife from it and gave it to Frank. He said, "Be careful of the blade."

The knife was broad, bevelled on one side to a razor-edge which curved to a point. let into its horn handle was an inscription in Gothic lettering. Frank read it aloud. "*Blut unt Ehre*. This is an SS knife."

"That's right. Chap gave it to me. Natty black uniform they wear."

"Blood and honour," Frank translated. "Swine. What do they know about honour? You were in Germany?"

"That's right."

"Nazi Germany."

"Holiday. Had a smashing time."

"You saw nothing wrong with going to Germany and fraternizing with fascists?"

"I was on holiday."

"Well, you'd better keep quiet about that."

"Why?"

"Just take my advice. Look, this isn't the OTC, There's no time here for playing Red Indians. That was a damn silly thing you did last night. It's nothing to grin about. I'm supposed to be looking after you. You wait for orders here and then you obey them."

"Sorry," Dick said. "Wanted to help. Shan't do it again."

"Good."

"Anyway, it was easier than deer-stalking,"

" Go on," Frank said. "You've been deer-stalking, have you?"

"Since I was ten. You couldn't walk up on a stag the way I did on those fellows."

"I suppose this was on the family estate? Taught by your faithful ghillie?"

"Something like that. I bet you'd go for it."

"Some of us never have the privilege."

"I know," Croft said. "It's a rotten shame." He brightened again. "It does come in useful."

"Listen to me," Frank broke out. "You can't ponce around doing what you like. This isn't a sporting holiday for gents. You stay with your company and do as you're told."

"Righteo," Croft said.

"Here —." Frank held out the forage cap. "Take this to Paddy. The company commander. Tell him what you told me. You'll get a hell of a bollocking. I hope you do. But he can use the information."

Croft said, "Righteo."

"And give him the pistol while you're about it. It's no use to you, you can hit fuck-all with a pistol."

"Righteo, dearie," Croft said, and went away to do as he was told.

Frank lay under a tree, looking at the sky through the foliage. Needles of sunlight flashed. The muttering in the sky rose as a string of gleaming grains high up moved across his line of vision, and fell as the aircraft disappeared. A shell crumped beyond the wood. Dick came back, stooped by his pit to pick up his rifle, and came across to Frank. Frank watched, covertly, his lids half-closed, as Dick examined the breech of his rifle, tried the action, took out the bolt and upended the rifle to squint up the barrel. He had done all this quickly and surely.

Dick said, "It's pretty mucky."

He turned the rifle over and looked at the heel of the butt. "There's no butt-trap. Where do I get a pull-through and some flannelette?"

Frank said, "What's a pull-through?"

114

Dick opened his mouth wide and uttered a happy, "Ha! — How long have you been out?"

"Long enough."

"Don't you clean your rifle?"

"What's all this in aid of?"

"A pull-through's a cord with a weight on one end and a loop for flannelette on the other. You pull it through the barrel."

"You don't say! Well, I haven't had the benefit of OTC training, not having been to a posh school. But I do manage to clean my rifle. O'Hagan's got a rod. And there's hot water at the cookhouse."

"Righteo," Croft said, and off he went.

When he returned he again came to Frank. "And what do you do for rifle oil? Nobody seemed to have heard of it at the stores."

"Didn't anyone tell you?" Frank sat up. "Bring my pack over."

Dick went to Frank's pit and came back with the pack. Frank opened it. He took out a square of brown cotton which looked as if it had been torn from some used garment, a hunk of bread, a tin of sardines and a jack-knife. He tore the bread in two and gave a piece to Dick. He pulled a tin-opener blade from its nest and opened the tin, holding the tin carefully level. He folded away the blade, pulled out another, spiked a sardine and gave it to Dick. He took one for himself and pushed it into his mouth on bread. In this way they disposed of the sardines. He gave the tin to Dick and said, "Careful. Don't spill it."

"Oh!" Dick lifted a delighted smile to him. "Crumbs! Now I call that clever."

He tore a strip from the rag, dipped it in the sardine oil and efficiently anointed the breech of his rifle.

Frank said, "You can do mine, too."

"Righteo!" Dick spoke, and grinned, as if he was delighted to do it. Oiling Frank's rifle, he said, "How long *have* you been out?"

"Nearly a year." Frank thought better of it. "A few weeks with the battalion." After a pause, "I expect you'll hear from your dad soon."

"Maybe he'll get down here."

"You never know."

"Or maybe we'll get to Barcelona. I mean, the two of us."

"To Barcelona? Not while a do like this is on. There's precious little leave at the best of times. Unless your dad pulls strings."

"He wouldn't do that."

"No. I'm glad. He's a good anti-fascist. Anyway, he seems to have brought you up the right way."

"My uncle Fred brought me up. He'll go daffy when he knows I'm here. He hates the Reds."

"I suppose he gave you a rough time, then."

"What for? The old bugger's very fond of me."

"About politics."

"Where do politics come in? I can't stand politics. Don't know a thing about 'em."

"For Christ's sake, then, what are you here for?"

"Well," the boy said, "it's a bit of a lark. Isn't it?"

It was a long moment before Frank could answer. "No. No, it's not. I wouldn't call it that."

Croft said, "I suppose you're here for the politics."

"Yes. I am."

"And all these chaps?"

"Yep. All of them."

"Well," Croft said, "don't mind me."

"It's a serious business here," Frank said. "Fellers get killed. We can't look after larky school kids."

"Steady on, old chap." Frank was taken aback by Dick's hard expression. "I was born to this. My mother's family are soldiers. And my dad was. I shall go into his regiment one day."

"Is that why he lets you stay here under age?"

"I joined off my own bat. He won't interfere."

"Maybe not. But he's a big name in this country. He can get you out whenever he likes."

"I told you —!"

"I know. But it's a help to know he can, if you get fed up with it." Resentment took possession of him. "These poor sods haven't got the option. If they clear out they're deserters."

"That's not my fault."

"No, but it's true. Churchill's nephew fought at Madrid. He was only your age. He was a brave kid, too. He was the only one alive out of a squad of eighteen men. I don't suppose he asked for it, but the British Government sent a destroyer to take him home."

"They won't send a destroyer for me."

"No," Frank said, "but, you see, you are different from us."

They watched a howitzer shell come over and drop. The explosion was muffled. Haxey came down the path from headquarters, his little notebook folded open in one hand. "All right," he called out. "Pay attention. I want all letters in by six o'clock. Meredith, Bob wants to see you about your wife's allowance. Taffy, you're to report to HQ. You're to go and see the doc."

Morgan said, "What for?"

"What do you think, you daft bugger? Your brain's gone soft with shelling. They're doing you a good turn."

Erickson called, "You'll get your ticket, Taff." There were shouts of encouragement and friendly derision from other men.

Morgan said, "When do I go?"

"Now."

"You won't see me for dust," Morgan said.

Yorky said, "I'll come wi' ye, Taff."

"No, you won't," Haxey said. "I want you. I want two men for a new shit pit. You and — Barnard, it's your turn for a fatigue. Get shovels and I'll show you where."

Tom Knibble said, "I'll get a shovel. Yorky, you go with your mate."

"No he doesn't," Haxey said. "I'm letting one skiver off. I'm going to see that this one works. You're too good-hearted, Tom."

*

Morgan went to headquarters. He did not come back, and late in the evening Yorky went to look for him. He came back. "He's not back from Brigade yet. Happen they've kept him."

"Happen he's on his way to Blighty," Haxey said. "I'll ask in the morning."

Late the next morning Haxey came back to the company. He said, "Morgan's copped it, lads."

Yorky was one of the men who came to listen. Haxey said, "He must have taken a short cut through the trees. One of those black pigs dropped right on him. A feller from Brigade found him by the crater."

"His fuckin' luck," said Scott.

Harris said, "It had his number on it."

"I'll get a shovel," Yorky said. "It takes a skiver to bury a skiver."

"I've saved you the trouble," Haxey said. "I helped the feller from Brigade to put him under."

"All right, then," said Yorky. "I'll save my strength for digging shit holes." He walked away into the wood.

Chapter 15

The crowds on the Barcelona bathing beaches were a dapple of bright colour between the city's edge and the sea. Shining brown bodies lay in rows on the mats, or rose out of rainbow spray to thump back into the water like dolphins. Emmy, with toes outstretched and fingers clasped under her head, met the heat as if engaged in sex. Her meagre body was encased in a jazzy black and white swimsuit. Her hair looked like straw.

Charlie reclined in a deckchair behind her. His white flannel trousers were sharply pressed. His pale blue shirt was crisp and spotless, with a Liberty foulard at the neck. His white hair shone like floss. The sun had done nothing to the waxen freshness of his face, in which no beard was discernible, not even in the pores, only a smooth blue shadow at the edges.

Emmy reached beck to caress his ankle, stretching to look up at him. "Charlie —." Her voice was saturated with idleness. "What a funny man you are. Charlie. Charlie Chaplin. Where are you from, Charlie?"

"I am a citizen of the Irish Free State. It's a lovely country."

"Hal Don't make me laugh! An Irishman now! You're not English. You're not American. You talk German like a German. You jabber away in Spanish."

"The gift of tongues, my baby. I am a little bit from here and a little bit from there. A universal man."

"And the hair on your legs is red, funny man. And you dress like an English lord."

"I'll tell you a secret. I am an English lord."

"Ha, ha! It was a lovely lunch, Charlie. When they see you they bring out a feast. Maybe you are a lord —. Charlie, you said you'd get me a visa."

"I am trying."

"Trying! Charlie doesn't try, he gets. Snap your fingers, Charlie, say the word, and show me a visa in your hand."

He snapped fingers. "Presto!"

"It's no joke. It's no *joke*, Charlie."

"You have to be patient, little one."

"Patient! That's what he tells me."

"He can't get you into the States?"

"He says it takes a few weeks. The war could be over in a few weeks. I could be in a concentration camp."

"He can hurry them up, a man in his position."

"Tell him! You tell him! He's got no time for me. He hasn't fucked me for more than a week."

Charlie said, gravely, "That is bad."

"I don't get a word from him. I suppose all he's worrying about is that boy of his. What about me?"

"He's a nice fellow but he ought to look after you."

"Yes, yes, he ought to. All this time I've stayed with him."

"But, you know, Emmy, sometimes I think, we don't count really, Europeans. An American can go across the sea and forget. Maybe Henry's not like that. He's a lovely man."

"Then let him look after me. You're right. What does he care about me? He'll be safe if the fascists come. He'll write a book about it and get rich."

"Ah, yes, his book. I shall be interested to read one day what he says about all this. Does he talk much about it?"

"He doesn't talk to me. I've got no brains. I'm only a fuck, and I told you that's not often."

"This one is going to be a big one, I think. It will go right back to his time in Russia."

"Yes. All his notebooks. All he has time for, his notebooks and the boy."

"You don't help him? Do a little typing for him, maybe? Does he let you see his notebooks?"

"He writes them with a pen. He types his articles. But the notebooks, it is every morning with his fountain pen. God knows what he writes in them." She kneaded his ankle again. "Charlie, Charlie, you could look after me. Nice man, Charlie."

"Nice girl."

In a child's sing-song, "Charlie, come into the bathing hut with me."

"Little one, I'll be honest. You don't come into my arrangements. Emmy, about a visa. I am not sure if I should raise your hopes, but I know a man."

"Of course you know a man. You can help me."

"He can help you. If he agrees."

"Of course he'll agree. You talk to him. How much does he want?"

"If it was only money I would bring you a visa tomorrow. He has to look after himself. He is in a dangerous trade. He has the police to deal with. If he helps a criminal or a spy he gets shot."

"Me a spy? Tell him."

"He will trust no-one, not even me. He will have to satisfy himself about you."

"Then take me to him. Take me right now."

"He is an elusive man. He changes his quarters. I have to find him. I have to make a safe arrangement. It takes a little time."

"Yes, it always takes a little time. I can't wait. I'm frightened."

"Emmy, if I do this I am taking risks myself. Don't annoy me."

"Oh, I'm sorry. I'm sorry, Charlie."

"You must wait."

"All right. I'll wait."

"And you must be discreet."

"I will be, Charlie."

"You won't say a word to anyone?"

"No, no. I promise you."

"No-one, not even Henry."

"Him? I'll be silent like the dead."

"Good." He put a forefinger on his lips. "*Stumm*."

"*Stumm, stumm, stumm*."

"Now I must drive back. Someone expects me. I'll drop you at the Majestic. Go and change."

She was on her feet like a child summoned, and scampered off.

*

Henry wrote in his notebook, *September 1, 1938*.

> Peter brought a letter from Dick. A scrap of paper on which is scribbled in pencil. *Wish you were here*. Peter says things are comparatively quiet for them. I was asked if I consented to Dick's staying there. I had to say yes.
>
> None of the Press corps has been allowed down there for a week but according to my contacts Dick and his friends are lucky to be out of it, if they still are. All accounts agree it's bad. The mountains which barred the Republicans' way to the Levante are now their last line of defence before the Ebro and Catalonia. They are hanging on against Franco's most massive concentration yet. He puts 200 'planes in the air at a time. Barrages with hundreds of guns to a mile. According to my source at Pedralbes, the Republicans are almost out of shells.

The most savage fighting. Spaniard against Spaniard. Internationals are only a small percentage of the Republican strength. The Spaniards like the word *valiente*. Plenty of valour down there and it is on both sides. Losses are truly dreadful. Spanish ferocity appalling. Part of me is stirred by valour but any man who was on the Western Front in 1917 must be a bit sick of it.

Of course it's not only Spain. Seen enough in my time and travels, conflict and cruelty everywhere. A human need as great as that to procreate.

If —. When the big war begins I see it spreading like a forest fire out of control. Armageddon. What will be the end of it?

Chapter 16

On the hill nobody knew much about how the war was going. Even to Frank it was for the moment a remote matter. His mental horizons were those his eyes saw. What his eyes saw was pleasing, an amphitheatre of mountains beneath an immense vault of sky. The heat was benign, sunlight gilded the air.

Every year, in his childhood, his mother had taken him to the seaside for a few days. She must have saved pennies all the year round to do so. There was a shadow in his memory which must be his father, a bricklayer, who had been killed by the collapse of a wall when he, Frank, was three. He had always taken what his mother had given him as unthinkingly as he breathed the air. It only occurred to him now among the mountains to reflect that she had used herself up for him. Indeed, until now he had not thought about her since the day when he had received those two letters by the same post to tell him that she had died. Now, on the hill, in the full morning, he felt something of what he had felt in his childhood, a wonderment at his presence in a far place and an incredulity at what had happened since his childhood to bring him here.

Frank was sitting by his foxhole sewing up a tear in his trousers. The shoddy cotton always split at the seams. A man came up the hill and stopped to talk with O'Hagan. The company commander pointed up the hill and the man came on towards Frank, limping a little. He was carrying a bulky sandbag. He went on past Frank and said, "Croft? Dick Croft?"

"Who wants me?" Dick was squatted on his hunkers by a petrol tin from which steam rose. He was stripped to the waist and he was using a stick to fish a sodden shirt out of the tin.

The man said, "I'm George Gamble. I'm at Brigade." An American. "Your dad wrote. He asked me to look you up."

Dick stood up. He held up the stick with the shirt hanging from it. "How about this? Not a louse left, I bet you."

"I'm glad to see you," Gamble said, shaking hands with Dick. "How are you finding it?"

"Not so bad. Nice of you to come." Dick started to wring out the shirt.

"Glad to do anything for your dad. He's a great fellow. I'm from Bennington myself. Do you know Bennington?" He was youngish, short, wearing glasses.

"Never been to the States. My dad says there's some grand fishing and canoeing in New England. He wants me to go there with him one day."

"You must go," Gamble said. "It's great." He turned to meet Frank, who approached, now wearing trousers again. Dick introduced Frank, and Gamble shook hands with him. Gamble said, "Seeing you here, Dick, I was thinking about another Henry Croft. He fought against the British, right outside our home town. That was in 1776. I guess you and your dad have more than made up for him."

Dick was putting the wet shirt on. "When l hear our chaps talking about the Lincolns," he said, "I sometimes think they must be on the other side."

"I guess every battalion thinks it's hard done by. I brought a few things." He gave Dick the sandbag.

Dick opened the top and looked into it. "Santa Claus." He showed it to Frank. "There's enough tuck here for a week."

"They're loaded, down there," Frank said, and to Gamble, "I'm told every day is Christmas at Brigade."

"Don't believe all you hear. The fat guys are all in the *Intendencia*. Listen, I can't stay. I brought Valledor over on my truck. I know he wants to get back." Valledor was the brigade commander. "I have a notion there's something in the wind. He's with your people now. I just wanted to introduce myself." He shook hands again with each of them. "Don't forget, come over and see me when you can. I'm in Supply. Maybe I do have a few goodies now and then. And remember, anything you want, let me know."

When he had gone Dick emptied the bag. There were a dozen tins of meat, fish and fruit, and a carton of Lucky Strikes. Dick said, "What say we pass some of this stuff round?"

There was something in the wind. O'Hagan and Haxey came back from headquarters and the word was put about to get ready. There was a lot of coming and going with ammunition cases. The men stuffed their pockets with cartridges in cardboard boxes. Bailey held out a bag of grenades by its sling and Frank took it. No enlightenment was offered. Little curiosity was shown.

The company set off on a hike in the dark. It soon became clear that they were alone. After a long time the word was passed back to be quiet. Soon after, they filed into a field near to the foot of a hill, in silence except for clinking of metal and the noise of clods and stones underfoot. The line came to a stop. The men sat down against a low, drystone wall. Some stretched out and slept.

Officers and NCOs conferred. Dick untied the ankles of his trousers and put the strings in one of his pockets. Bailey came back. He said there were some fascists on the hill. The men waited. The darkness was thinning. O'Hagan broke the quiet in a low, clear voice. "Right, lads."

He stepped over the wall. Frank went forward with the line. Rifle at the trail, he hurried on. Haxey ran along the line, behind the men. He called, "Come on, come on, for all you're worth," and went to the front. O'Hagan was out in front, at the left of the line, running hard, and the men went after him and Haxey at full pelt.

Frank had no thoughts. He was preoccupied by the effort of breathing, the impact of his feet on the ground and the bag of grenades bouncing against his hip. He could not hear any sound except that of the men running. The ground began to rise. His head was down and he could not see up the hill. It had seemed to be low enough at the start but the top seemed a long way off now. The climb became steeper. His legs slowed. Effort hurt. Breathing came to hurt. He still heard nothing but the sound of the advance, except for spatters of a not-loud whip cracking, which he knew to be the sound of small-arms fire. He was toiling up the hill now, breathing to fill painful lungs, seeing nothing but the ground, then another drystone wall. He dropped behind it. Haxey had got down, and O'Hagan, and all the men were doing so.

Now Frank heard the small snap of single shots from above. The wall hid the hilltop. He could only see the paling sky. The thumping of his heart subsided but he still felt a little sick. Haxey scurried past, stooped low. Frank heard him say peevishly to Bailey, "It should have been an hour earlier."

Twenty yards to Frank's right the wall ran into a rise of the hillside. Haxey was looking that way up the hill at a faint trail that ran to the top. O'Hagan went to Haxey's side and Frank, unbidden, went with him. Haxey went up the track. Near the top he cried out and came rolling down. Frank slung his rifle and ran up hill. His head was down. His fists went like pistons. At the top he stood astride and started to throw grenades.

Tom Knibble's voice came to him from nearby. "Frank, you're just asking to be shot."

A quick glance back, then he threw another grenade. Tom was lying a little way down, with Dick Croft. He had a hand on Dick's shoulder. Frank threw his last grenade, turned and jumped, exuberantly. He landed on his backside and slid down to his two friends. They went back down the path. Haxey was sitting at the end of the wall, wiping blood from his cheek. He said, "What did you see?"

Frank said, "Nothing. I think they've gone back behind some rocks."

O'Hagan said, "Sounds like they're pulling out." He started back toward the far end of the line.

Haxey said to Frank, "You're a bit of a show-off on the quiet."

There were men moving at the other end of the line. They went out of sight. Down the hill Frank saw a body lying in a brown mound and a second with limbs flung askew. A man was helping another man slowly away. A lot of men were asleep. O'Hagan appeared at the top of the hill. He called, "They've legged it."

They all went up to the top, disorderly. They found no enemy dead, only a lot of cartridge-cases and many neat piles of excrement. Scott went down the hill with some helpers to attend to the wounded and bury the dead. O'Hagan said, "It was only a patrol. There should have been some of our Spanish on this hill. Where were the bastards?"

A company of Spanish came later in the morning and took over the hill. All the way back, Frank trudged with the seat of his torn trousers hanging open. Tom called him The Ragged-Trousered Philanthropist. Dick said, "A bare-arsed baboon, more like." To Frank, he added, "You were an idiot. You're the one who's supposed to keep me out of trouble." Frank said, "Don't do as I do. Do as I say," and felt good.

*

Frank and Dick looked forward to a rest after a night of exertions, but soon after they were back in their positions Haxey sent for Dick, who came back to say that he was going out on a patrol that night. After the night's encounter, and Dick's earlier report, it was obvious that the enemy must be about in strength. The patrol was to locate them. On the way Dick was to show where he had encountered them. Frank said that he would go along.

Segal, the corporal who was to lead the patrol, woke them soon after midnight. Syme, a steel worker from Clydebank, was with him. After the four of them had washed some bread and tinned meat down with Spanish brandy, each pair retired under a blanket for a final smoke.

They set out along the track. As Dick had told Frank, it led to a main road. There were fields on each side of the road. Beyond the fields on the far side of the road, at some distance, was a range of low hills. There was no sign of enemy occupation here. To the left the hills opposite them came nearer to the road. Segal pointed to the hills. The enemy were not likely to be on the plain. He led them to the left, through the fields that bordered the road.

Now they walked slowly, with a high, careful step, putting their feet straight down so that they did not dislodge stones. Less than a mile ahead of them, across the road, the white ruins of a village glimmered on a low knoll. It took them an hour to come level with it. They were in a vineyard. They went carefully between the vines, putting leaves gently aside to avoid brushing them. The road was bordered by a hedge of dense shrubs, navel-high. A sharp, sour smell of crushed plaster increased in their nostrils, infused with the sweet taint that Frank recognised as the smell of dead. Segal stopped and stood at the hedge, looking at the village. Syme, Dick and Frank did the same.

All four men kept still. They watched and listened. The knoll across the road was covered with broken walls in which black holes gaped at the patrol. The village had been captured in the advance and soon lost. Segal was looking beyond it, to a spur of the hills which came to within perhaps a kilometre of the village. The road in front of the hedge looked bare and, even in the dark, dangerously conspicuous. Segal looked at them and nodded. They followed him to a gap in the hedge and went through it. He crossed the road quickly and a spasm squeezed Frank's heart when the corporal went into a narrow, steep, cobbled street. Syme and Dick followed. Frank went after them.

Silence here was not possible. They clambered over fallen masonry. Rubble crunched underfoot. Ruins were a maze on each side of them, each angle of jagged walls enclosing a wedge of blackness. Frank flinched as a big, black, swollen rat scampered across the street in front of him. He heard the crunch of boots not their own and a shout, "*Manos arriba!*" and he went over sideways into a doorway, hearing a blast of firing close over his head.

More shouts as he pressed himself down among piles of rubble. Tramping footsteps. Frank glimpsed a man filling the doorway, the snout of a machine-pistol. He pressed his face down, not daring to move the hand which held his rifle, then he obeyed the order to stand up. The man was bareheaded. A large cloth badge was sewn into the breast of his shirt. Someone came up on a spring behind the man, embracing him. The man screamed and pitched forward. Frank saw Dick start away, and went after him. Gunfire echoed in the street, men shouting, but Dick had gone back into a doorway and Frank followed. The firing stopped. Someone was giving orders. He moved and ducked from one broken wall to another, behind Dick, keeping away from the street. Dick stomach-rolled over a ledge and Frank went after him. The bare road was beneath them. They jumped down and ran across. A man had been posted to their left, a rifleman. He fired in the moment that Dick hurdled the hedge, holding his rifle high. Frank, unarmed, fell through it to the sound of three more shots.

There was no more noise behind them but they ran hard through the vines, until Dick, ahead, slowed down, stopped and turned back, breathing hard. Frank dropped to the ground. Dick sat next to him, thrust his dagger into the ground, pulled it out clean and put it back into the ankle sheath. he said, "They got the other two."

Frank said, "They were Falange. I saw the badge. They must be up on that spur."

"What a performance," Dick said.

They made their way back to the company, reported to O'Hagan, went to their pits, lay down and slept at once.

Chapter 17

Frank became aware of someone shaking him and woke up to bright sunlight. Dick knelt on the edge of the pit, grinning. "Hungry?"

Frank had to go through a spell of eye-rubbing and stretching before he said, "What are you on about?"

"Are you hungry? Can you manage some scoff?"

"That's a daft question."

Frank started to sit up, Dick pushed him back. "Breakfast in bed, milord? What would milord like? Egg and bacon? Spot of kedgeree?"

Frank sat up. "You are a fathead."

"How about this then?" Dick lifted back flaps of sacking from a package and showed thick slices of ham.

"Where did you get that lot?"

"From our friend Gamble."

"You've been down to Brigade?"

"Call me early in the morning, mother dear. I was made very welcome. In fact he wants us both to go down for a little entertainment."

"When?"

"Tomorrow, when we're off the hill. Got bread —? Give me your mug, then, and get your teeth into this lot. I'll go for some coffee —. Eat up, dearie. Dick will look after you."

*

Gamble lived in a lean-to shack built against a sandstone slope; three walls of adobe covered in scabby, smeared whitewash, holes for windows, an entrance closed by a blanket and a roof, sloping down, of cracked and faded tiles. Inside, on the dirt floor, stencilled crates were stacked at the back. Against a wall was a camp bed which Gamble had made, a wooden frame on blocks with sandbags nailed between the struts. There was a small wooden table. Otherwise there were only boxes for furniture and Gamble's belongings to give the place a domestic touch.

Gamble sat on a box, winding the handle of a small portable gramophone which stood on another box. "I hope you don't mind Jolson. He's not too schmaltzy when he does those old jazz numbers."

He rested the soundbox needle on the rim of the record and pushed the switch. A swishing. Jolson began to sing "Swanee, How l Love You".

Gamble's guests sat on the floor with their backs to a wall. Frank said, "That's the first song I can ever remember. I think my mother must have rocked the cradle to it."

"She must have rocked you a bit fast," Dick said. "I think that's when your brain got poggled."

"He's run away from school," Frank said to the others, "as you may have guessed."

Gamble said, "Help yourselves. Don't be shy."

Dirty-looking bottles filled with red wine and stopped with paper stood in the corner near Frank. On a box in front of the guests was a carton of cigarettes and another of candy bars. Frank reached for a bottle, unstopped it and upended it to his mouth. A giant stooped in the doorway. Gamble said, "Ernie, hello —!" and to his other guests, "This is Ernie Gold from the Lincolns. Ernie, meet Dick Croft and Frank Brendan."

"Glad to meet you." Gold slouched in, hands in pockets, an amiable giant. He was so big, broad and bulky that, with his brown, abundant, curly hair he called to mind an outsize bear. He leaned, shoulders hunched forward, to look down at them. "Hi, Felipe. I didn't think to see you at the bottle."

Felipe was drinking. He was a sergeant, the chief linesman in the brigade signals section. The boys had seen him about as an interpreter. Felipe said, "You see something new every day, Ernie. It takes a man to drink and a pig to get drunk."

Gold settled down next to him. He said, "That's meant for us, you guys."

Felipe gave him the bottle and said, "Nothing personal."

Gamble said, "Our fellows get drunk because they're not used to wine. You people are."

"Sure," Felipe said, "but what do you think Spanish people say when they see foreign soldiers fighting and being sick on the pavement and pissing against the walls?"

Gold said, "That's only a few."

"It only needs a few," Felipe said. "Foreigner has always been a bad word in Spain."

Gold said, "That comes hard after what we've been through. We're only here to help you."

"Ernie, you are loved for it. Our people have shown that often enough. But we are only human. We will still be going through it when you go home."

Frank said, "Who says we're going home?"

"Everybody knows."

"I wish I knew," Gold said. "Wondering doesn't exactly make for a happy soldier."

Gamble put on another record, Louis Armstrong playing "Saint Louis Blues". They talked about people in the brigade. Gold reminisced about past leaves and how he had not had a woman for a long time because he couldn't do it in a cathouse and it was wrong to take advantage of the poor girls in their warpaint who grabbed at a guy on every street corner down the Ramblas. Felipe sang a couple of bitter lines from the song about the girls of Barcelona who walk the street to sell their meat. He spoke about how it was before the war and soon was off into his childhood. Mother's huge pot of fish stew bright yellow with saffron and hot with spices. The balcony full of caged songbirds. The fiesta. When everybody danced the *sardana*. Dick made them all laugh with stories of his holiday adventures on the estate, out with Tam, the head keeper, one night, out with Robbie, the poacher, the next. Gamble played Bessie Smith, Robeson, Schnozzle Durante and Galli-Curci. Six empty bottles stood in the corner. Gamble said, "Listen to this now."

He put on a record. It span, swished, through the thick, hoarse, muffled gramophone sound came notes clear as glass. Gold closed his eyes and murmured, "Jelly Roll."

They listened to the stomping rag rhythms, the chords chopped from the keyboard, runs of pure notes, chilling sharps and flats, a melody picked out in fluid transitions of mood, now carefree, sounding in the imagination through smoke, clatter of glasses and bray of hoarse voices, now, through a trill, poignant, suddenly in exotic time, the tragic Spanish tinge, Gamble sat and listened, tapping a foot, musing. His guests sat in a row on the floor, their heads back against the wall, their eyelids dropping. All of them felt the same tiny shivers of ecstasy. All had gone into the other world where suffering is transmuted and a little joy is to be had.

*

They walked back along a path through the wood. Dick said, "Nice chap."

"Sincere. The other one, too. That Gold."

"I liked him. Seemed too nice to be a communist."

"What the hell do you mean?"

"Ha!" This was a big laugh. "Take a joke!"

"It's all very well laughing, but you have to be serious sometimes. You must have seen that all the best men here are communists. Don't you ever ask yourself why?"

"Oh, come on, you're going to ask me to sign the pledge."

"I'm only asking you to think about things."

"Give it a rest, dearie."

They went on. Frank said, "I expect you'll carry on at Oxford after this —. All being well."

"Haven't given it a thought."

"By God, if I —. I won a scholarship to Cambridge. St John's. I used to ride there on my bike and stand in King's Parade leaning on the saddle and looking at those colleges —."

"Why didn't you go up?"

Frank was silent for a few paces, until, "I could loathe you. You and your Winchester accent."

Dick was all interest. "Have I got an accent?"

"No, not really."

They strolled on. Dick said, "That chap Gamble, is he a Red?"

"A communist? No, he told me he wasn't."

"And the other chap, Gold?"

"I don't know. Felipe is."

"Decent fellows."

"Yes."

"Pretty decent lot altogether out here."

"I reckon so."

Dick looked at him sideways, slyly. "Even the communists."

"You're trying to rag me."

"Well, " Dick said, "I did rather used to think that they were all smelly little men with beards, and tarts with sandals and dirty feet. And mostly Jews."

"Now you know better."

"Well," Dick said, " I daresay there are exceptions."

"Doesn't it occur to you to ask why quite a few of this decent lot are members of the Party?"

"Ah, yes, this is where I'm supposed to ask you why and then you give me the lecture."

"It wouldn't do you any harm."

"Kindly spare me it."

They came out of the wood and took the path down to headquarters. Dick said, "You were up to your neck in it before you came out here, weren't you?"

"Yes, I was."

"And you could have been having the time of your life at Cambridge. That's what I call a silly ass."

"All right, I'm a silly ass."

"What do you get out of it?"

"The Party —." A few paces on, "I don't know. I think it was when I found out that I was among the finest people in the world. You needn't grin. Listen. I'll tell you. I was in Paris when the *Front Populaire* came in. I was so happy. I was walking along the Rue Saint Jacques and I saw a girl selling *Humanité*. That's the Party newspaper. I just looked at her face. She looked so — well, this is what I'm trying to tell you. She looked so noble —."

"Did you chat her up?"

"No, I didn't want to —. Well, it was like looking at a picture. I didn't want to —." He broke off.

"Then how do you know she was noble? She might have been an absolute cow."

Frank said, smiling, "You're bloody hopeless, aren't you?"

Dick said, cheerfully, "That's right, lovey."

They were crossing the headquarters clearing. The secretary looked up from his table and called, "Over here, you two. We've been looking for you."

They came to the table. Dick said, "What is it, another patrol? Do you want us to bring back Franco's goolies?"

The secretary said, "Frank, I've got a job for you. Letter from Peter." He held out a sheaf of papers. There's a JSU conference in Barcelona. Here are your credentials and the rest of the bumph. You're a fraternal delegate."

Frank took the papers, and looked at the top sheet. "I'll have to be off pretty sharp —. It's a two-day conference. How long do I get?"

"I'll give you three days' leave, you lucky little bugger. *And* you —." This was to Dick. "You're to go as well. You can thank Peter for that. I reckon he must owe your dad a favour. Go and tell Paddy. Come back down here at seven, and I'll get you away on the truck."

Chapter 18

Noisy crowds of strollers surged up and down the Ramblas. Early evening sunlight gilded the grey stone of buildings. A pearly light was full of bright colours, foliage of trees, flower stalls, girls' dresses, banners. Frank and Dick walked up from the waterfront. They had come in on a train from Tarragona. Their uniforms were patched and dirty. Frank wore a beret on the back of his head, showing the three-point star badge of the Internationals. He could not expect to be noticed. The many-coloured stream was dappled with the brown uniforms. There were compositions by Goya on the benches: cripples in uniform. Other Internationals came past in the crowd, one on crutches, one with an empty sleeve, one with a patchwork purple-and-pink-rubber face. The whores at the corners of side streets wore teetering high heels, peroxide hair *en bouffant* and chalky white masks gashed with bright red. Clusters of children assailed the strollers with begging-cups and supplications. Frank and Dick walked jauntily, with pleasure. Dick said, "Clock the birds!"

He was throwing looks to right and left as they walked. Near to the corner of the Plaza Catalunya he at last uttered a triumphant whoop. He strode away from Frank's side. A few yards ahead he came level with a girl who had just turned away from them after coming out of an office building. Dick and the girl walked side by side at a smart pace. Dick's head turned to the girl. He was talking. She kept looking ahead. Then her head turned toward Dick. Her face, and his, eased. They stooped and now faced each other. Dick was smiling, talking, beguiling. The girl's head went back and she laughed. Dick took her arm and turned her toward the centre promenade. Frank saw her face. She was a pale, striking beauty, with glossy black hair. She used no make-up that he could discern. She wore a spotless white blouse and a black skirt. Dick led her to a café table. He was inviting, expostulating. She was shaking her head but laughing. Then came a truce. There was an earnest exchange of words. Dick laid a hand on the table as if to confirm a rendezvous. He saw Frank waiting, lifted a happy grin to him and waved. He shook hands with the girl, most formally. She turned away and walked rapidly toward the square. Dick came back to Frank. He was radiant. He breathed in deeply and gave out a long, happy sigh. "Ten o'clock tonight."

They went into the Majestic. Frank recognised the elderly reception clerk. He began, "Do you remember —?"

"It is a pleasure to see you back, *Señor* Brendan. A room has been reserved for you gentlemen."

A shriek behind than made them turn. Emmy was at the foot of the stairs. She ran to them, arms open. "Darlings! Oh, you darlings!" She hugged Frank and screwed her lips on his cheek. He wiped lipstick while she kissed Dick. "Wait till your father sees you! Charlie, Charlie, look —."

Charlie was standing beside a club chair. He came and shook hands with them. "Boys, I tell you, Henry is looking forward so much. How are you both?"

They talked. Emmy glanced at an ornate little watch on her wrist and screamed. "Oh, my *God*! Look at the time. Charlie, come on —. Boys, you haven't got a bath with your room. Use ours." She gave Dick a key. "Oh, wait till your father sees you."

The boys went upstairs. For a while they prowled about Henry's rooms. It was a pleasure to walk on carpet, to see their reflections in polished furniture, to try out armchairs and sit on the edge of a spring mattress. Frank looked approvingly at himself in a cheval mirror. There was a tap at the corridor door. An aged waiter came in. They admired his dress suit. He set down a tray with a bottle of Dubonnet, a soda syphon, a bucket of ice, two glasses, a dish of sugared Spanish cakes, a plate of sandwiches and two packs of Camels. "With *Señor* Charlie's compliments, *señores*." He bowed, wished them a good appetite and went out.

Dick said, "I'm famished," and in the time it took Frank to eat two sandwiches, finished the other four.

They took baths and pampered themselves in immense, fleecy towels. They dressed, stretched out in armchairs by an open window, looked down on the palm trees and smoked Camels.

Henry walked in. He looked tired but lit up as Dick raised a bright face and called, "What cheer, Dad!"

Henry maintained his New England composure. "Hallo, Dick, Frank. It's good to see you both. How are you?"

Dick said, "Top of the world, Dad."

Frank said, "We're fine. You two talk. I've got some 'phone calls."

Downstairs, he rang Peter to say that he was in. His next call was one that he had looked forward to. On the way here he had rehearsed in his mind himself (that glance in the long mirror!) confronting Colleen. He was confident. A girl answered, "She's not here. She's gone to Paris. This is Sadie —. Who is that —?"

He remembered Sadie. He said, "A friend. Thanks." and hung up.

He went upstairs to tell Dick and Henry that he was meeting Peter for dinner. Dick walked to the door with him and said, "Hey, mate! I've just remembered. That bird!"

"What about her?"

"I must have been batty. I don't want to leave Dad this evening. You have her."

"Thank you, I'm not short of a girl."

Dick said, "Oh, hell!"

"I'll tell you what," Frank said, "I might be able to change things round a bit. I'll try and see her."

"Oh," Dick said, "Don't let her down. She's a dear. It wouldn't be right."

That evening Frank had a long talk with Peter about political matters, in the canteen at the Colón. He cut back to the Ramblas just before ten o'clock. Air raid sirens were sounding. The street lights were out.

The girl's name was Encarnación. She was at the appointed table. So was her mother. Frank was neither surprised nor disappointed. Encarnación, this afternoon, had looked like a nice girl. Most of the nice girls of Barcelona were good girls. 'Planes could be heard. The guns on Tibidabo were firing. It was enough for him to sit at a table with a pretty girl on a perfumed, romantic night, to the sound of distant guns, wearing a patched front-line uniform and an IB badge.

The old lady was a tiny handful in black, with a face brown and lined like a winter leaf. She told Frank that one of her sons had been killed in the Aragon. The other was across the Ebro. Encarnación was a typist in the City Engineer's department. He exchanged decorous talk with the two of them. The sound of 'planes had gone away. Most of the talk was about better times. He walked home with them. The All Clear sounded. At the entrance to their block he shook hands with the old lady, then he gave Encarnación the pack of Camels and shook hands with her.

Dick and Henry were still talking in the lobby when he arrived back at the Majestic. The two boys went to bed after one o'clock in the morning. A chambermaid was sitting on a chair outside their room. She rose to meet them and told them why she was waiting. The boys went into the room. A few minutes later Dick handed their army clothing out to her. At six in the morning she tapped on the door and gave Frank a neat parcel. It contained their uniforms, washed, darned and pressed. Pinned to the outside of the parcel were a red carnation and a note, *To our valiant combatants of the Ebro.*

*

Next morning, Dick went to the beach with Emmy and his father.

At the conference hall Frank was back in another existence so familiar and cherished that the battlefield vanished from his mind. To walk up the steps on to a platform banked with flowers and to be seated with the youth leaders, the famous general, the government minister, looking out over the crowded, buzzing assembly, was to be restored to a position in life to which, so young, he had attained.

Behind him, in great white letters on a field of red, was the watchword of the day: *Resist! Resist! Resist!*

He did not listen (he never did when he was to speak) to the other speeches, only hearing the noise of them booming from the amplifiers while in his head he rehearsed his own.

He stood up, as always breathless for a moment then confident, in his hatched, faded, front-line uniform, giving forth phrases assembled like toy bricks, no effort required except to deliver them to the back of the hall. His voice echoed about the hall and bounded back to him. Fervent greetings. Youth of Britain. Combatants. Testifying with their blood. Solidarity. Youth of all countries. Heroic people of Spain.

A tumult of applause. For him.

After the morning session he was talking with some of his old colleagues of the JSU when, over the heads of the crowd, he saw a face that he recognised. The Prussian Guardsman, that one, Hans, who had sent him to the battalion, was talking to a young officer who had his back to Frank, while he looked to and fro over the bobbing heads as if for Frank to whom, on seeing him, he raised a hand briefly. Frank, noticing the departing officer's profile, thought, as he had before, of Tyrone Power, of whom so many young Spaniards were the spitting image.

Hans was in a grey civilian suit, this time one of decent cut, his shirt collar open at the neck. He came across, put a hand on Frank's arm and interrupted the conversation. "You made a good statement to the conference. Come with me." To the rest of the group, "He is needed. Excuse him."

Frank walked through side streets with the German, not asking any questions. Hans made commonplace enquiries about his life with the battalion and told him, plainly as one who had kept an eye on him, that he had worked well. Hans led the way into a small restaurant. There were a few small tables covered in red check oilcloth, at which workmen were eating. Frank followed Hans through a bead curtain into an empty back room. They sat, opposite each other. An elderly woman came out of the kitchen. Hans said, "*Salud*, Carmen."

She said, "*Salud, coronel*," put out cutlery, went back to the kitchen without another word and returned with a basket of bread and two plates of dried beef and rice. Hans said to Frank, "Wine? l drink nothing in the day."

"Not for me."

Hans broke a bit of bread, put it in his mouth and ruminated. He swallowed the bread and said, "Your friend has come with you, eh?"

"Yes."

"Henry Croft's boy. I am glad he is your friend. Is he a good soldier?"

"He's very good." Frank had felt a stir of pleased surprise that Peter, evidently, had thought he mattered enough to have talked to Hans about him and Dick.

"I am sure his father is pleased to see him."

"He is. Do you know him?"

"I know about him, of course. Where is the boy today?"

"He's at the beach with his dad."

"Good. They will both enjoy that. You did well to make friends with the boy. His father is very important."

Frank laughed. "I didn't make friends with him. It just happened."

"It happened well. You know, for his father's sake you must look after him. You must keep a good eye on him."

"Don't worry, I shall."

"How do you find the boy? What level of understanding does he show? Is there anything more than his father's bourgeois liberalism?"

This made Frank laugh at length, remembering. "Not even that. He's completely non-political."

"No-one is non-political. Everyone acts and chooses."

"I know, but he simply doesn't think in political terms."

"In his own terms, then, what are his attitudes? After all, he is here, he is an anti-fascist."

"Since he's here, he is," Frank said. "He said he'd come for a fight, and as his father was on this side it was good enough for him. It's the sort of thing the young English gentleman goes in for."

"And he is a young English gentleman."

"Well, an English upper-class schoolboy. Rugby football and knocking policemen's hats off on Boat Race Night."

Hans smiled with him. "That sounds like a progressive activity to me. Perhaps no? Well, have you been able to teach him anything?"

"I shall, l hope, but there isn't a lot of time for that in the Pandols."

"Nonsense, I am an old soldier, in the trenches there is nothing to do but talk."

"I know, but he's a great joker. It's very difficult to get on to anything serious with him." Frank saw that he was putting himself in a bad light. "I shall. I shall, but I don't want him to feel I'm getting at him. I mean, I do like him. I must make him politically conscious."

"Of course —. You know he came here directly from Germany?"

"Yes, he told me." It was becoming clear what Hans' job was. "He was on holiday there."

"Who goes for a holiday to a fascist country?"

"The English do."

"Reactionaries. The friends of Hitler."

"No. No. All sorts of people. There's a workers' travel association that still runs holidays to Germany. I know quite progressive people who go there because of the youth hostels and the hospitality and they just say they've had a lot of fun." He saw Hans' face and became a little desperate. "All right, they know that very likely there's going to be a war, but they don't take it seriously. The English don't take anything seriously. All Dick says about Germany is that the girls were smashing. He wears an SS knife. He said a chap in a natty black uniform gave it to him. He's completely innocent."

Hans chewed another piece of bread, reflecting. Then he said, "Never mind. He has voted for us with his feet. You are going back tomorrow?"

"Yes."

"What are you doing for the rest of today?"

"I shall be at the conference in the afternoon."

"No need —. No, no. I am your superior officer, you know. No need to go back. The report was what mattered. The discussion this afternoon is rubbish. I am ordering you to go and enjoy yourself — on the beach, with your friends."

"I thought they'd rather be on their own."

"They will both be glad to see you. As for you, never neglect your friends. Learn to put people before everything."

"Of course. Yes."

"We can learn from people as well as teach them. Especially from a man in Croft's position."

"I know that."

"I am speaking from a Party point of view. I am speaking to you as a Party man. You must not forget the work you have been given."

"— You want me to watch Henry Croft?"

"That is not your responsibility. But you are close to him and to his son. You might learn something of significance. When people are at ease, enjoying themselves, they are expansive, they reveal themselves. Of course, he is a friend. We value him, of course. But if we have to be on our guard with our own comrades, we certainly must not be less so with others, even the best of them."

"I know. It's simply a question of vigilance."

"Just so. When you are with someone like Croft, you treat him as a friend, respect him, yes, but you remember that he is an American, a bourgeois, and that in the end a man is what his class is. In the end it may be that the better we know him the more we like and trust him. You may say that you are being vigilant in his interest as well as in ours. But remember, always, you are a Party man. In the last resort, no personal feelings. Duty first. I know you understand."

"I do."

"Good. You can reach me at any time. Hans, care of the Red Aid —. Now, enjoy yourself with your friends."

*

Frank found his friends still at table under the awning of on open-air restaurant. Dick was in trunks, Emmy in her swimsuit, Henry divested only of his jacket. Henry ordered another bottle of white wine. Frank told him about the conference.

They found places on the beach; at Emmy's insistence, in the full glare. She would not swim. Her costume was not for wetting. Frank was too drowsy to swim. Dick went into the water. Henry, watching him chopping out to sea with a wake behind him like that of a torpedo, said, "His mother taught him when he was two. We took a villa that summer at Antibes. Our last summer together."

Frank said, "Mine didn't swim. Never had been in the water. Girls didn't in Oldham when she was young. I learned at my grammar school when I was eleven. The school swimming bath stank. The water wasn't changed all season. Imagine it, all those boys. But I was crazy about it —. Henry, why did you join the British Army?"

"I'll tell you. Do you know, when Dickens was six, he read all those books in the attic? — Fielding, Richardson, Defoe and all that? Well, when I was six I had all of them out of my father's glass-fronted bookcase, and more. When I fell in love with those books I fell in love with England."

"My mother was a great reader," Frank said. "The other women in the street used to call her the school-teacher. Actually she was an office cleaner. She used to take me to the public library every week. When I was small she read to me. We used to go for walks along the Lea towpath. It's an industrial river, all backs of factories. We talked about books and I don't know what else."

Henry said, "What do you mean to do after this?"

"That's for the Party to say. I like journalism best. I've always liked writing."

"If ever you want a start in the newspaper game, I figure I could do something."

"How do you know I'm any good?"

"I've a notion you are. I'd see you had your chance, anyway."

Dick shook cold drops over them. "What do we do now?"

Frank said, "Why don't you all come to the conference dance?"

Emmy cried, "Ah, marvellous!"

Frank said to Dick, "All the girls will be chaperoned. They're like that in Spain."

"Not the communist girls, I bet."

"Especially them, and especially if they've got boys at the front."

Dick said, "Wait till they see me."

Emmy said, "You gorgeous boy. Can you dance? I can't wait to dance with you."

Henry said, "Dinner comes first. Tonight we dine at the Ritz. We're Charlie's guests. He won't be there. He says it's our night. Tactful fellow."

The head waiter met them as they went into the Ritz restaurant, and a bottle of Moët Chandon stood in an ice-bucket on their table. They feasted.

The conference hall was hung, for the dance, with strings of patriotic bunting. Beneath the flutter of colours, in pallid lighting and intense heat, Frank span and stamped with one pretty girl after another. He saw Dick whirling past, always with the prettiest, except when he was in Emmy's clutching embrace; and Henry, always faintly smiling. Uniforms and frocks and the flags made a kaleidoscope swirl, to the racket and rhythm of the band. Frank felt tireless, transported. An electricity went through him and he sensed it in all the others. Gaiety became a fever. To him, it was the Duchess of Richmond's ball.

He felt let down when the music stopped and people ebbed away to the doors; but a little later the sweet intoxication ran in his blood again as he and Dick, with Emmy linked between them, were stepping out on the pavements, he and Dick whistling jazz tunes, Emmy humming and singing. Frank was a fine, fluting whistler and he showed off. Henry walked, smiling, behind them.

In Henry's sitting-room they emptied a bottle of Charlie's Scotch. Frank sprawled in an armchair, replete with contentment. Henry said to him, "This is good, this is good. Tonight is very, very good."

Frank looked up at Henry's thin, intelligent face, which was lit now with pleasure. Emotion spread in him. He was happy with his friends, tonight.

*

The newspaper men at the Majestic had chipped in to make sure that Dick and Frank went on their way well fed. There were eggs, bread, pâté, rusks, cakes and real coffee on their breakfast tables.

Emmy came down to eat with the boys. Henry had started wo:k early. She told the head waiter to send a pot of coffee up to him. The boys went upstairs with her when they had finished gorging. Henry was writing in a board-covered notebook. He glanced up as they came to his table. He said, "My diary. I'll be with you in a minute."

Henry's briefcase lay with its flap open. Three other notebooks with the same marbled covers were tipped out on to the flap. Frank saw more inside the case. He looked down at one, and read aloud from the label, in a questioning voice, "Armageddon?"

Henry said, "The last battle of the nations. The Day of Judgement."

Frank put a hand on the notebook. "Do you mind?"

"Go ahead." Henry resumed his writing.

Frank picked up the notebook and sat down. He read, turned over pages and read more. When he looked up, Dick was sunk in an armchair, reading another of the notebooks. After a little while Frank went back to the table to take another. Emmy was in the bedroom, banging wardrobe doors and singing one of last night's tunes. Dick looked up from his book and said, "Here, you read this."

Frank took the notebook from him and read. He read for a long time, from this and other notebooks, until Henry finished his task, gathered up the notebooks, and locked the briefcase. Henry said, "If you boys don't object, I'll walk across town with you."

They were to get a lift back on a truck that was going down to the 15th Brigade.

Frank said, "You go on down with Dick. I have to call in at the office. Peter's got a bag of letters for the battalion."

Peter had told him last night about the bag of letters but Frank had a new and urgent reason for going to the office, one that made him hurry, his breathing quickened by intense resolve. Once there, he put a sheet of paper into a typewriter and began:

"You were right. We must never take anybody or anything for granted. Croft has a briefcase full of notebooks in which he has accumulated the most appalling collection of lies and slanders about us. To begin with his diary entries while he was in the Soviet Union, he has an entry for December, 1934, in which he says that Comrade Stalin was responsible for the murder of Kirov, and purports to justify this with all sorts of so-called facts and deductions. He also (June, 1936) retails a rumour that Maxim Gorki did not die a natural death. In August, 1936, he comments day by day on the trial of Zinoviev and Kamenev. He puts together a cock-and-bull explanation of why they confessed to their crimes so fully and why they were so robust and vigorous. He further attempts to question the fairness and humanity of Soviet justice by listing all sorts of tortures he alleges to have been committed at the Lefortovo prison by the comrades of the NKVD. In writing of all these matters, he again and again refers to information from mysterious sources which he does not identify. He clearly had many illegal contacts in the USSR."

His letter took up four quarto pages. He sealed it in an envelope, addressed the envelope to Hans and left it at the Red Aid office.

*

The truck drove south past troop convoys and marching squads of recruits. In the pine woods between the road and the sea they glimpsed the huge army camps and men in uniform swarming among the trees. They turned into a side road at Castelldefels and drove to the foot of a hill which was crowned by high walls surrounding a crenellated castle of red stone. This was the International Brigade prison. He had been there before with letters from Peter and he had one to deliver now.

"Hey," Dick said, "Clock the meatface!"

The sentry outside the closed gates was massive. He had a submachine-gun slung at his shoulder. On his belt were a big holster and two grenades.

Frank said, "They're all Germans."

The truck stopped. Frank got down and said, "I shan't be long."

He went up the slope to the gate, parleyed with the sentry and showed a pass. The sentry called through the bars. Two more heavily-armed men came from a hut inside. A loud bray of voices came to Frank from the courtyard as the men opened the gates.

Frank went in and followed the path to the castle entrance. Across the courtyard to his right a crowd of men milled about, prisoners at exercise. Three more sentries faced them with submachine-guns at the ready, keeping them back from the path.

A few faces turned towards him. He paid little attention, except that one face, perhaps twenty feet away, caused a scratch at the edge of his mind so that, almost at the castle door, he paused and looked back. He saw what had made the face stand out from me others, a look of intense, almost horrified recognition, the same feeling that smote him. He heard the man's shout.

He went in and delivered the letter. He came out a few minutes later and his step, as he walked back towards the gate, was hurried. He looked straight in front of him. But above the hubbub of talk the man was shouting again, and he had come forward, ahead of Frank, so that he was struggling with two of the guards, a few feet from the path. Other prisoners were shouting now, encouraging him, abusing the guards. The man was frantic, freeing a hand and waving, his face bright red with desperation, as the guards pushed him back into the crowd. Frank walked straight on past. Behind him he heard the raucous, despairing voice, shouting, "Brendan! Brendan! Frank! It's Morgan! Morgan! Frank —! Stop! Fucking bastard! Bastard!"

*

The road climbed into the hills. Dick sat on a bale of comforts which Charlie had given them for the battalion: chocolate, cigarettes, soap, razor-blades, chewing-gum. Frank lay on a folded tarpaulin, his shirt off, in the sun. Dick said, "There's a sandwich left."

"You have it."

Dick ate it. He said, "Frank. That stuff of Dad's. In his diary."

"What about it?"

"Well, you read it."

"Some of it."

"It's all about Russia."

"Well?"

"Pretty hair-raising, isn't it?"

"It's all rot."

"My dad wrote it."

"I'm surprised he fell for tosh like that."

"My dad doesn't fall for tosh. You know that."

"He did in that stuff I read."

"He wrote down what he saw."

"He didn't see all those things." Frank was sitting up now. "He says in the diary, people told him these things. It was just hearsay."

Dick spoke doggedly. "My dad is one of the best reporters in the world. I read his articles. He's found out all sorts of important things. He's always been right. He doesn't fall for any old story."

"He has done, in the stuff I read. Who would have told him stuff like that in Russia? Enemies. He's swallowed a load of enemy propaganda, a pack of lies."

This silenced Dick but Frank saw his sulky and rebellious expression. He said, "I suppose you're thinking about the Moscow trials. You know about them, I suppose?"

Dick had begun the conversation idly. He spoke now with bitterness. "I do read the papers, you know. Your old Holy Joe Stalin has shot about two-thirds of his own government."

"They confessed." Frank met Dick's obdurate look and raised his voice. "They confessed, didn't they? They were traitors. They owned up."

"My dad says they did it to save their wives and kids."

"They did it because they knew they'd betrayed the Party. Life was nothing to them without the Party. It was the only way they could make amends to the Party."

"Are you like that, too?"

"Like what?"

Dick put out his arms and imitated a *salaam*.

Now Frank was bitter. "You don't understand. Nor does your dad. He'll never understand. He's a bourgeois. He looks at everything through bourgeois eyes."

"What's special about bourgeois eyes? They can see as well as any other. Bourgeois. All you can do is say words. You weren't there. My dad was. He saw."

"He thought he saw."

"He saw!" This was a shout.

"All he can see is the surface. He doesn't understand history. He hasn't got perspective."

"And you have?"

"Yes, I have. Dick, history is a science. I've been taught."

Dick was more worked up than Frank. He was breathing hard and he looked fierce. "I'll tell you what, mate," he said. "You're the one that's swallowed the propaganda. You're words from the neck upward, that's all you are."

"The truth is too much for you. You're what you are. Winchester College."

"You think you're clever. You think I'm thick, don't you?"

"You certainly give that impression now."

"Do you know what my dad said about you?"

"Please tell me."

"Last night, after he'd had a talk with you. He said to Emmy, you were so naive, he felt dreadfully sorry for you."

"Thank you for telling me."

"He said he didn't blame you. He said he liked you."

"I'm much obliged to him."

"He said how could he wonder at a green schoolboy swallowing it all when he's just following all those great minds of the West that lick Old Joe's boots, all these famous poets and whatnot. He said they're just as naive and they've got no excuse."

"Well," Frank said. "I never knew you could put two serious words together. You're almost intelligent. But you're dead wrong. If only you'd let me explain."

"Get bollocksed," Dick said. "Get fucked. Get bloody fucking double-fucked."

They were silent after this, for an hour, each on his own side of the truck. Dick sat frowning with his lips compressed. Frank looked away, at the passing scene, simmering with a succession of rages.

He cooled down in time and decided that he must not give way to his worst feelings. He had to deal with all sorts of people, the victims of all sorts of illusions. Dick had good qualities, It was up to him, Frank, to be patient, never to be provoked, to find what Dick's own concerns were and to cultivate them, show Dick as time went on that those concerns could only be met in the revolutionary way; unless (his own anger rose again) Dick was just a young aggressive animal, a class enemy whom chance had brought for a little while over to our side. No, he liked Dick, he must not despair of him, or of any soul. (He did not use that word in his thoughts.) It was his duty to try, and try, never discouraged, to win Dick for the truth.

Looking, after all this cerebration, at Dick's mute angry face opposite him, however, it was not easy to break the silence. An hour had gone by and the passage of time made it ever harder to say anything. Frank's chance came when the truck slowed down and came to a stop in front of a crude road block, a pole lying between trestles. It was manned by a vigilance patrol of five youngsters, younger than Frank had ever seen in army uniform. They were armed with a variety of discarded army rifles, some bigger than themselves. They gathered round the cab and their leader, a boy who could have been no more than thirteen years old, officiously examined the driver's papers, then stepped back and waved to his comrades to lift the pole. The truck started off, and as it drove away, the children cried, in high voices, "*Adelante, adelante, a la victoria!*"

Frank and Dick had watched the goings-on in silence. Frank said, "They're taking them out of the nurseries now."

Dick said, "Poor kids."

Frank suppressed his wish to explain to Dick that it was right for these children to help for their own future. The light note must be maintained. He said, "When I was a kid I liked to play soldiers."

Dick said, "We did. The OTC was a real Fred Karno's army."

So their conversation resumed; but in occasional fits and starts, and always commonplace and constrained.

*

They crossed the Ebro at night. Beyond the hills the sky was lit by flickers of white light. The noise grew as the truck approached the front. It was still dark when the truck crawled down a rutted lane towards the familiar bulk of the Pandols. The noise of guns was loud and continuous. The hills appeared and disappeared in front of flashes and fiery glares. The lane entered a wood. Men were hurrying to and fro in the darkness. Lanterns blinked in a farmyard. At the back, a column of men forming up looked like a single, surging mass. The truck stopped. When the driver switched off the engine they heard others, many others by the sound of it, throbbing in the dark. The boys went on foot down the road. A big truck confronted them. Others were behind it. Their engines were running. The back of every truck was filled with armed men. Gates, the Brigade Commissar, stood by the first truck, talking to someone in the cabin. Frank shouted, over the noise of engines and distant guns, "We're British. What's up?"

Gates said, "Get rifles. Come back and wait here." He returned to his conversation.

At doorways looking on to the farmyard trucks were being loaded. A storeman broke off from his work, cursed them and found weapons for them. They came across Gamble, busy at his truck. He said, "There's been a breakthrough. That's all I know. That's the Canucks waiting to pull out. The Lincolns are ready. Your people are coming up."

The Canadian trucks drove away. The first of the British trucks pulled up in front of Gates. Fletcher, the new commander of the battalion, leaned out of the window. He and Gates talked. Frank went round to the far side of the truck and gave the bag of letters to the commissar. Cooney said, only, "There's been a breakthrough. Join your company."

They ran along the line of trucks. There were shouts of greeting from their comrades. Hands hauled them up into a truck. It was packed. Tom Knibble said that they had chosen a fine time to come back. Yorky wanted to know if they had had any cunt. Frank said, "Wouldn't you like to know?" but what had seared him in the moment he saw Yorky was the memory of Morgan, red-faced with desperation, shouting his own name and Frank's. Dick had opened the bale and was giving out Charlie's gifts. The truck began to move.

Chapter 19

The man lying on the camp bed with an arm across his eyes might have been asleep, except that each time a sound was heard outside the room he lifted his arm from his eyes and turned his head to look at the door. After a few moments he would resume the appearance of sleep.

The room had no windows. Its walls had once been painted in a matt cream colour but this was patchy and invaded by stains of pale brown damp which revealed that the windowless room was underground. Along one side of the wall it was apparent that shelving had been removed, leaving lines of paler surface and ragged holes in the plaster where screws had been wrenched out. In places there were pencil scribblings on the wall. Examined closely, these would turn out to be columns of figures, the remains of hasty calculations or names of different fabrics with figures against them. This was once, one might conclude, the basement stockroom of a textile business. The stout, wooden door was painted green, and had a strong steel lock, presumably once a safeguard against theft. Its former use did not explain, however, the spyhole drilled about five feet from the floor; nor why in the ceiling, from which much of the lining paper had been torn away, the rose of an electric light fixture was sealed off and another light had been fixed, a bulb of dazzling power under thick glass inside a black iron frame.

The room was empty but for the bed and the man lying on it. He had a bolster for his head but no blanket. He was a big man, with thick grey hair now uncombed, his collarless shirt covering a pair of massive shoulders, his trousers, without belt or braces, opened at the waist from a mound of belly. There were no laces in his shoes.

His head turned at a brief scraping noise in the corridor outside. Its position, and the intentness of his eyes, were those of one interpreting what he heard. The guard had moved his stool. The guard sat down again. Now there was silence. From somewhere above came the muffled thump of a door closing, then the tap of footsteps (lightweight shoes, he could tell that, not the boots of another guard) coming down the bare wooden staircase to the basement. The footsteps came along the corridor, singing louder on stone. They stopped. No voices, that meant someone known, someone in authority. A key was thrust into the lock, the heavy mechanism clashed and the door swung open. It was lined with metal on the outside. In a frame was a card with the prisoner's name: KOSTYREV N.V. The prisoner pushed himself up and put his feet to the floor, sitting to face his visitor; behind whom the door was closed and locked.

The prisoner said, "You? What have you come for?"

Charlie smiled. "*Servus*, Ludwik." He sat on the bed next to the prisoner, who remained hunched forward, unmoving, frowning at the door. Charlie took out a packet of Chesterfields, shook the pack so that cigarettes protruded, and held it in front of the prisoner, who did not move. "Come," Charlie said, "you need it."

Kostyrev, the small-time journalist, sat as if no-one were in the room with him. Charlie said, "Come on, you have to take what you can when you can. Keep your nerve and your strength up. Do I have to tell you?"

Ludwik (a real name, obviously) kept his mouth clamped. Charlie shook out a cigarette, put it in his own mouth, found a lighter with his free hand, snapped it and lit up. He put the lighter away, inhaled, and breathed smoke out. The smoke thinned into the stale air and filled the room with its aroma. Charlie put the packet down between himself and Ludwik. "We have both had a good run of luck eh? Nineteen years. One fine day it runs out for each of us."

No reply. Charlie said, "For me, too, who knows when. Ludwik, I can do something for you —. I can see that Valya is looked after. And the child."

Ludwik turned a face distorted by grief and anger. "Scoundrel! Bag of shit!" His hand, scrabbling at the packet, shook. He thrust a cigarette between his lips and waited, glaring at Charlie, drawing in with a great spasm of breath in the moment that Charlie lit the cigarette for him. He exhaled, took the cigarette from his mouth and relaxed again into his slumped position.

"I mean it. I'll send them money. I'll get them away to America."

"You'll trick them as you did me. Leave them alone. Have you no humanity left?"

"I will help them. They are not safe in Paris. You know that. They won't be safe this side of the Atlantic."

"They won't be safe on the moon, if those devils go after them."

"Then what can we do for them, Ludwik? You're an old Chekist. Think."

"Nothing. Not a damn thing. Unless they decide that she is no use to them, and no threat."

"Unless I get them away, new passports, new identity, trail covered. Ludwik, you know me, I can do it, I can do anything, you know the things I've done, I can do it again for you."

"For me." Ludwik spoke with a flat derisiveness.

"For you."

"Like you sent the message that lured me here. Eh, Fedya?"

"As you would have done."

"I confided in you. It was you who reported me, wasn't it?"

"No.

"Liar. Filth."

"There was no need for anyone to report you. They don't rub us out for what we've done. Soso has no more use for us. We have destroyed our thousands and our tens of thousands and our millions for him. Now it is time to execute the executioners. No witnesses against him. He must stand well with posterity. The father of his people. He doesn't need us old Chekists. He has factories turning out his new NKVD, the robots, the men of the new breed."

"Why do you come and talk to me like this?"

"Why not? There are no microphones in this wretched cellar. We're not in the Lubyanka."

"What more are you supposed to get out of me? A confession? What am I supposed to confess? Come on, tell me. What fantasies now?"

"Ludwik, they don't want confessions from us. Silence, that's all. Nine grams of lead here." He tapped the back of his neck. "That's all."

"Go away, then. Go away." His outburst delivered, Ludwik turned his back on Charlie and smoked, like one whose thoughts were far away.

Charlie left him to himself, lit a cigarette and enjoyed a few long intakes of smoke. Then, softly, "Ludwik — Valya. The child."

Back to him, Ludwik murmured, in a deep, reflecting voice, as if to articulate thoughts. "It's not from you —. This offer. It comes from them, doesn't it?"

"You don't believe what I say. You're too deep in bitterness. But we are friends from boyhood. I don't forget the times when we swam together in the Vistule, preached revolution at school. I will make sure that Valya and the child get away. I will."

"By courtesy of the Cheka. Don't smother me with chicken fat about our boyhood. I would rather not remember that —. What's the price? Come on, you said, we're old hands. To business. What do they want of me?"

"What do they always want?"

"Names? Whose names, for God's sake?"

"Is it God, now?"

"*He* talks of God. Six-Six-Six. It's always God with him."

"Who?"

"The Boss."

"Soso? He is Six-Six-Six?"

"The number of the Beast is Six-Six-Six. It's well known that he says, 'Thank God,' and 'God forbid,' and 'God help you.' Ah, — God help us all. Whose names do they want so urgently that they can't wait to torture me in Moscow, but I have to speak now?"

"The Brigades, Ludwik. They're concerned with the Brigades."

"Oh, leave me alone. How many of them have we shot? Hundreds? More? How many are crammed in that prison? Innocent men. Brave men who came in faith. Names! Now they want more?"

"They always want more, Ludwik."

"I have done this work since December, 1936. I have created an entire apparatus. I had to deal with forty thousand, fifty thousand men coming in. I took their passports for us to use. I had them watched. Our men are everywhere in the Brigades. We have shot hundreds of suspects —."

"Spies and saboteurs."

"Innocent men. Now they want more? Still?"

"Ludwik —." Charlie was all patient, kindly expostulation now. "There must be enemy agents. That is self-evident. If you deny something so undeniable, you are inviting suspicion. And if, in spite of all the vigilance of your excellent apparatus, hundreds of enemy spies have been subsequently exposed, what do you think they must have concluded in Moscow? That you are a fool? You? With your record? Or that you have deliberately let spies through your net. Perhaps you have shot innocent men to divert attention from the real spies who still operate."

"Fedya, you don't believe this drivel."

"It is what they believe that matters. The thesis has been adopted that you not merely admitted spies into the Brigades, you set up an enemy network of your own and are their controller."

"Ha!" Ludwik threw back his head, mouth wide open, and uttered his derision in a slow, anguished, "Ha! Ha! Ha! Ha! Ha!"

"They want the names of your people."

"Ha! How many? Fifty? A hundred ?"

"There must be people in key positions. So it is said. Give them ten, Ludwik. Six. It may satisfy them."

"Oh, yes, when they have finished with the six they will have six more names from each, and six more from each of those. You see, it is the work of Six-Six-Six."

"Never mind Six-Six-Six or the men you name. In the Brigades, they are probably dead men anyway. At least save your own wife and child."

"Give me another cigarette." When that business was completed Ludwik drew himself up into the angle of the walls at the top of the bed, legs outstretched, facing Charlie. His gaze now was calm and thoughtful, as was his voice. "Fedya, Fedya, what has become of you?"

"What has become of us all, Ludwik?"

"Do you ever think of 1927, when we heard of the rising in Shanghai? We were in Amsterdam, and what a party we had."

"Yes. You danced on a café table. Like a great big bear."

"And 1926, even, when the British workers began their General Strike, and we thought, at last, at last, in the citadel of imperialism, the workers will seize power. Ha! I was in Baku. Where were you?"

"Berlin. Such illusions we had, Ludwik."

"Illusions? It was for the Revolution. The Revolution."

"Which did not come and will not, ever. Not as we dreamed of it. The British workers didn't want a revolution in 1926, they were against a revolution, they would have taken up arms against a revolution —."

"What are you saying? The revolution will not come?"

"Oh, listen to the True Believer. Heresy! Rank heresy! Ludwik, this is your chance, denounce *me*!"

Ludwik said, dully, "Don't be a fool, Fedya."

"That has been our opium, the word 'revolution'. We have known that ours was —." He paused for a word.

Ludwik said, "It was being betrayed. By Six-Six-Six."

"No. No-one betrayed it. It betrayed itself. It betrayed us. What we brought to birth was not what we wanted. We brought to birth something unknown to us."

"Fedya, I am looking death in the face, but I do not spit on our glorious October like you. I still have my memories."

"Delusions. Opium delusions. Cowardice."

"Cowardice now? With our records?"

"It is a coward who blames Soso. Wicked Soso, spoiling our beautiful revolution. We committed crimes as monstrous as his. We are as soaked in blood as he is."

"*We* are?"

"When I was passing through Kazan in 1919 I met you. You were dog-tired. You told me that for three weeks you had been sitting in the courtyard of the Central Prison with your thumbs on the buttons of a

Maxim gun, shooting. Your thumbs were sore. You showed me them. Turn and turn about with other idealistic comrades you were shooting, from morning till night."

"Enemies."

"*Ts, ts, ts,* such enemies! All the middle classes, every clerk you could lay hands on, school teachers, shopkeepers, wives, children, old parents, never mind whether they had done anything or not, they belonged to the unreliable classes. And did you spare the workers? Any worker who was not a dumb slave of the Party, to the wall with him! Everyone who belonged to another revolutionary party, Social Revolutionaries, Anarchists, Mensheviks, to the wall! You complained, you were deaf from the gunfire in that small space, you couldn't sleep at night, it even upset you that you were impotent."

"And you? Did you act any differently then ?"

"I did the same. I know what I am. I know what the revolution is."

"We had to. We would have gone under if we had not. Everything was against us. That we won was the greatest miracle in human history. Or so others would have called it. We Bolsheviks make miracles."

"Hear the ring of pride! In the face of death the Old Bolshevik proclaims his faith!"

"I don't regret anything, Fedya. We were a fortunate generation, we young revolutionaries of 1917. We saw the October Revolution. From all over Europe we flocked to Russia. We fought in the Red Army. We took part in socialist construction. Some went back to their own countries to establish communist parties trained in Lenin's principles. Some of us founded the finest intelligence service on this planet."

"Bravo! Then what have you got to complain about? You've done a good job, You've served your purpose. A trifle out of date, perhaps. Time to replace you with the new model."

"It is for the past that I have no regrets. I repudiate the madness and tyranny that oppress the Fatherland now."

"You can't, Ludwik. You can't. You created it. I created it. Lenin created it."

"No." This was a shout.

"Steel yourself, my old friend, digest a little blasphemy. Lenin was Stalin's father."

"Vladimir Ilyich was a good man, a great man, he was kind, he was cultured —."

"Ludwik, Ludwik, you simplify, you think that only the brutes do evil. Kind, cultured people who strive to do good, do evil. In the name of

Utopia. You and I have done evil. We swept multitudes out of our way, and out of this life, because they seemed to stand between us and Utopia. And then we found that our Utopia was a mirage."

"Fedya, I am sorry for you."

"*You* are sorry for *me*?"

"I have my memories. You can't rob me of them whatever you say. From what you say, you have nothing. What have you got to live for? Why are you doing all this?"

"What I have to live for, is to live. There is no other reason for living, old friend. I do my job because it is a job. Perhaps there is more than that. What I have seen come into being in the country that we have made our own, is power. Such power as the earth has never seen. It is curiously exciting, satisfying, to participate in that power, even if one will one day be destroyed by it. Of course, that is what the new men live for, those who are stepping into the shoes of our murdered generation. They know no more of the October Revolution than the Christians do of the crucifixion. They have no idea what was hoped for. They only know that their country is great and that they are part of its greatness. Well, that's enough. It won't be the proletarian revolution that conquers the earth, but the new power. And it will."

"You don't believe a word of that," Ludwik said. "You are sufficiently old-fashioned to have to produce an ideological justification for yourself. The truth is that you are a rat, a time-server and a lickspittle whose only motivation now is to buy his own life with those of others."

"I am here to save your life, and Valya's, and your little boy's. You may not wish to live, but let them live, Ludwik, let them live." Ludwik did not speak. Charlie went on, "They are not in Paris."

"What?"

"They are in Moscow."

"Liar. I had a letter from them three weeks ago."

"It was posted earlier. We saw it, of course. They received a note from you in reply telling them to leave for Moscow at once. You told them who to see at the Paris Embassy to arrange the journey. You wrote that your life depended upon it."

Silence, heavy upon the recumbent man. Then he said, heavily, "It was written in my own hand, of course, a perfect likeness. The technical department is very good —." He nodded, to himself. "Very good."

"You can save them yet. You can. You really can."

Ludwik, still shut up with himself, muttered, "Devils, devils, devils!"

"Names, Ludwik —. Six — names. Then you can go home, see Valya and the boy —. And, who knows? You'll have at least a chance."

Ludwik, without looking up, mumbled, "A chance."

Charlie stood up. "I'll tell them to give you a pencil and paper. Six names." He stooped over the bed. "It should not be difficult. You can always give them mine for a start." He touched Ludwik's forehead with his lips. "*Schluf, mein kindele, schluf.*" He straightened up and went out.

Chapter 20

The convoy sped towards the sound of the guns. The road was a ribbon of quiet, its surface faintly phosphorescent. Low, wooded hills on both sides were black. Soon, the fires and the noise were to one side of them, far away; a little later, they saw and heard the battle on both sides. Dawn was breaking. The entire front seemed to be spewing up noise and smoke around them. There was a spurt of smoke and fire among the trees not far from the road, and two more. Another salvo of three fell close to the road behind them. The shelling found the road and continued.

The trucks slowed down and, one by one, turned into the shelter of trees and stopped. The noise of motors ended and there was only the din of explosions. Cab doors slammed, footsteps slapped on the road, officers came along shouting, "All out! All out! Move!"

The boys jumped down and stood stamping their feet on the road. The days were still hot but the September dawn was chilly. Neither Frank nor Dick had anything to say. They were looking about them, trying to make sense of what was happening to them. Frank could hear grenades cough, not far off, small-arms fire, screams and desperate, shouted commands, faint but sharp.

Shells fell on the road and among the trees, making the air reek. When an explosion was near the ground jumped underfoot. More orders were being shouted. Files of men were moving off through the trees. O'Hagan hurried toward the company, shouting, "Come on, let's get out of here."

They moved off. A track through the trees went slightly uphill. The ground was soft. Strange stretcher-bearers came past with their loads, heads down, ignoring the company. Groups of dishevelled soldiers stood about like street idlers, talking among themselves in Spanish. Yorky said, "They're the buggers that broke."

Frank called out in Spanish, "Where are your lines?"

A Spaniard turned to glance at him, turned back to his comrades and said something, and they all laughed.

The track emerged from the trees and ran in a cleft up a hillside. Frank could see the summit of the hill not far above. Shells exploded on its flanks. Spanish stragglers were still coming back, and wounded. A smashing explosion at the front of the company made him totter. He went on, and soon skirted a large, stinking crater on the far side of which was a messy heap with two outflung legs. O'Hagan watched the men come by. He said to them, "Haxey."

The battlefield smell grew. Bodies littered the slopes. Frank passed a cluster of them stiffened in grotesque positions. O'Hagan, walking alongside his men, pointed and shouted, "Get in under that ledge."

He watched them. A steep bank protected at least from shells falling higher up. When they were all lying under it he went off. He came back, called them on to their feet and led them across the slope to another partially-sheltered ledge nearer to the summit. They spread out, shovels were brought up and they dug in. For a change, it was easy in the soft ground. They settled down.

In reserve, they listened to the battle over the hill, but were not diverted by it from their own small preoccupations. They emptied their bladders and bowels, ate, smoked, scouted around for boards or logs that might give a little head cover or talked of things that were not to do with war. After a while, most of them, most of the time, slept.

Frank was able to do this. In a cradle of earth he had no being; until he was aware of a grip on his shoulder, shaking him. He opened his eyes. Dick, kneeling at the edge of the pit, shouted, "Are you all right?" The effort of the shout made Frank hear the now dreadful uproar of bombardment that surrounded them. Dick must have seen Frank's incomprehension, for he made a gesture at the ground behind him. Frank looked. A crater still smoked where two foxholes had been, Syme and Tom Knibble in them. Frank shouted, "Get down, you fool."

Dick ducked away out of sight. Frank flopped back into the pit, face downwards, and put his arms round his own body, pressing the ground, which every few moments trembled. The bombardment moved away. As soon as Frank's head was clear he went to Dick; who was still dazed, no merriment in his eyes, no bloom in his smudged cheeks.

They learned a little about the battle from wounded coming back. There were attacks coming in all day, furiously pressed, the wounded told them, and before each onset a barrage like the one that had fallen on the battalion. Yorky said that it was the worst he had ever experienced. Erickson, the new commissar, came along the pits, asking men if they were all right, and exchanging banter; but he said to Frank, "It's the flanks we're worried about. If they're overrun, we're done for." Frank knew that this was in confidence. The men showed their usual lack of curiosity and were better left so.

Someone shouted, "*Avión!*"

Frank huddled down in his pit. The engine noise suddenly shouted overhead. He saw eight twin-engined 'planes, quite low. He brought his rifle up to his shoulder and followed round, firing ahead of the 'planes. He could hear the whole battalion firing. One 'plane sheared away from the others. Its wings tilted more steeply. It slipped out of sight. He heard a great explosion. The men were all cheering. The 'planes went away. Frank saw strings of bombs falling from them, on to fields already obscured by the smoke of shelling.

The battalion had no rest from the sound of engines. 'Planes attacked them ten times in the day. All the while shells fell, and flights of mortar bombs, and once more the full barrage shifted to hit them. Frank saw a lot of British wounded, now, going down the hill.

There was a new climax of bombardment in front of them. Not only wounded came back but Spanish stragglers who hurried away between the pits of the British and took no notice of shouts. There was a stir in the pits. O'Hagan came along the line with Erickson, to tell the men to get ready.

They did not have to move. The Lincolns came up for a counter-attack. They passed through the lines. The customary jeering was exchanged with the British. The Lincolns went out of sight. Their wounded came back in a growing stream. British soldiers went up over hill to help the American wounded back. Frank gave a shoulder to an American with a smashed hand. He asked how it was going.

"We're still over there."

"There's a lot of you chaps wounded."

"There's a damn sight more dead. The fascists are coming over again. God knows if we can hold on."

The American went on his way. So many more wounded came back that Frank wondered if there were any of the Lincolns left. But they stayed over the hill. The British were not sent for. Most of them slept. Frank wondered what was happening on the flanks.

Chapter 21

An open car stopped outside the Majestic. Henry Croft sat next to the army driver. The driver got out, came round to the pavement and opened the door. As Henry stepped down he thanked the driver. In the lobby, he made sure that there were no messages and went upstairs.

Emmy was out. He bathed, changed his clothes, typed out his story and went to the Press Bureau. Victoria was waiting for him. When he had 'phoned his story, they left together.

They walked downtown to the waterfront. Victoria looked trim and cool. Her face was youthful, the glossy grey cap of her hair an enhancement. She walked at Henry's side, serene, patrician in a jacket and skirt of cream linen, the jacket over a blouse of fine lace. Under whatever dispensation she lived, Henry thought, she would be an aristocrat, one of the upper set.

She said, "Did you have a good day?"

"It was very interesting. I'm grateful to you for setting it up."

"I wanted you to go," she said. He had been out all day, visiting small farms to the north of Manresa. "I hope you will send a story about the private farmers and the way we help them. It will show the Americans we are just like them."

"Didn't you see my story tonight? That's what I wrote."

"Oh, Henry, thank you. You are a good friend."

They strolled through the crowds, the mélange of voices, the clacking of wooden soles, the little explosions of laughter. Henry said, "It sounds like carnival time. You'd never know how things were."

She walked with face uplifted and spoke serenely, "That's the Spanish people."

"They just don't face reality."

"Perhaps they prefer to think of what it will be like in the future when the people have won."

"That's how you think, Victoria, not how they think."

"Don't you believe in a good future?"

"Victoria, for God's sake, that's opium — your opium. The immediate future for these people is hellish."

"You don't begin to understand, you good, middle-class, New England American. As long as we fight we haven't lost. As long as we haven't lost we can believe in victory."

"That's communist theology, Victoria. It's a kind of madness."

"It's a madness that has inspired us to perform the impossible many times. It will see us through. It will, Henry."

He was fascinated by the gaze she turned on him. It was a look he had had before from communists, calm, utterly certain. He said, "It's like talking to a marble statue. And of course you make me feel a scoundrel."

"You don't need to feel that. You're all right. You'll learn."

He guided her to a table on the restaurant terrace. "If the catch is in, we'll have sea bass," he said.

A waiter brought *tapas* and sherry, and greeted Henry by name. When he had taken the order and gone, Henry said, "Well, now, Victoria, one good turn deserves another. I went and looked at your farms. I want to go to the front."

"I'll see what I can do. No, Henry, I will. This time it's a promise. But you may have to wait till things quieten down at the front."

"Will they ever? How long can you hold on down there?"

"As long as we have to."

"Here we go again."

"I'm being strictly realist, Henry. Maybe you looked at today's tapes. The Czechs think it is going to be war. The Soviets have let it be known that they will aid Prague. The armies are all mobilized."

"You are praying for a European war to save you —."

"We're not praying for it. It's coming."

"You're praying. It's your last hope. And I tell you, everyone else in Europe, except the Nazis maybe, everyone else dreads it, I dread it. My God, another Great War?"

"It is coming. Others will have to face it as we have had to do."

"It looks like it but, you know, I wonder."

"You wonder?"

"I wonder if it is coming. At least, as soon as you think."

"What else? They'll let Hitler take Czechoslovakia? That's not possible."

"I think they may do even that if it buys them time. If Chamberlain and Daladier see any way to avoid fighting, they'll take it. They know it will only put off the evil day, but they'll settle for that. They're not villains, Victoria. They're not wicked capitalists striking a devil's bargain with Hitler. They're like their people. They crave for peace."

"I don't believe the people are such cowards."

"If war is avoided, believe me, there'll be celebrations in the pubs of London and dancing in the streets of Paris."

"If so, will be a feast of fools."

"Surely, and in my heart I'm just as much a fool. I feel I could sell my soul for a year's respite. Shameful, isn't it?"

"If someone like you talks that way, then we're truly alone."

"Now you know why I ask if it's all worth it."

"Henry," she said, "we must stop now, or we'll spoil a good evening. Did the driver take you to Montserrat? I told him to."

They talked about that.

*

It was after eleven when Henry looked into the dining-room at the Majestic, found some of his colleagues and sat down to talk with them. Two hours later he went up to bed. Emmy was still out.

He was not surprised in the morning to see her bed unoccupied. She came and went as she pleased. After his bath he dressed, in the same suit that he had worn last night, which he had hung on the bedroom door; then went to get his diaries. He opened a wardrobe door. His briefcase was not there.

After a moment of thought he opened the other leaf of the wardrobe doors. On Emmy's side there were only unused hangers on the rail. None of her shoes were on the top shelf. There was nothing on the floor, where she had stored her old white suitcase. He wandered about the rooms, looking. He dropped into an armchair and remained there for a while, in thought.

Downstairs, a girl clerk, Luisa, was at the desk. He said, "The *señorita* went out yesterday. She didn't leave a note and I'd like to know when she'll be back. Did she say anything?"

"Not to me. I was on all morning. Pepe was on all day —." She called, "Pepe!" The old doorman came to the desk. He said, "Yes, *señor*. She went out yesterday morning. I cannot say what the time was, but it was in the middle of the morning."

Luisa said, "She certainly did not speak to me. I did not even notice her."

"Did she have any cases with her?"

Pepe said, "Two, *señor*. l wanted to call a boy to carry them for her. I was surprised when she said no."

"Was one of them a briefcase?"

"I can only recall that one was white and one was dark — black?"

"She was alone?"

"She was when she left. I watched her go up the street. I was surprised that she carried her own bags. A car was parked by the corner. She got into it and it drove away."

Henry said, "I suppose she will telephone. If she does, please take a message. I have to go out."

He had an appointment at the port with the agent of a Greek shipping company. He watched a cargo of cereals being unloaded from one of the company's ships, the last, he was told by the agent and the ship's master, that the company was running to Spain. Too many ships had been sunk by the blockading Italian submarines. It was an old story. There were more and more signs in shop windows: "NO FOOD TODAY". Henry did not bother to make notes. His mind was busy with another matter.

He hurried back to the Majestic. Luisa was at the desk. He asked her, "Is she back? Is there any message?"

Luisa held out an envelope to him. She said, "This came a little after eleven o'clock."

His name was on the envelope, in Emmy's angular, Teutonic handwriting. He tore the envelope open and took out a leaf of squared paper torn from a ring-backed notebook. He read, *Gone to friends. I will be in France when you read this. Love, E.*

"Who brought this?"

"A little boy. Is there anything wrong, *señor*?"

"No. No — thank you."

He turned away for a few moments, beset by multiplying worries. Then he asked Luisa for a telephone and rang the Ritz. Charlie told him to come over.

In Charlie's room, he explained what had happened and gave Charlie the note. Charlie handed it back. "She could have been a little more forthcoming."

"I'm paralysed by this, Charlie. She's taken me completely by surprise. I'm worried for her. But there's also my briefcase. I can't tell you how much it matters to me. I can't see what to do. I can go to the police. I don't want to lodge a complaint of theft. I'm just an idiot who complains that his girl has run out on him. Can you imagine, in the middle of a war?"

"She only took the case? No money?"

"Not a peseta. I carry all my cash on me. For God's sake, I wish she had taken something. She should have asked me. She was welcome to it. Why should she walk out without a word? Did she give you any hint of this?"

"Not a word. In fact she made a date with me for tomorrow at the beach."

"I don't get this. Why should she go now? I was waiting for a visa to come through for her. She knew that."

"Maybe that is it," Charlie said. "The visa. She talked to me about that. She thought you were stringing her along. She was very bitter."

"She knew me better than that."

"She was getting desperate. She knew things were going badly at the front. She was afraid of ending up in a Nazi concentration camp."

"Why didn't she talk to me? If she wanted to go, she knew I wouldn't stand in her way. I could have got her out to France at least. How is she going to do it? You can't get past the frontier controls without papers."

Charlie reflected. "Maybe she is not going to France. Maybe it is bluff. Or maybe somebody has made promises on which he can't deliver."

"Who? She was always telling me that she had no-one except me. And she could have said you, of course."

"Of course. But she did have someone, eh? Someone was waiting for her with a car."

"That's what I can't figure."

"Henry," Charlie said. "You do know what she was like with men?"

"Yes. Yes, I know. She was free to do what she liked."

"You know she would lie down for any man who promised her something?"

"I guess she would, yes. That's what she means about friends?"

"I think so."

"Why did she take my case?"

"You said it was valuable."

"No, no. I didn't mean that. There was nothing in it she could sell."

"She may not have known that."

"Of course she knew. I kept my diaries in it. She saw me working on them every morning. I need them. All the stuff I brought out of Russia is in them, all the inside stuff I've collected in Spain. They're useless to anyone else."

"Would she realise that, I wonder? She's greedy, she's sharp-witted, and she's a little pinhead. I can imagine her filling up with some crazy resentment, about the visa, who knows? And suddenly she makes up her mind to walk out with your case, just like that, *punkt*."

"Then she wouldn't have written that note. She'd have left me to sweat."

"I don't think she would know quite how to play it. She is a little slut but she is not a bad sort."

"Wait," Henry said. "There's more to come." He told Charlie about the man he had found in his hotel room, and about the scratch on the lock of the briefcase. "That's why I keep thinking there's some dirty business going on."

Charlie nodded slowly, as if agreeing, but then said, "No. No, my friend. Stop and think. Some time ago you found a black beetle in your room. I have had that experience, too. So have your colleagues. You must know. A routine attention. Have you any other grounds for suspicion?"

"No. No, I haven't."

"Then you must keep your head, my dear fellow. Forget about the bogeymen. Be careful not to make false connections. To be frank, you are in a banal situation. I prefer to look first at the most banal explanation. I understand that girl. I can see her now, she gets angry, she tells herself you don't appreciate her, you take no notice of her, you're stalling her about the visa, and suddenly she gets a great idea, she'll throw a scare into you, she'll run away and out of spite, she'll take the precious diaries."

"But, look here —."

"Wait." Charlie held up a hand. "She gets one of her boyfriends to take her away. Perhaps he has even said he will get her out of the country. Then she gets cold feet, she starts to feel sorry, she sends you a nice little note. What do you say?"

"What can I say? Whatever she's done, I'm helpless. Unless you can do something."

"My dear old man, of course I can. I give you my word. I have contacts. Even in France, if she has crossed the frontier. I can put out feelers. Unofficially, not to embarrass you, I can put a word in the ears of certain members of the police. I think I shall find her, and maybe not far away. And then I prophesy that she will be greatly relieved to give back your diaries."

"Whether you're right or not, you're a good man, Charlie. Thank you."

"We are friends. Say no more. But you must be patient for a few days."

"I guess I have no alternative."

"Now have a drink," Charlie said, bringing out one of his golden bottles from a cabinet. "And try to relax."

Chapter 22

Frank saw a pine copse blown out of the ground by one salvo. This was on the second day. The battalion stayed in reserve. The explosions came like metronome strokes, all day, with intervals when they quickened into a blur of noise. Behind the shelling was the unending sound of enemy 'planes. Frank was keyed all day for a crescendo of that noise to warn him each time another attack struck from the sky. Once, for an hour, he looked across the plain to a patch of sky that was darkly speckled with aircraft. There must have been a hundred of them. He saw the multitudinous fall of bombs, the smoke and flashes on the plain and heard the continuous rumble. That was where friendly troops were supposed to be coming up to secure the brigade's flank.

All day long he heard the cry repeated, "Stretchers!" Men went away. No sound came from a shallow pit behind him where Burke lay wounded. Burke had said, "I'm done for. Let me stay with the boys."

Somewhere down the line the little Spanish runner screamed for a long time, all the afternoon. Frank was at a point of tiredness when his mind was insomniac but his body was like lead and his eyelids kept closing. He had not drunk water or eaten for twenty-four hours. The heat smote him. White dust was plastered in his sweat and seared his throat. His bowels ran (he used a corned-beef tin) all the more perhaps because he was so frightened. He did not stop being frightened. He knew now what it was like to be at breaking-point *all the time*.

Barcelona hardly ever came into his mind. When it did, it was on another planet. He did not think about Dick, whom he only glimpsed occasionally.

Early that day the Canadians went up to put in an attack. They went over the hill and a terrible barrage came down on them. All through the morning their wounded streamed back. The news was that the Canadians had recaptured all the lost positions; but the fighting did not diminish.

When it was dark the British went up, into a landscape that was beyond the limits of Frank's imagination. Wherever he looked, the dead were thick. It was hard to find any weapon pits, the ground was so cratered. Bodies had been heaped as ramparts in front of shellholes. Another day came. The Canadians were still somewhere in front, still, from news gleaned, pushing on. Shells continued to fall on the British. In time, they came under fire from the flanks, too.

Frank saw his first tanks next day. Four of them came up a slope, at him directly it seemed. He held the leading tank in his rifle sights and kept up a rapid fire at the black aperture in its front. The noise of rifle fire was deafening. It sounded as if the whole battalion was firing. He heard the heavy machine-guns join in. He pushed in one clip after another, nerving himself to keep his fire aimed and steady. The ball of his thumb was cut in ribbons by the sharp edge of a badly-made magazine platform. Through the stock he felt the rifle grow hot. The lead tank swerved away. The others followed. On the slope he saw the lead tank tip over and vanish from sight. The three others scuttled away. He heard men cheering. He was too tired, hoarse and drenched with relief to join in.

It was dark. Sleep tried again and again to swallow him. But O'Hagan was shaking him, "Come on, come on."

On his feet, he was able to exchange a few words with O'Hagan. The Canadians had gone on for a kilometre and were holding fast somewhere up front. The battalion was now in a neck of captured ground and fire had come from the flanks. There were supposed to be friendly troops out there, O'Hagan said. Hadn't they come? Had they skedaddled again? No-one had told him.

O'Hagan was to take half the company out to the right, to try to make contact with friendly troops. Frank could not count the stooped figures moving around him in the darkness but there seemed to be very few.

Dick came to his side. Dick's face was pale and haggard in the gloom. He went in front of Frank without speaking. The line of men moved down the slope. The dead lay around them like a regiment asleep. Frank saw a shape tilted in front of him, black stamped against the thinner darkness in sharp, mechanical lines, giving off a gleam here and there. He smelt oil and metal. It was one of the tanks he had seen today, small contraptions, scout tanks probably. It canted steeply into the ground, a thin-barrelled machine-gun pointing upward from the closed turret. A track had broken. He passed it and saw that the surface was scarred by rifle bullets.

It was behind him, and the smell that grew now was of things burned. They were coming down to level ground, among a wilderness of thin, splintered pine-trunks, charred black vegetation craters, bodies. He heard a loud snap and the gnat drone of a bullet. A busy cracking began. Twigs fell. Earth danced in front of him. There was an impact of great pain upon his head above the right temple. He came up from a deep place. He was face downwards, his arms hung down and his hands dragged along, it must be, the ground. He was riding something that heaved under him, some animal. His cheek lay on the animal's back. Wetness trickled on his head. Nausea swept over him. He was annihilated.

*

He opened his eyes. Daylight dazzled him and thrust pain into his head. He was lying on his back. He lay with his eyes lightly closed, getting used to the red glare inside the lids. He took long, deep breaths. He was sick. His head throbbed to the pace of his heartbeats. He opened his eyes. He looked up at branches and leaves laced into a sort of roof. He heard someone groaning, someone else muttering. He turned his head to one side. He was in a shelter of branches. Three wounded men were lying alongside him, variously bandaged. A medical orderly knelt beside the farthest of them. He turned his head the other way, saw boots, two legs in breeches, a face looking down at him. He wrinkled his eyes at the face. It was Eddy. Eddy bent down to him. "The hero is awake, is he?"

Frank rummaged among thoughts. Eddy said, "I should have had you out of it. Even before you went on leave."

Frank put a hand to his head. A surprise. There was nothing more than a plaster taped to his shaven skull. Eddy laughed. "Nothing much, eh? A thick skull. It bounced off, your friend said."

Frank was able to mumble, "Friend?"

"Your friend brought you in. Croft."

Frank made the effort to look about him. Eddy must have seen. He said, "He has gone back. They have made some sort of a flank. They are having a bad time down there."

Frank listened to steady shelling. At last he managed to put words together. "What happened?"

"Nothing very good. The other two battalions are finished. Yes, I think they must be. There is not too much left of the British. But they are holding fast." Frank was attentive to the shelling, not the voice. Eddy said, "Hill 356 is in the Republic again."

"Hill 356." This was muttered.

"For a few days. Then it will change hands again." Eddy squatted down. "Frank, can you understand what I'm saying?"

"Yes."

"I an going away. I will not be coming back. You are hearing me?"

"Yes."

"Someone will come. Till then, if you have anything to report, write to Hans."

"Hans."

"You are not to go back into a company. I said, you are not going into the line any more. Understood?"

"Yes."

"I have arranged it with headquarters. They will find you things to do. As —," he lingered, relishing the next words, "— a dogsbody. You know what they mean, eh? A dogsbody?"

"Yes." He had not heard shells explode so abruptly, so cleanly before.

"Listen."

"German gunners. Eighty-eight millimetre. A very good gun."

"Dick?"

"Dick. Your friend. He went back. Maybe you'll see him when it's over. Maybe." He rose up. "You have a good sleep now. In a war you have to think about yourself. We'll talk again before I go." Eddy turned to the orderly. "Look after this fellow. We need him." He went away.

Chapter 23

Nobody (the guests told each other) could remember a party in this wartime city like Charlie's goodbye party. It looked as if the entire smart set was flocking in to the Ritz: government people, army people, diplomats, party people, business people, the Pressmen and all those well-dressed women who had come from everywhere to follow the camp.

Charlie had taken a salon: gilt chairs, tall vases of flowers on low, ornate tables, evening sunshine streaming in through tall windows and a pianist playing soft Palm Court music. It looked, too, as if Charlie had emptied his private cornucopia, bottom up. Whisky flowed at the bar in the corner. Waiters went among the guests with trays, offering caviar on toast and champagne.

Charlie was everywhere among the chattering throng, showing his splendid teeth in an untiring smile, shaking hands, answering questions; always, one might have guessed, the same question, always Charlie laughing, flashing back at them the same answer, "Paris. Where else?"

Henry came in, looking washed out. A lot of people were leaving. It was time to go on to dinner. Charlie stood at the door receiving farewells. Henry said, "Hello, Charlie," and waited.

Charlie shook a hand, clapped a back, kissed a woman and packed the party off with a friendly sweep of his arm. He turned to Henry. "Better late than never."

"They repatriated a trainload of Internationals today, invalids. Nearly all of them were blinded or amputation cases. I went with them in the train as far as Gerona. I came straight from the station —. This is sudden, Charlie."

Charlie stayed him with an upraised hand and turned to a departing couple, a picture of entire, absorbed attention to them. Henry went into the room. He took a drink, looked around. He exchanged greetings: a smart uniform here, a black suit there, people in the know, but he was not in a mood to tackle them for news. He saw Victoria with the Mexican consul. They were talking about Diego Rivera when he joined them. Henry said, "You praise Rivera for his politics. I prefer to enjoy him as a painter."

Victoria said, "The aim of socialist art is to *mobilize* those peasants..."

The consul laid a hand on her arm. "Henry knows about that, my dear. He knows Rivera and he knows Mexico. I cannot say the some of other American reporters."

Henry reminisced about a visit he had made to Mexico City in 1927 when the American newspapers were reporting riots against the Calles government. "The other papers called them Bolsheviki. I found that what they were rioting against was the new diphtheria vaccination. I guess none of the other newspapermen spoke Spanish. Not that they cared. I sent a report to the State Department about it. Mr. Kellogg liked to hear from me."

Victoria said, "Henry, I have good news for you. I've heard from the Army. They're letting you go to the front."

"That's wonderful. When?"

"Very soon, that's all I know. They'll telephone you."

"I'll drop everything when they do. I hope they'll let me go to the Internationals." To the Mexican he said, "My boy is with the 15th Brigade," and to Victoria, "I haven't heard from him. All Peter knows is that they are in the line."

The mob was thinning. Henry excused himself and went back to Charlie. He said, "Some party!"

"Well, why not?" Charlie stretched his shoulders back, relaxing. "I can't take it with me. I do things in style, eh?"

"You never said anything about this the other day. Why are you going? When did you decide?"

"When? I don't know. It has been in my mind. Why? It is time for the rats to leave the ship. I see prospects elsewhere."

"Do you always go out on a big party?"

"That's way it is with me. A bigger party is nearly over, old friend. It is time to get out —. Don't you think?"

"If you feel that way."

Charlie turned to a waiting group. He shook all the hands, kissed all the offered female cheeks and went with the party to the door. Fatigue weighed upon Henry. The depression which had drained him since Emmy's flight had worsened this evening, after the journey with the cripples. He went to the door and put out a hand, "Well, Charlie. This is it."

Charlie took his hand, completed the clasp with the other hand and said, "Stay a little."

"I guess I'm done up. I'll hit the hay as soon as I've eaten."

"Stay. Eat with me. Only the bar-flies are left. I'll tell the *maître* to attend to their gullets." He went to the head waiter, talked and came back. "I've ordered room service. Come."

Henry walked out with him. "To tell the truth I'm not very hungry."

"You can pick at some cold cuts."

In Charlie's room they could hear loudspeakers down the street giving forth the Riego hymn. Flags dotted the fronts of the buildings opposite with colour. Charlie pulled an armchair to the low glass table. "Come, sit. I can see how tired you are."

He went to the cabinet and poured a lot of whisky into each of two large crystal goblets. He set a glass down in front of Henry, sat opposite him, leaned back and stretched his legs. "So. *La commedia è finita*. Almost."

"There's a lot of fight left in them yet."

"True. *Ma digo io che è finita*."

"I guess so."

"It is time for the supers to leave the stage."

"Unfortunately the actors can't."

"You and I are not actors." Charlie leaned forward. "Henry, you should go, too."

"Surely — when my job's done here."

"It's done, Henry. Believe me. Leave. You're too big to waste your time waiting for the end."

"I saw the beginning. I guess I have to see this out."

"You should be in London and Paris and Berlin, where they are already playing the overture to the big drama."

"Time enough when the curtain's down on this one. Where are you going?"

"Paris. Paris *la belle*. I shall have good times there."

"You have good times everywhere, I imagine. And then? After Paris?"

Charlie took a sip and savoured it. "Where there's a dollar to be made."

Henry drank, scrutinised Charlie, came to a decision and put down his glass. "Charlie, — this is a time to he honest. It's now or never. Every time I have ever met you, Charlie, I have tossed a mental coin. Are you an agent or aren't you?"

"Me?" Charlie's smile, over his glass, was at once sweet, surprised and questioning. "An agent? You mean some sort of secret service man?"

"That's what I mean. I guess I've made up my mind by now."

"But why, Henry? What on earth makes you think that?"

"I don't know. The nickel has dropped that way. If so, of course, there's no question about who you're working for."

Charlie watched him, silent, amused; then, sobering, "Henry, forget this nonsense. You must get out."

175

"Not yet. To tell you the truth, I feel as if I belong here."

Charlie emptied his glass, a slow absorption of liquid into himself. When the whisky had gone he set the glass on the table, stood up, went to the window and after a few moments turned to face Henry. "Henry, I said, must. You are in trouble here. It's not safe for you any more."

"Why must? What is this? What sort of trouble could I be in? And how do you know?"

"Don't press me. I hear things. I can't tell you more, do as I say, pack, and get out, quickly. Do you hear me?"

Henry considered. "I think I know what you're getting at. It isn't entirely news to me —. Do you know anything about this Emmy business?"

"Never mind Emmy. I'm talking about you. Go."

There was a tap at the door. A waiter pushed a trolley in. He put a bottle of white wine in a bucket, platters of cold meat, white rolls and a bowl of salad on the table. He arranged napkins, cutlery and condiments. Charlie waved him out. After the door closed behind him, Henry said, "I told you, I have a job to finish."

"It is finished, my friend."

"I guess we fellows in the Press corps are the witnesses. We have to see the tragedy out."

"If you stay you won't see it out."

"Look, if you know something, tell me. Emmy comes into this, doesn't she? And my diaries. Tell me and I'll deal with it. I'm an old-fashioned American, Charlie. I won't be scared. I stand on my rights. For God's sake, I can ask the government for protection."

"The government can't even protect its own people."

"I know Negrin, Del Vayo —."

"The people I'm talking about don't care about the Spanish. God Almighty couldn't stop them."

"I guess Washington could. Wait till I tip off the Department."

"You could wrap yourself in the Stars and Stripes, Henry. They wouldn't care."

"All right," Henry said, "You're an agent, their agent. The question is, why are you telling me this? Have you got orders to scare me out of the country?"

"I'm trying to scare you, but nobody ordered me to. I want you to go to France. You shouldn't even show up at the frontier. I will give you a route and a man to take you over."

"This doesn't figure. You want me to believe that you're double-crossing your own people, for me. Why?"

"Just do as I say."

"This man you spoke about, this guide. Suppose he squeals on you. You'd be finished."

Smiling, Charlie shook his head.

Henry said, "Charlie, you are inviting me to step into a lunatic world. Much as I like you, you're no altruist. Why are you doing this? For all I know, the trap is right here, and you are setting it."

"It's no trap. You'll have to trust me."

Henry was silent. Charlie stood in front of him, meeting Henry's assessing eyes. He said, "The truth is, my friend, I am already finished."

Henry broke a silence. "So that's it. That's where you're going."

"*Na rodinu.*"

Henry nodded. "Some Fatherland! You're on your way to the cellars."

"Just so."

"Why don't you run?"

"I don't want to run."

"No. I've heard. None of you run. It seems you all go."

"I'm telling *you* to run, Henry."

"It's a nightmare. You. And me. You run, for God's sake. Don't worry about me. There must be someone I can talk to. I'm a friend, a newspaper man, I've done nothing outside of my job. What else am I supposed to have done?"

"Tell me, what have *I* done —? Henry, you're in the lunatic world like me. You should see the bill of accusation against you! He spied in Moscow. He collected information from oppositionists and traitors. In Spain he has wormed his way into the confidence of people in the highest positions, he haunts the military headquarters for what he can ferret out, he goes to the hospitals to get information from the wounded, he was caught spying in a battalion area at the front. Oh, yes, they know about that. Everything. You're a spy. They've decided. It's quite possible they have a confession already from some wretch in the Lubyanka that he sold military secrets to you and carried out acts of sabotage on your instructions. Don't tell me it's crazy, because I'm going back, my friend. I'm going back there."

After a few moments Henry spoke. "It's crazy all right, but I've heard it all before. I was at the Moscow Trials."

"That's why they are after you. The stuff about Spain is half pretext, half paranoia. By this time they've got to thinking crazy over there. But

177

it's for what you unearthed in Russia that they've fingered you. Just one example, your account of how the confessions were obtained."

"I see you've read my diaries."

"Yes. After all my experience of human folly, I'm surprised, I'm forever surprised at how few are the voices in the West raised to expose the Trials. Some are mystified by the confessions, but look how many accept them as genuine. All those famous liberal reporters, great intellectuals also, even diplomats. And of course it is all tied up with bigger matters. The need to make a treaty with the West against Germany, trust, peace, war. You are only a little man, Henry, with a little voice, but they like to be thorough and you have to be silenced."

"I see —. Well, they've got the diaries."

"It is all still inside your skull. They mean to deal with that."

"Now tell me where Emmy comes into this. What has happened to her?"

"She was offered a ticket to the Argentine and a visa in exchange for the diaries."

"Where is she now?"

"Nowhere."

"Oh, my God!" Henry rose, went to the window and looked out for some moments. "Poor girl," he said. "Poor girl." He turned round. "I believe you. But I can't jet out. My boy is down there on the Ebro. I know your people. Relatives are hostages to them. If I say a word out loud, even to my colleagues, if I make a move, I endanger him. I have to keep quiet and get down there to see him. I'll figure out some way for the pair of us to get away."

"I shall not be here to help. All the same, I will leave you the name of the guide."

"Thank you."

Charlie went and refilled the glasses, "So, you see, we are in the same boat, my dear Henry."

"You need not be. Cut and run. Spill the beans."

"Really, old man," Charlie said, "a fellow has to live up to his code, eh? Let's drink to that." He held out Henry's glass.

Standing by the window, Henry said, "I'm sorry, I'm not up to that sort of play acting. Maybe you fingered me. And maybe her too. Did you?" A few paces took him to the door. "I'll say goodbye, Charlie." He paused for a moment. "I hope you make out somehow."

Charlie said, "*Proschai.*"

Henry went out. His last look took Charlie in, standing there, smiling a little, the two glasses in his hand. Henry closed the door and went downstairs. Victoria, like most of the other guests, had left. He went after her, to hurry up his pass to the front.

Chapter 24

Erickson came away from the telephone. He said to Frank, "The trucks'll be up any moment. You can come out and help."

Frank said, "Righto."

He lifted the blanket and looked out of the headquarters dugout. It was in the base of the hill, under timbers and at least ten feet of earth. Across the clearing outside, the Spanish *aiutante* was talking with Cipriano, the commander of the Spanish company. The headquarters interpreter and four Spanish riflemen were with them. Erickson said, "That was Gates on the line, he's sent us a hundred and thirty-two men. Cipriano can take half. We'll have to spread the others out among our lads."

"If they're anything like the last lot of Spanish reinforcements we're better off without 'em."

"No we're not. The lads are half-dead on their feet. There's always trenches to dig and gear to hump. We'll have to make do with what we get." At the back of the cave a runner was talking to the telephonist. Erickson said to him, "Get your mates, Ted. You'll have to take these buggers up to the companies."

The runner went out. Erickson was acting as battalion commissar while Cooney was away at a conference. He said, "I could have thanked God for those lads that came in last night. I nearly cried when I had a good look at them. Young MacNally could go blind with those eyes of his. Barnard's wound's come open at the edges."

"MacNally said they volunteered to come. They all seemed glad to be back."

"They're not glad. No bugger's glad. They're just better men than Jesus Christ and his saints." Erickson was talking about fourteen British who had come back from hospital. "I don't know where we'd be without a few like them coming back."

In the distance the enemy guns were like a continuous knocking of hammers. The duller detonations of arriving shells rumbled among the hills. The brigade had been relieved but the front was close at hand and alive with the enemy offensive. Pain darted behind Frank's eyes. He had only a small dressing taped to his skull but a twinge occasionally stunned his mind for a moment.

Erickson said, "I can hear the trucks. Come on."

Frank was a headquarters man now. He had got hold of a pistol which he wore in a big holster on his belt, and a black leather jacket with a fur collar and a zip fastener. He was grateful for its fleece lining when he went outside. The weather had changed overnight. He had come outside this morning to see a grey sky and black clouds around the peaks. The air was cold and a chill wind prowled.

The first truck came into sight. Behind were two more. All were packed with men. Erickson signalled to the drivers to come in under the shelter of the trees. The trucks stopped. The Spanish officers were shouting to the men in them, who scrambled down. These were unarmed. Four armed men, their guards, stayed in each of the trucks. A great deal of activity followed. Cipriano called the recruits round him and made a brief attempt to hearten them. Erickson spoke a few words of welcome which were interpreted. A sorting-out began. Most of the draft, as usual, were pitifully young, all the more pathetic for their over-large uniforms and for the assortment of improvised packs, cheap suitcases, musical instruments and other possessions that they clutched. The unhappiness and bewilderment in their faces did not diminish during the speeches. There were some older men with them, who kept together in groups, and who were otherwise distinguished by the portions of unfamiliar uniforms that they wore. These looked self-assured enough, and contemptuous of what was going on. Cipriano was asking the reinforcements about their training. He listened to answers, turned to Erickson, said something and shook his head. There was more talking. Erickson came across to Frank. He said, "This is the worst yet. All that lot there are deserters. Most of them'll be off again. And them others over there are prisoners of war. Christ! They'll be over the lines before you can say 'shit' — if they don't shoot our lads in the back first."

Frank said, "I'll get round the companies and see they're watched."

"We'll have to arm 'em with the others. See to it, will you?"

Frank said, "I want their names first."

"Fuckin' get 'em out of here before the 'planes come over. The whole lot of them."

Frank said, "Righto."

The trucks were moving off. Cipriano had picked out a contingent and marched them off. Frank selected twenty of the remaining youngsters, those who looked the brightest and steadiest, to go as carriers to the machine-gunners. He knew not to take risks by letting any of the ex-prisoners near to the precious guns. These, with the remainder, he divided up into three parties. He told the runners to take them to the rifle companies.

Ted, the runner, pointed to a man who had stepped out of the crowd and who waited on his own under the trees. Frank went to him and said, "*Vaya con los otros.*"

The man was shortish and thickset. A forelock and thick eyebrows of shaggy black hair intensified the frown on his creased, doggy, darkly weathered face. He was bareheaded and there were no badges on the limp, worn-through military jacket over his shirt. All his clothes hung loose on him. He said, "I'm not fookin' Spanish. I dare say you can tell a fookin' Scouse when he talks to yer."

"Too true," Frank said. "Are you back from hospital?"

The newcomer took a *carnet* from his jacket pocket and held it out. Frank took it and looked through it. He gave it back to the man. "Glad you're back, Dugan."

Dugan said, "Where are the machine-guns? I'll get back to my mates."

Frank pointed. "Up there, behind those trees. Go for a rifle first. Armoury's over there."

After, Frank went to each of the company commanders. He talked to them about the reinforcements and asked them to send him new muster rolls on which the names and next-of-kin of the reinforcements would be shown. When he came back to headquarters he said to Erickson, "There's a chap just come back to the m.g.s —."

"Dugan. I know. l saw him."

"He's come back from a punishment company."

"I wish they'd kept the bugger. He's a bad element."

"What did he do?"

"Trotskyist."

"Jesus! What? Was he open about it?"

"They never come out in the open. Not the ones we get. They just make trouble. That's what he did."

"He should have been shot," Frank said.

"He would have been, just about anywhere else in the IB. He was lucky it was this battalion."

"I suppose we shall have to keep an eye on him."

"Let's hope he's learned his lesson. He's a good machine-gunner. It's not easy in them punishment mobs, you know."

"I've never come across them. I've seen the jail."

"We ran into one of 'em the night before we crossed the Ebro. I reckon those lads would a damn sight sooner have been in the clink. They'd been there for weeks, sounding the river bed and putting patrols over the other side. Suicide job. A bullet for anyone that didn't toe the line. They were all sorts, every language you could think,"

"He's lucky they let him off."

"They had to. We need every man."

Frank sat down to his typewriter. There was an unfinished sheet of speaker's notes in it, for the company commissars. "I'll get on with these," he said.

*

From the time of Frank's arrival at the front he had been able to sleep and wake at will, each bout of sleep a blackout into which fatigue dropped him; but since his concussion he had not slept well. The twinges of head pain were not frequent or serious but he found himself waiting for them, awake. When he slept he dreamed in snatches, and though he could not recall the dreams when he opened his eyes they left him unsettled.

He went to Brigade early and called first at *Trasmisiones* to listen to the radio news from Barcelona. Enemy attacks had been repelled with heavy casualties. Ernest Hemingway had sent another message of support for the Republic. A delegation of French priests touring Catalonia praised the facilities given to the Church. Girl workers at the Francisco Ferrer clothing factory had produced a record number of uniforms in the previous month. The British Cabinet was meeting to discuss the Czech crisis. Downing Street was pessimistic. Informed sources in London expected war.

Frank was in the Brigade Commissar's office and had just taken his speaker's notes from the duplicating machine when a runner, who had been looking for him, told him to report to Lieutenant Kulich in the autopark.

He had seen Kulich about. As a Brigade observer Kulich came up to the British sometimes to lead the battalion into positions. His peaked cap, said to be the highest in the brigade, well back on his head, the stub of a cigar clenched between his teeth, he would stalk in front of the leading company, thumbs hooked into his belt, ignoring both the shellfire and the men who followed him. Frank found him in the autopark, standing by a big open Buick, talking in Spanish with the driver across the open bonnet. He turned to Frank. "Hello, Brendan. Eddy told me about you." So Kulich, too, was SIM. "You in HQ now eh?"

"Yes."

"I told Erickson to see you don't stick your neck out any more."

184

"I won't do that."

"They keep you busy?"

"Yes."

"What do you do?"

"I've taken over the documentation. I'm to help Erickson get out material for the commissars. That's what I came up about this morning —."

"I know. I just rang the British to ask for you."

"And I shall give a hand generally. I'm going out with Hooky today scrounging fresh meat."

"Scrounging?"

"He barters for it."

"Don't go too far. I want you back here tonight at ten o'clock."

"Here?"

"That's what I said. Right here in the autopark. I told Erickson you'd be away for twenty-four hours."

"What for?"

"You be here. Ten o'clock. We'll push off as soon as it's dark. You better get back now. Erickson wants you to get that mule party moving."

*

Night had already fallen at ten o'clock. The clouds were piled in startling black mountains above the broken skyline, deepening a darkness that was speckled with flashes and fires and shaken incessantly by the sound of guns. Kulich sat in the back of the car, the big collar of his greatcoat turned up, chewing an unlit cigar. The driver started the engine when Frank appeared. Kulich said nothing. Frank was hardly aboard when the car started to move.

On the road there was the usual night-time stir of foot soldiers moving up to the line and coming out, and ghostly trucks flitting past. Ahead of them Mora was dark and quiet. Before they came to the town they turned off to bump along a track that climbed a shoulder of the low hills facing the river. Kulich did not speak. His head back against the cushion, he seemed to be occupied by fierce, private thoughts. Frank did not break the silence.

He saw ahead the small bulk of a house against the hill. Something in front of the house that obscured his view turned out to be a camouflage net stretched over the roof and covering a small courtyard in front of the house. The car stopped under the net. Kulich and Frank got out. Faint streaks of light showed round the edges of a blacked-out window. The door was open. A woman waited for them.

Kulich said, "Marta, hello!" and shook hands with her. He flipped a hand at Frank. "Brendan."

Frank shook hands with her. She was tiny, grey-haired and bright-eyed, a woman in her fifties. She wore an apron over her dress. She ushered them into a room. She said, "Take brandy. Help yourself. Then you will eat."

Marta: Frank remembered the name. Marta went into a kitchen. Kulich poured two glasses of brandy. The room had a parquet floor, a fireplace and walls done out in rustic style, three big armchairs, bright rugs and a lot of china knick-knacks. Kulich called out to Marta, "How have you been?"

"Fine." She came into the doorway. Her accent was slight and pleasant, "You look well. You haven't brought any clothes to sew?"

"Not this time. You did a good job. I guess we could call you a technical specialist."

She brought in a tureen of soup. After, she served a roast chicken with rice, and put out wine and fruit. She had been to Paris since she last saw Kulich. He, it was clear, had memories of the place. Names and gossip passed between them.

Frank had a tiny bedroom to himself. Kulich took a long and noisy bath. Frank gave up waiting for the bathroom and went to bed. Nothing had been said to enlighten him. He slept uneasily on the spring mattress. The room was too warm. He listened to the war in the distance.

In the morning they had white rolls, butter and good coffee. Frank and Kulich went outside. It was a cold, grey day. Kulich smoked a cigar. They looked out through the garnished netting at the Ebro. Kulich reminisced about the April retreat when he had been hauled out of the river on the far bank, naked and nearly dead. They watched an air raid on Mora. The 'planes appeared and disappeared among the clouds. Two fighters came down and streaked low over a road. Kulich looked at his watch and said, "Maybe he's sitting this one out in a ditch."

Frank asked no questions. Soon after they had gone back into the house a car drew up outside and Hans came in. He was in uniform. He greeted the two men briefly and went into the kitchen with Marta. He came back and said, "I cannot stay long. Sit down. We will talk."

Marta brought cups of coffee on a tray. When she had gone, Hans said, "You have both heard the talk about a withdrawal of the Brigades. I have not called you here to speculate about this but to make certain things clear. Is there much talk about it in the battalions?"

Frank waited. Kulich said, "The Lincolns are buzzing with it. A lot of bad talk. The Spanish in the battalion keep hazing our boys about it."

"They are hostile? There is someone inciting division?"

"It doesn't need anyone. I wouldn't call then hostile. They're kind of ironic. Yeah, contemptuous. I guess they are bitter. It's the contempt that upsets the American boys."

Hans looked at Frank. "What about your people?"

"The Spanish aren't as integrated with us as they are in the Lincolns —."

"I know, I know —." Hans cut him short. "And in the Spanish company?"

"I don't know about them."

"You should. Listen, both of you. The talk about withdrawal is to stop. Do you understand? Kulich, you must knock it into their heads at the Brigade. Make the battalion leaderships understand. This rumour must be denied. It must be stopped. There will be no withdrawal."

"Sure," Kulich said. "It takes the heart out of them. I guess it does."

"And you —." Hans turned on Frank again. "I have heard nothing from you since Eddy left your battalion."

"We've been in the line," Frank said. "You know what sort of shit our lot's been taking."

"This rumour, it is not affecting their fighting spirit?"

Frank, beginning to feel harassed, said, "I don't know what they feel like under that sort of fire. I'm at HQ now. It's at your orders. I reckon I'd feel sick if I had to go in against machine-guns and I thought we might be pulled out tomorrow."

"When they come out, do you hear subversive talk?"

On a sudden rush of feeling, as if tears were coming to the back of his eyes, Frank said, "What do you mean subversive talk? They grumble. Of course they grumble. The British always grumble. There's something wrong when they don't. Yes, they do talk about a withdrawal among themselves. They do feel sick at having to go in again and again. But I'm not going to pass on every grumble to you and get a lot of bloody fine lads punished."

Hans eyed him, for a long moment. Then, unexpectedly, he smiled, a slight smile that softened the lines of his mutilated face. He said, "I am glad you value your comrades. But what you must know is this, both of you, and all political workers in the 15th Brigade. The talk of a withdrawal must make no difference to our work. We must maintain vigilance to the utmost. Suppose, let us suppose, that the day came when the Brigades were disbanded. There are certainly still spies in the ranks —." Suddenly, "You agree, Frank?"

"Yes. Of course. It stands to reason."

"Then the spies will be allowed to go, with the others. To work against us in their own countries. We must expose them here, where the conditions are favourable for exterminating them."

Kulich said, "That makes sense."

Hans said to Frank, "So cherish your comrades by all means. I remember the British frontfighters in France. Here, too, they are second to none. But on condition that you redouble your efforts to expose the bad elements. Vigilance, vigilance to the end."

Kulich chewed a cigar. Frank said, "I agree."

"When you suspect, you report. No weakness."

"Of course."

"Good." Hans reached into a briefcase. He brought out a sheet of paper clipped to a photograph. "Here —." He gave it to Frank. The picture was an enlargement from a British passport photograph, with the top of the embossed Foreign Office stamp showing in the bottom right hand corner. Frank recognised the face that looked up at him. He said, "This man came back to us yesterday. His name is Dugan."

He read the typewritten notes on the sheet. Biographical details. Born Liverpool, 1906, unemployed, active in unemployed workers' movement, joined Party 1934, unmarried. Enlisted IB October 1936, wounded Brunete, returned battalion August 1937. Unmasked as Trotskyist and defeatist July 1938, transferred punishment company. Hostile activities not detected during previous Party membership. Frank said, "I knew from his *carnet* where he'd been. What exactly had he done?"

"What it says there." Hans took the paper back. "He has to be watched. He might spread his poison again. He might desert. When the front situation permits we will take him back."

Frank said, "Have all the men in the punishment units been sent back?"

Hans said, "All, now."

"And the men in prison?"

Kulich said, "I was up there last week. All the 15th Brigade men are out. We've had to scrape the barrel, the Brigade's a husk. The Lincolns and the 59th aren't fit to fight. We're taking two companies from your battalion to reinforce them."

Frank said, "I hadn't heard."

"They're moving today."

Frank said, "There's a man of ours in the prison who hasn't come back yet. A man named Morgan." He caught their looks. "I saw him on my way back from Barcelona."

Kulich waited for Hans to answer. Hans said, "He will not come now."

Kulich said, "They're all back. I told you." More gently, he said, "Maybe they sent him somewhere else, Frank. It happens."

Frank said, "Of course."

"You are at headquarters now," Hans said. "Do you see much of your friend Croft?"

"Not for a day or two."

"Don't neglect him. I hear he is a good soldier."

"He is. And the men like him."

"Do they? Has he gained some influence with them?"

"It's not a question of influence. They just like him."

"I see that you like him, too."

"I suppose I do. He brought me in when I was hit."

"He was your friend before that."

"Yes. Why?"

Hans smiled. "I am glad you are his friend. Do you have influence with him? Do you educate him?"

"I try." He saw Hans' waiting, expectant smile. "He's got a mind of his own."

"You once thought him naive."

"He still is, politically. But he's, well, he's tough. He's stubborn. His mind's made up."

"By his background. The son of a rich family."

"By his father."

"Henry Croft. Yes." Hans took a clip of papers from his briefcase. "We come to this." He showed the papers to Frank, who saw the four pages of his own letter denouncing Henry. "This was very good. Has the son read the diaries?"

"Yes. Some of them, anyway."

"You have discussed them with him?"

"Yes."

"What is his attitude?"

"He believes them. We had a hell of an argument about them."

"And after that?"

"Nothing. It was just the once."

Kulich broke in. "So here he is, in the battalion, believing all this poison. A guy who carries an SS knife. Why didn't you report this argument?"

"I didn't take it seriously."

"You didn't?" And at his incredulous, accusing voice Frank felt a knife of terror in his own entrails. He was digging a pit for himself.

"You don't understand —."

"OK," Kulich was speaking quietly but intensely, "he brought you in when you were hit. But has he talked about any of this stuff since?"

"Not to me. I hardly see him now."

"Not to you. But to all these guys who like him?"

"How could he? They're Party members, most of them. Never mind about liking him. If he breathed one word out of line I'd damn soon hear about it."

It was Hans' turn to intervene, gently, "They are having a bad time now, yes? In and out of action all the time. No rest. Nerves frayed by these rumours. I have seen it myself, at such a time even Party men become demoralised."

"How can you call them demoralised?" Frank's spurt of anger was fed by confused fears, for himself, for his friend. "They're fighting like heroes. Ask Gates. Ask him —!" He indicated Kulich.

"Sure," Kulich said. "But guys in that state are easy meat for a diversionist."

"He doesn't talk politics, you take my word." Frank still spoke loudly, angrily. "He's too tired, like the rest of them. I only see him when he comes back. I wish you could. He looks ten years older. I can hardly get a word out of him. I just make sure he's all right and give him some cigarettes. Don't sit there and talk to me about diversionists. Just wait till we get a breathing-space and I'll talk to him. He's only a kid, I'll win him round. Leave him alone. Leave him to me. Please!"

Hans was smiling again and nodding benevolently. "Of course. You spoke up then like a real Bolshevik. Good. Good. Young Croft is lucky to have a friend like you. Eh, Kulich?"

"He sure is," Kulich said.

Hans said, "We have confidence in you. You will teach him. You will watch over him. And you will let us know now he develops." He closed his briefcase. "And now we will eat. Marta has cooked something good for you before you go back to your duty."

Chapter 25

During the night Frank heard a pattering outside his cave; then the rain dropped like a cataract. It slackened toward daylight. A steady downpour continued. He went out to a dark dawn. Water rushed among the gravel underfoot and brimmed over the edge of the path to splash among the bushes.

The morning was cold. The rain had stopped. The air was still damp. At headquarters Frank was writing an article called "After the JSU Conference" for the Brigade newspaper, *Volunteer For Liberty*.

He had only a telephone operator and a couple of runners for company. Erickson had gone up the hill with the officers. The battalion had been put on standby. Frank typed. The operator was talking, scribbling, listening, speaking again. He put down the instrument. He turned and said, "Listen to this. The chap at Brigade heard it on the radio this morning. Negrin made a speech at the League Assembly. He said he was ready to withdraw all foreign volunteers in the Republic, if —."

Frank said, "Shut up —. I said, shut it." A stride took him to the operator's table. He snatched the paper away from the man and glanced at it.

"I was only telling you —."

"We know about that. It's talk. That's all it is. Do you want this to get around and upset everyone?"

"They're entitled to know —."

"They're entitled to know nothing. They're on standby and they're going to be in the shit any minute. Do you want to go with them —? If I hear a word about this business and it comes back to you, you're in trouble —."

"OK, OK." The man was anxious and placating.

"And that goes for you two," Frank said to the runners. "And for that silly bugger at Brigade. I'll see that Gates hears about him."

He knew it was hopeless to threaten or warn. He went out into the clearing. An enemy spotter 'plane was bumbling around under low clouds. An old acquaintance by now, the little high-winged monoplane went round and round. The baked earth in the clearing had gone soft. Where mules or men had trodden it was miry. He walked on to grass. It squelched under his espadrilles. Water came up through the worn rope soles. The 'plane buzzed away. Frank watched, knowing what was to happen. A black blob fell from the 'plane, trailing smoke, a message canister. He walked up and down, refreshing himself with the cold air, waiting. The first shell landed over the hill. The second went wide, into the woods. Two more, then a salvo dropped on the woods. The shelling continued. The 'plane was back overhead, circling.

He went into the dugout and finished the article. The shelling had stopped. Erickson and the officers came back. Frank left the dugout. He walked up the path, along the ridge past his cave, and up the steeper path, among dripping trees, to the company lines.

His old company was encamped among the trees at the head of a long slope. Going up to them, he passed the machine-gunners who were busy with their weapons and stores. He saw Dugan, seated on a log, and went across to him. Dugan was intent upon the cartridges that he was checking in a belt. He tested their seating, one by one, carefully. Frank said, "Hallo, Dugan. Everything all right?"

Dugan glanced at him sidelong. "Why shouldn't it be?"

"I reckon you're glad to be back with your mates."

Dugan said, "I reckon so."

Frank sat next to him on the log. "I saw in your book where you'd been. Was it bad? How did they treat you there?"

"So-so."

"I haven't been out here long, but they say it can be bloody rough in those companies." Dugan kept his eyes on the cartridge belt. Frank said, "I don't know much about these things. What was it all about?"

"Nothing much."

"I don't understand," Frank said. "They send you away to a mob like that and you say, it was nothing much?"

"That's right."

"You're a volunteer. They had no right."

"Don't tell me," Dugan said. "Go and tell some fucker else."

"You must know why they came down on you."

Dugan said, dismissively, "Ask me."

"I'm asking you."

"Look, *moosh*," Dugan said. "I'm busy. It'll be my fault if the gun jams."

"Oh, right," Frank said, and stood up. "How are you off for fags?" He took a packet from his tunic.

"I'm all right."

"Take the packet."

Not taking his eyes off the belt, Dugan pointed to a flat stone. "Leave it there."

Frank put the packet on the stone. "Anyway, I'm glad you're settling in. I'm just a sort of odd bod, at HQ. I'm supposed to help people. If there's anything I can do, let me know."

Not looking up, Dugan said, "All right."

Yorky, drinking from a tin mug, was looking down the slope as Frank came up. He said, "You're too late for a brew-up."

Dick and Harris were also nursing mugs of coffee between their hands. Twigs still smouldered in a small alcove of stones. The pockets of the three men bulged with cartridges. Their rifles and gear were against a tree-trunk. Dick said, "Get a mug. We'll give you a slop of ours."

Frank said, "You drink up. I'll get some down below. Everyone all right up here? You didn't get any of that shit?"

Harris said, "Not this time. That bugger up there hasn't spotted us yet." The 'plane was still droning round and round the hill.

Yorky said, "You've got nowt to worry about down there, with the bloody hill on top of you."

"You're dead right," Frank said.

"You wouldn't have an umbrella to spare?" Dick said.

"The Chinese used to go into battles with umbrellas up," Harris said. "That's what I read in a book when I was a kid. I remember we all thought it was real funny."

"Have you all got ponchos? I can fiddle you some from the stores."

"We done that already," Harris said. "Great fiddlers, us three. Old King Cole. He sent for his fiddlers three. You wouldn't know what we're on standby for, would you?"

"Not a thing. They were all in a huddle round Fletch, then they all got busy."

"Ah, well," Harris said. "We'll know when we get there."

"We will an' all," Yorky said. "We're the bloody fire brigade, we are."

"That's about it," Frank said.

Yorky threw out a "Ha!" He said, "Look who's talking. You won't be there. How did you work it?"

"I didn't work it."

Dick said, "You're green with envy, Yorky."

"Frank's only a youngster," Harris said.

Yorky pointed at Dick. "This one's younger."

Harris said, "He's a political worker. They need political workers down there."

Dick said, "He's our man in HQ. He can tell us all the good news."

Yorky said, "Can he tell us when we're going home?"

"When we've won the bloody war," Frank said.

Yorky said "That'll be the day —. I saw you talking to Dugan down there."

"That's right."

"Right surprise to see him back."

"You know about him?"

"Know about him? I were sleeping next to him when they took him."

Dick said," What's this about?"

Harris said, "Feller in the machine-guns back from a punishment company."

"Punishment company! That's a turn-up! What else don't I know about?"

Frank said, "When was this? What happened?"

"July, when we were up at Falset, before this lot started. A lot of the lads were right browned off. We were out in the fields, you see, under sergeants, and the officers fucked off into the bloody village, and lived indoors, they had an officers' mess and lived like kings. At least, so we heard. We were living on bloody chick-peas. We had nowhere to go and they never got up anything for us to do. But they put the village out of bounds to us. One night about twenty of the lads went into the village. They went to the brothel. That was out of bounds to us poor buggers. They got into the villagers' club and had a right royal booze-up. Then they all got put under arrest."

"There was a lot of sympathy for them," Harris said. "And Dugan spoke up for them, even though he was a Party member. I was at the Party meeting. He said they ought to be treated compassionately —. They were in the end. But the commissars were all for making an example. Dugan wouldn't be shut up and said he had a right to raise it in an open battalion meeting."

"And a right bloody cheer he got from the lads," broke in Yorky. "They shouted and cheered like Bingley Brass Band. He went on about all the complaints the lads had. And the next thing you know, about two o'clock in the morning I wake up. Someone's bending over Dugan and whispering to him. They go away and that was the last we see of Dugan till the other day. He knew me, I was his mate in hospital once, and he told me where he'd been. I don't think he's said a word to anyone else, the poor bugger's that scared. It was Haxey as took him away."

"That poor bugger," Harris said.

194

"Well," Dick said. "This beats Banagher. Just for opening his mouth, was it?"

Frank said, "He was a Trotskyist."

"A what?"

Harris said, "Trotskyists make trouble."

"That's what they call you when they put the black on you," Yorky said. "It's after this feller Trotsky."

Dick uttered a big laugh. "Trotsky." He looked up and shouted, "Trotsky!" His voice resounded among the trees. Men turned to look. Dick cupped his hands round his mouth and uttered a mightier shout, "Trotskee-ee! Trotskee-ee! Up Trotsky! Good old Trotsky!"

He stood there laughing, and for these moments looked like his old, shining self. He beamed at Frank, and cried, "Put me in irons, comrade."

Frank said affectionately, "Idiot!"

Whistles were shrilling. Voices took up a cry, "*Avión!*"

They could hear the beat of engines coming at them. The entire company became immobile under trees. The roar and throb became immense, enclosing. They heard the fall of bombs. Overlapping detonations shook the ground and the trees. They all stood still. The engine roar did not diminish. A second salvo of bombs exploded, a third and a fourth. The noise began to dwindle. Frank stepped out from under his tree. Four vees of bombers were going away, one behind the other, five 'planes in each. Smoke began to come up over the trees. From down behind the hill they heard voices calling, "Stretchers!" "Stretchers!"

*

Erickson was to take a defaulters' parade that evening. The commander and the officers were too busy getting ready for a move. He had to wait until another air raid had ended, another big one, fifteen German 'planes. It was the eighth since dawn and there had been two more shellings. Frank, waiting with Erickson, had six dead to report to Barcelona. Eleven wounded had been taken away.

Two men were brought in. Both had bruised faces. They had been fighting. One of them called the other a fucking ignorant Mick. Erickson gave this one a dressing-down and made him apologise to the other. He told both of them that there had been too much fighting, he was going to put a stop to it. At this point the signaller called to him, holding out the telephone. "It's Brigade."

Erickson was at the telephone for a few minutes. He came back to his table, sat down and said to the two men, "Next time I'll put you on digging for a week. Get back to your company now. You'll get your bellyful of scrapping tonight."

When the men had gone he said to Frank, "Run up and get Croft, will you? Right away."

"What for?"

"Get him."

He was still at his table when Frank came back with Dick. He stood up and said, "Dick, I'm sorry. I've bad news for you. Your father is dead." Dick looked straight at him. Erickson said, "It came through on the 'phone. Your dad was coming up in an army car. They were heading for Brigade. They were strafed from the air. Your dad was hit, in the head." Dick still looked at him in silence. "They're going to bury him this evening. They want you down there. I can't come with you. We're waiting for orders. Frank, you go along." He came out from behind the table. "I'm sorry about this, Dick. I'm truly sorry." He shook Dick's hand.

Frank and Dick went out. Frank began, "Oh, Dick, I'm so sorry —." Dick did not seem to have heard.

*

The battalion truck dropped them at the autopark where a car was waiting for them. The journey from the autopark was not a long one. A couple of miles down the road they were in a winding stretch between banks when the car slowed and turned in to a farmyard through a gap in the bank.

By the door of a barn stood a deserted truck. Next to it, also empty, was a staff car. In a field to the right of the farmyard a party of soldiers gathered round a pile of fresh clods, four of the men with spades, six more lounging upon rifles, an officer with them. That must be the grave.

Kulich came out of the barn. He said, "Good, here you are. Let's get on with it —. Croft, I'm real sorry about this. Your father was a real friend. He was one of us, and that's the way we're going to see him off." He shook Dick's hand, turned, and called, "OK"

Four men came out of the barn with a coffin on their shoulders. It was wrapped in a Stars and Stripes flag. George Gamble walked alongside. He looked upset. Behind came a soldier carrying a bugle, another with a camera and a young lieutenant in a raincoat: Spanish by his cap badge and by the way he wore the coat across his shoulders like a cloak.

The party stopped at the graveside. The photographer busied himself. The pallbearers lowered the coffin on to cords held by the gravediggers.

Gamble pulled away the flag. The coffin was a plain box of planks, the nail heads gleaming. Kulich stepped forward. He straightened his cap and looked around him. "We are here to honour a fine man, an American, a soldier of the Republic." He aimed his voice beyond his listeners. "From the first days of our fight he has been with us, never flinching, always faithful. He was often to be seen in the front line of battle, whatever the danger. Now a fascist bullet has struck him down. Let us send him on his way with this simple message. Goodbye, old comrade. When the flowers of peace blossom again in a free and democratic Spain, you will be among the heroes remembered. We pledge ourselves to follow your example. Goodbye, Henry. Goodbye, soldier." He cleared his throat and called, in a lower pitch, "Right, men."

The gravediggers lowered the coffin out of sight. The burial party officer gave orders. A volley was fired over the grave. The bugler played Taps.

Throughout the proceedings the photographer had been busy. Frank had, all this time, been only half attentive to the burial. Something was familiar about the Spanish officer. It was the raincoat that teased Frank's mind. He found himself trying to define the colour, which he had seen before, cream — dirtied, was it, or faintly yellow? — and to unearth a memory of those big lapels, that belt and the way the coat did not fall sharp and straight as he might have expected but looked full and soft, oddly seeming to come out slightly from the waist down. The grave was being filled in. Kulich came to them, with the Spanish officer. He said to Dick, "This is Antón. He was your dad's conducting officer."

Antón spoke good English. He shook hands with Dick. "It was bad luck. The 'plane missed the car. One bullet, that was all. It is always the best ones who have the bad luck."

Kulich said, "Henry didn't look good. You wouldn't have wanted to see him. I know where to get some fine black rocks. We'll raise a cairn. I'll send you a photo."

Throughout this Dick said nothing. Gamble came. The flag was folded under his arm. He shook hands with Dick. His lips moved for a moment but nothing was audible. He nodded to Frank and went to the barn. Kulich and the Spanish officer followed. The grave was filled in. The burial party went to the truck. The staff car and the truck left.

The Brigade driver took Dick and Frank back to the battalion. Frank tried again. "Dick — words don't mean much —."

This was when the car had set them down. Not looking at him Dick said tiredly, "Yes. All right," and walked away towards the company lines.

Erickson told Frank that a hill had been taken by the fascists. It was called Hill 485. Sixteen hundred feet, that meant. Two companies had already gone to the other battalions. The remaining companies went out on trucks, in the dark.

It was raining when Frank went to bed. The wind came up. The fall of the rain on gravel and the blustering of the wind were loud, a steady noise in the foreground that muffled the continuing noises of battle. Frank woke early with head twinges. He was depressed after the night's dreams. As usual they were unremembered, all except the last. In this he was in a classroom, the Arts Sixth classroom of his old school. He could not recall who the other boys were, or who sat in the master's chair, but he remembered sharply and painfully who had been sitting at a small desk under the windows: his mother. She was silent and she did not move. That was all he could retain of the dream. Of the earlier dream fragments nothing came back; but he was convinced that she had been in each of them, a silent presence.

Chapter 26

It was possible to follow the spreading of the enemy offensive by the spreading of the noise and its increasing violence. Detonations sounded nearer and made impact on the body as well as on the eardrums. Explosions winked like heliographs on mountainsides. Evanescent grey puffs of smoke appeared over treelines and sometimes the smoke climbed in a black pillar to the clouds. It was embracing, this unseen battle into which the companies had disappeared.

Nor did the battle spare the battalion. An air raid scattered the headquarters men while they were lining up for breakfast. After that the 'planes came back almost hourly; and one could look out from the hill to watch 'planes attacking all round. They were the masters, they dotted the entire sky, their noise incessant. Against it sounded at unpredictable intervals the big guns around Gandesa before the crash of their shells shook the air and the ground in the battalion area.

As Frank went about his duties, he had a curious, recurring experience. An image from the last of his dreams appeared sometimes, in front of whatever scene he saw, a picture of his mother, transparent but clear. He thought it must be in his mind but, for moments at a time, at intervals, he could swear that he saw it physically. He had other things to think of and each time he dismissed it. It continued to bother him.

He was at headquarters typing an ammunition indent for the secretary. Something pushed him forward with great force. His cheek hit the typewriter which was falling away from him as the folding table collapsed under him and the oil lamp went out. He lay face downward under thumps on his back that became a weight upon him. Someone was shouting. The typewriter lay on its side in front of his face. More voices now. A match scratched. He found that he could move and that the weight was not imprisoning. The oil lamp was burning again. He stood up, tottering, and shed lumps of earth. Ted, the runner, had blood on his face and was talking in an edgy, excited way. Frank had no idea what Ted was talking about. Two soldiers came past, carrying the telephone operator. Ted helped Frank to go out of the dugout. The fresh air was something to drink in.

He staggered across the clearing and turned to see what the headquarters men were pointing at and talking about. He saw a crater on the slope above the dugout. He went to the edge of the clearing and sat down heavily on the wet bank. His face hurt. He touched it and saw a little bright blood on his fingertips. His right cheek was the place that hurt. His fingertips found contusions. The ache in the jawbone must be a bruise.

Erickson was in the clearing, ordering men away. They dispersed. Erickson came to Frank and enquired. His voice came from a distance through thickness. Frank stood up. He felt his heart running as fast as an electric bell. He turned quickly away from Erickson and vomited. Erickson told him to go and rest.

Frank went to his cave. He went in past the blanket hanging in the entrance, took an electric torch from a shelf at the side, switched on to see his way to the lantern that hung from a spike hammered into the wall, lit the lantern with fingers that shook and dropped matches, and subsided on to the pile of dried alfalfa heaped under a blanket against the wall. The cave was one of those that peasants had lived in. The back part was divided off by a crudely-mortared wall of hewn rocks with an open doorway in the centre. Frank had put up spikes to hang things on, and two shelves. Two empty crates made a table and seat. For a soldier, it was a bijou residence.

He stretched himself out on the alfalfa bed. His cheek smarted. He slept on and off. His head twinged on and off. His jaw ached on and off. He saw his mother on and off. He looked at his wristwatch. Nearly an hour past noon. He stood up and was giddy. He put out the lamp and went out of the cave. Poor daylight was enough to dazzle him. He stood on the narrow path and vomited into the bushes below. The 'planes were still in the sky. The loud noises of battle all round made him giddy again. He started along the track towards headquarters.

*

He turned a corner in the path down and saw Erickson standing in front of headquarters talking to a man in a raincoat. The wearer of the raincoat turned as Frank approached and said, "Hallo, there."

Frank said, "Hallo."

Erickson said, "You've met Antón."

Frank said to Antón, "You were with Henry when it happened."

"Correct. That was a sad affair — true?"

"Antón'll be with us for a few days," Erickson said. "Look after him, will you. Show him round. He'll tell you what he wants."

"I am here as an observer from the Staff," Antón said. "You know, I was due to come down here when they told me that Croft was to come. The plan was for me to accompany him around the Brigade, then send him back and go on with my own duties here." His raincoat hung open, showing a smart tunic, polished belt and loaded holster. Frank's attention was on the raincoat. "Poor fellow. But here I am."

There was an American touch to Antón's speech. It was the flared fall of the raincoat that fascinated Frank. Then he remembered something about it.

Erickson was saying, "He can kip in with you," and to Antón, "Frank has organized himself a home from home up there. He's nicked a load of mule feed for beds. You'll sleep well on it."

Antón said, "I'm sure I will. I'm grateful."

Frank said, "*De nada*. Come up. I'll show you."

They went up to the cave. Frank carried Antón's valise. On the way Frank said, "Have you been to America?"

"Two years. I was in Minnesota. Agricultural college."

"I wondered if you'd been to Moscow."

"Oh?" Antón stopped on the path, turned and smiled at Frank. "What made you think that? Have you been to Moscow?"

"No," Frank said. "It's a long story. Silly, really."

They went on. Frank said, "I joined the YCL when I was fifteen. I went to a meeting and someone heard me speak and invited me home. Pat Allbright was there. He's one of our Party leaders. He's a really great man. I was quite hostile then, you know, all for socialism and all that but I believed lots of anti-communist rubbish as well. Pat took an interest in me, and I went to see him a number of times, and he recruited me. He's always been a friend since then. Well, more than a friend. He's been like a Dutch uncle to me, he really has."

"Maybe. But when are we going to get to Moscow?"

"Well, Pat wears a raincoat. I realised today that it was the same as yours. But, you see, Pat was in the Soviet Union for a few years. He went to the Lenin School, and than he was sent to the military academy in Leningrad. That's the point about the raincoat. It's very warm, isn't it? I think there's kapok in the lining. He told me that only the military wore it over there."

Antón laughed. "And anyone else who can pull a string or two. You're quite a sleuth, aren't you? I was there, but you know why?" He smiled as if inviting complicity. "To study agronomy. That's all."

"Oh, sure, sure." Frank tried to invest these words with the tone of one sharing the joke.

They went into the cave. Frank said, "The alfalfa was stored here. It's on boards. The damp doesn't come up. There's plenty for both of us. I'll get some more planks and fix up a bed for you over there." He indicated the opposite wall. "You can hang things up there."

"I can see. Great." Antón said. "I'll take the room."

"How long are you here for?"

"That remains to be seen. My orders will come through on the telephone to Brigade."

"What do you want to see here? If you want to see the battalion in action I'll get you up to the companies."

"Not just yet. I'll stick around and learn about your experience, organizational stuff. Maybe I can read the war diary."

"I'll get you that."

"You know," Antón said. "You ought to go to Moscow one day. It's an interesting place."

Frank said "Oh, I want to. I want that more than anything else. It 'd be just about the greatest experience on Earth. I hope they'll send me there one day."

*

Antón went back on some errand to Brigade. Frank installed a set of bed-boards in the cave for him, with planks resting on crosspieces. He piled alfalfa on the planks and left two folded blankets on top. Giddiness returned. The effects of the morning's concussion had recurred in waves throughout the afternoon. He lay down again.

Voices roused him. They went past, in snatches, low, gruff, against the tramp of feet on the gravel. He went to pull back the curtain. Dusk was turning to night. Riflemen were coming up the path, walking with long, effortful steps, some wearing their waterproof ponchos, others in stained, tattered shirts and trousers. He did not talk to any of them and none of them looked his way.

When they had stopped coming he went down to the clearing. Erickson said, "The truck's gone up for the next lot. Ernie's a good lad, he's running right up into the shit to bring them out. The poor buggers are so tired they can hardly put a foot forward."

Frank waited. Each time the truck came back he watched the men getting down. Another line of scarecrows started to straggle up the hill. At last he saw a few faces from his old company: O'Hagan, who went across to Erickson and a group of officers, then, two glum, fed-up tramps, a young one and an old one, plodding in silence side by side like Weary Willie and Tired Tim in the pink comic paper, Yorky and Dick. Frank stepped forward and held out something. Dick turned a streaked, drained face towards him, twitched his mouth, took the chocolate bar and went on. Frank saw him break the bar in two and give a piece to Yorky.

Each time a truckload came in, more men were directed to a group outside HQ, walking wounded who had stayed with the battalion. Bandaged, showing rusty bloodstains, some were standing, some sat slumped against the wall, a few stretched out and slept on the sodden ground, arms round their heads. Comrades tended the wounded. From time to time a shell came over and burst in some comfortingly distant place. No-one took notice of these.

Erickson conferred with officers. A sorting-out began among the wounded. Erickson said to Frank, "Some of these lads'll have to go. Get 'em down to Brigade. I'll arrange for them to be taken on from there. Get back quickly. We need the truck."

Frank rode in the cabin of the truck. Fourteen men were in the back. On the way to Brigade he watched shells explode off the road. The truck drove straight into the autopark. An ambulance was waiting. Frank and the driver climbed down. Soldiers joined them to help the wounded to the other truck. A shell exploded with the particular crash of close proximity. Gamble appeared, carrying a sack. He said, "Erickson told us these fellows haven't had anything. I guess a shot of this won't do them any harm." This was a bottle of Spanish cognac which he handed up with some loaves, hunks of cheese and tins of sardines. "I'm afraid it's all we can do just now, boys. They dropped an ashcan right behind the cookhouse."

Another ashcan dropped nearer than that. A cabbage-head of black smoke appeared behind the workshop, then flames and smoke while men shouted. The ambulance went off. Frank said, "I have to get back."

"I'll come along. I've a bone to pick with your damn quartermaster."

Frank turned to get into the cabin. Gamble, scrambling up into the back, called, "Up here. Come on."

The sat side by side with their backs against the back of the cabin. Alongside the road shellbursts leapt up like greetings. Gamble said, "That was a bad business yesterday. I'm so grieved about Henry, I can't tell you."

"It was rotten luck."

"Yes, like that Spanish fellow said, fellow who looked like Tyrone Power."

"Antón? He's with us now." From this moment Frank's mind had to cope with the shock of what Gamble had just said as well as to what Gamble went on to say.

Gamble said, "You sure need some beauty treatment." Frank's cheek was discoloured and patched with dried blood. A dark bruise ran along his jaw. He still had a plaster on his head. Gamble pointed to the noise of battle. "You weren't up there?"

"I got this at HQ."

Gamble sat with his own thoughts, then said, "I never liked that Kulich."

"He wears a fancy uniform."

"I don't like the way he talks to people. It's nasty, kind of. He's always the boss."

"He was all right yesterday."

"The last time he met Henry he bawled him out. It was on the Pimple. Kulich bawled him out in front of all the officers. For no reason at all." He paused, following a train of thought. "He's a funny guy altogether, that Kulich. He comes and goes when he likes. He can take a car whenever he likes." Another hesitation; as if each new statement required a further decision. "Frank, I saw Henry. I mean, I saw Henry's body." Frank waited. Gamble said, "Well, wasn't it all done very quickly? Why didn't they let Dick see the body?"

"Maybe it was better he didn't."

"Maybe."

Frank looked sidelong at Gamble. "What do you mean?"

"The first l knew of it was when Kulich turned up on his own. He went to the workshop first and told them to knock up a coffin. He took it back on the truck. What he wanted from me was the flag. I couldn't find it. He told me to bring it down the road. I asked him what it was for and he said Henry was dead. Hell, I got there, and Kulich was outside with the burial party. He went into the barn. Massie, that's the lieutenant from the Lincolns, he talked to me for a minute, and then I went into the barn just as they were lifting Henry's body into the coffin, Kulich, that is, and this Antón fellow. l was behind them, kind of. Kulich called out to me to wait right there. I waited at the door and he took the flag from me and told me to go and see the grave was OK. I mean, Massie was there already."

"Well?"

"I saw the body when they lifted it. The bullet had taken the top off Henry's head."

"It would, wouldn't it?"

"The entry wound was in the back of the neck."

"How could that be?"

"That's it. It's the angle. A bullet from a 'plane travelling upwards? How could it be?" With his hand he illustrated a 'plane's shallow dive.

They were both silent for some seconds. Frank said, "Wasn't there an air attack?"

"I don't know," Gamble wailed. "Sure there were air attacks. You don't have to wait long to hear one of *them*. I heard the 'planes coming down, and maybe it did happen when Kulich said, about an hour before I saw him. Maybe this is all crazy. Maybe I've got no right to be saying this. But it's all in here." He put a hand to his head. "I can't get rid of it."

"Did you see the body again?"

"No. When Kulich sent me to the grave I wasn't needed there. That was obvious. I went back in but they'd nailed the lid on the coffin."

"Perhaps you imagined it. Perhaps he fell back and his neck got damaged."

"It was an entry wound. I know an entry wound. I *saw* it." He was near to tears. "It was a big one, too. Not a clean puncture like an m.g. round. You ever seen a pistol slug hit at close range?"

After a moment, Frank answered. "You don't know what you're saying."

"I do. I do. Maybe I shouldn't have said it. *I* don't know."

"I can't believe it," Frank said. "You've got something wrong somewhere."

"Maybe l have."

"Have you talked about this to anyone else?"

"Only you. Of course, I wouldn't want it to get to Dick, not for worlds."

"You'd better not talk about it again. I think it is crazy. Forget it. That's what you've got to do."

"I wish l could. Oh, sure, it's crazy. You're right, it's just crazy talk. I must be going cuckoo."

"You're overwrought. We've all been having a bad time. Get some sleep. You'll forget it."

"Sure. Maybe you ought to forget it too."

"Don't worry about me." It was raining. They had arrived. They climbed down. Gamble said, "I'd better find that storeman of yours. I'm tired of his tricks. I only have to turn my head and there's another sack of stuff gone." He limped off towards the stores.

The rain came down heavily and the wind rose. Frank went straight to his cave. The blanket dropped on the noise of wind and rain and the more distant noises of battle. Frank dried rain off himself and sat down.

Tyrone Power.

The raincoat had distracted him. He had though himself so clever to have spotted it. It was not the raincoat that had prodded at his memory. It was Antón himself. Tyrone Power. Antón was the Spanish officer Frank had seen in Barcelona, at the JSU conference, talking with Hans.

Quickly now the names came together. Antón. Hans, Kulich, Marta (Peter saying to Hans, "Remember me to Marta.") All those names and then Henry. Henry. And then Frank remembered his own letter to Hans, denouncing Henry.

Chapter 27

The weather lightened and the grey days were shaken by the roar of enemy 'planes, which filled the sky like a starling swarm. At Brigade, Frank picked up a rumour that the Listers had been blasted off their mountain positions. There was other news, a German ultimatum rejected by Prague. Westminster Abbey in London open day and night, full of people praying for peace. The battalion was roused up once more in the night: shouts, bustle, hurry, but no surprise. Some buggers had fucked off or been overrun somewhere and the fire brigade was needed. The trucks sped off into darkness and disappeared into that hammering commotion.

Frank had no work to do next day. Antón was no trouble. He had gone off, as he did often, to Brigade. Frank set off through the woods to climb a nearby hill from which he might catch some glimpse of the battle.

He was in a vague, wretched mood. The news about the Listers unsettled him. Once out of battle he had started to think about the war and he felt cold and hopeless. There was a headline in the latest issue of *Volunteer For Liberty*, "On the Final Road To Victory". He raged at it. It put him into such a tumult of bitterness, scorn, derision and rejection that he felt ill in his bowels. Unwonted, astonishing questions appeared in his mind. How could his comrades deceive themselves so? And others, the faithful men? Impermissible questions: he hoped that the tramp and the climb and the cold air and the calm of being alone would clear his head of such wild things.

His head hurt, too, although he had taken off the dressing. He had lain awake for a long time last night, tormented by a jumble of thoughts that refused to become coherent or comprehensible. For an hour or two towards dawn he had drifted into a fitful and superficial sleep, in which faces appeared that, without waking him, jolted his heart with shocks like electricity.

One face was Henry's. Oh, that business! Each time he reckoned up his discoveries, they let loose terrible thoughts in him, wrong thoughts. Thoughts? That was hardly the word to use for the fragments of perception that tumbled about inside his head like the multiform patches of colour in a kaleidoscope. He would go to pieces, he would go to the bad, if he let this business take hold of him. He had to put it away from him. He must think only of the struggle.

But there was another face that gazed at him out of the darkness and struck a strange grief into him. His mother. That nuisance, who had lately kept intruding into his dreams. Even in daytime her face sometimes appeared in front of him, a transparency, wan, gentle, ever young, reproachful. At home he had always rebelled against what he had called (knowing himself to be unjust) this silent nagging. He had told her briefly that he wasn't going to Cambridge. She had taken it in, smiled wonderingly and said, "You must do what you want." It must have been heartbreaking for her. His education had been her passionate concern. When he was small his mother had stood with him at the gates of the grammar school and said, "That's where you're going, my love." He had disappeared into the revolutionary world and told her almost nothing about it. He had never had the courage to explain himself to her. Of course, she saw the pamphlets and newspapers that he brought home, she saw his articles (and read them all, and cut them out), she saw him announced to speak at meetings; but she did not ask questions. She said once, "You're a good boy. I'm sure you know what's right." She must have been terrified.

He reached a summit. He looked out over a sea of mountains. The noises were a tale that he could read: the sustained, swelling overlay of detonations diminishing into a faint clamour of small-arms fire then resuming, the aircraft thunder loud for a while from one quarter, then another; but he could not see the planes now because of the clouds.

It would have been better if he had made a clean break with her. But he had never brought himself to leave her home finally. He had travelled a lot, and for weeks, sometimes months at a time he had occupied the spare divan in some comrade's flat, but he would turn up at home for a day and a night, or move in for a while, welcomed with that wan smile and no questions. Of course, it had all been because of not wanting to hurt her. It had never occurred to him then how often and terribly he had done so. This was what so upset him now.

He stayed on the hill until late afternoon. He was repelled by the idea of food but he felt hunger pangs. On the path down he was hardly aware of his surroundings. He remembered her in hospital. She had only known that they had taken a little lump away and she did not know that she was dying. At least, she had behaved to him as if she did not. Now he doubted both these things. The visits had been dull. He had not known what to talk about and had kept an eye on the ward clock all the time. All that he had told her (cowardly again) was that he was going away for a while on business. She had just smiled at him. He had only written one letter to her from Spain, an attempt to reassure, telling her that he was doing a safe civilian job. Then she had, amid all those flattering excitements, gone out of mind; until the morning when he had opened those two letters in Peter's office, one from the hospital and one, a bitter, accusing little letter it was, from the woman next door. It only now occurred to him to ask, who had buried his mother? What could have happened?

Oh, he had been amiss in the matter. One must care for people. The Party insisted on that. He should have talked to her about politics. She was an intelligent woman. She had taught him the letters of the alphabet before he even went to infant school, and read books with him, and on their walks together they had talked about all manner of things. He should have educated her. He should have brought the local comrades to see her and look after her. They would have offered themselves to the lonely woman as friends and enlisted her with his encouragement as a comrade. The simplest of souls could come to a heroic stature. Maxim Gorki's *Mother*. Every cook would learn to govern. She would have had friends, then, to be with her in her illness and to bury her. *Who had buried her?*

Unwelcome thoughts. Demoralising, unmanning thoughts. A little boy is separated from his mother in a crowded store. He is hollow with fear until he sees her again. Frank recalled that feeling, experiencing it now. For the first time he realised that she was not waiting for him at home. She was not there. She did not exist. Rain stung his face. Pestilential woman, loving, accusing! How to make her go away? And there was the other face, Henry's.

*

The companies came back in a darkness that was pitchy beneath unbroken clouds. Frank stood with Erickson and the commander, counting, waiting for the next truckload, looking for faces. Faces were missing. O'Hagan was not there, nor was Yorky.

Later, Frank went up the hill. Rain was dropping in thick, glistening rods, smashing and bouncing upon the ground, rushing loud in loud orchestration with gusts of wind and constant slam of artillery. He picked his way among sleepers who lay like mummified dead in tiny excavated caves and pits flimsily covered with canes and foliage. He found Dick, inert as if punches would not wake him, swathed in blankets and ponchos (whose?) with more ponchos tied into the branches of his shelter. Frank left him.

He had hardly finished drying himself when Antón came into the cave. He was wearing, now, using the sleeves, his raincoat, the garment sodden, its collar turned up. He took off his cap, shook it and put it on the big crate. "Bad. Filthy."

"The companies are in."

"I know." Antón unbelted his raincoat and sat down. He undid the flap of his holster and took out an automatic. "The road is a mudbath." He released the magazine. "I hear they took the ground back."

"I don't know."

"Another hill."

"Yes."

Antón glanced at the pistol, closed it again, tried the action and put it back in its holster. "Your friend has come back."

"Yes. I've been up there." Frank glanced up. "How do you know? I didn't see you down at HQ."

Having, soldier-like, seen to his arms first, Antón took his towel from a hook and wiped his face. He did not take off the soaked raincoat although water from it was spreading into the blanket beneath him. Frank said, "Your bed's getting soaked."

Antón stood up. "I have to go."

"What? To Brigade? It's pissing down."

"I am leaving you. I have been called back to Barcelona." He went to open his valise. He had put out a book and a framed photograph of a girl. He reached for these.

Frank watched him putting them away. "You mean, now?"

"Yes, now. I must report there first thing in the morning."

Frank took this in while Antón continued to pack his few things. Antón said, "Frank, your friend is to come with me."

"Dick —? What for?"

"Orders." Antón closed the valise. "There is to be a memorial service in Barcelona, for Henry Croft, at a Protestant church. Croft was a greatly respected man. It will be a big occasion. There will be delegations from the Army, all the parties, all the mass organizations. The Press corps and the consuls will be invited. Negrin may come. Of course they want the son to be there." He glanced at his wristwatch. "I shall have to start at once. Go up and bring the boy."

"I can't wake Dick. He's dead to the world."

"You will have to."

"Let him have his sleep. Brigade can send him up tomorrow."

"There may not be time. I don't know when this service is taking place. I was ordered to bring him tonight. Go for him now."

"How long will he be away?"

"I don't know about that." Antón lingered for a moment, studying Frank. "Perhaps you shouldn't expect him back." He met Frank's stare. "He is a young boy. He has done more than enough here. Perhaps they think he is better out of it." Frank's gaze did not leave his face. He said, "All right, I'll tell you something. There will be an announcement any day now. The Brigades are to be withdrawn."

Frank sighed, but his intent gaze did not flinch. Antón said, "Keep your mouth shut till it's official. I'm trusting you. But you see, there would be no point in sending the boy back. Would there?"

Another lag of silence, then Frank said, "Let me come with you."

"That's not possible. I've no orders about you. You are in the front line. Don't carry friendship too far."

"The battalion will give me a few days. Let me ask."

"You are being ridiculous. You are a Party member. Behave like one."

"Where will he stay in Barcelona? After the service. I could meet him there."

"How do I know? You are not coming. You will not follow. You will stay at your post. You will tell the men that he has gone back to England. That is an order."

"From whom?"

Antón took a small wallet from his pocket, opened it and showed it to Frank. On one side, his photograph. On the other, a printed legend under the heading *Servicio de Investigación Militar*. "Go. Bring him down to headquarters. I shall be waiting by the car." Frank stood in a sort of torpor. Antón said, "You will have time to say goodbye to him there."

Frank put his bare feet back into his soaked espadrilles. He buckled on his belt, slipped a poncho over his head and went out in silence.

He stepped into a dark so dense that he could only see the edge of the path by the blackness beyond the phosphorescent torrent. He could hardly hear the guns for the blustering and wailing of the wind, the loud shaking of trees and the water noises. He made his way uphill, feeling the bank on his left for guidance.

When he had rounded the bend in the path he stopped. He turned and placed himself so that he could look back toward his cave, and waited. Soon he saw movement down there. Antón emerged, a shape

211

darker than the darkness, and went away along the ridge. Frank hurried after him.

Antón could have heard nothing in the rain until Frank had almost caught up with him and he had hardly begun to turn his head when Frank put his pistol to the back of Antón's neck and fired.

Antón fell forward. He lay with his head toward the edge of the path. No second shot was needed. Frank stopped, used both hands to turn the body over, heaved again and the body went over the side. It crashed a little way down and stopped. Frank lowered himself at the edge of the path, felt down with one foot, then let himself down, using hands and feet, until he was next to the body. It was held by a bush. Frank pulled at the feet until he had freed it. He worked it down the slope and dragged it into the bushes. When it was deep in the undergrowth he climbed the slope and looked back, to make sure that the pale raincoat could not be seen. The bushes were as dense as wool. Frank was sure that even in daylight they would conceal. He climbed to the path again. He scraped at the gravel with a foot where Antón's head had lain. He stood for a while letting the downpour strip mud off him. He went back to his cave and inside, stripped, dried himself and rolled up in his blanket. For some time there was chaos in his mind; then he slept without dreaming.

Chapter 28

When Frank went out early next morning he was struck at once by the quietness. There was no sound of guns. The rain had stopped. The sky was lighter, whitish clouds jostling like an ice pack, with puffs of smoky black blowing beneath. From the path, he could see no sign of Antón's body. The mass of bushes on the bank beneath the path appeared solid and undisturbed.

He walked down to headquarters. Antón's car was parked under the trees behind the cookhouse. With luck, no-one would give a thought to Antón, at least for a while. Frank only thought of the immediate future. Brigade would assume that Antón was here. Here, they would assume that he was at Brigade. His prowling to and fro had been taken for granted. But, something might go wrong. Suppose a telephone call from some mysterious rear establishment to Brigade set people hunting for Antón? Suppose someone, Hans, it might be, was waiting for him at that house on the Ebro? Suppose —? Frank did not much care. He felt emptied, peaceful and indefinably content. He did not know if he had acted upon a false suspicion, and about this, too, he did not care. If not to save Dick, then to avenge Henry. What if he had killed for nothing? That was a small matter down here, where he had seen good men die by foolish mischances. Nor was he much concerned about himself. At times in the fighting he had been in intense terror of death but for the most part he was past caring.

Soon after, he was talking with Erickson outside headquarters. The battalion commissar was back and Erickson was now in command of the company. Gamble's truck stopped on the other side of the clearing. Gamble got down from the cabin and saw them. He waved and turned away to confer with the battalion quartermaster. Two men came from the cookhouse and started to unload sacks from the truck. Gamble came across to Frank and Erickson.

Frank said, "It's quiet. It's been quiet since I woke up. Do you reckon we've stopped 'em?"

Erickson said, "Not them."

"Valledor says they're regrouping," Gamble said. "Here, look at this."

He had taken a *Frente Rojo* from his pocket. He gave it to Frank, who unfolded it. It was the day's issue. He looked at a block of black type in the centre of the front page then read, his lips shaping words, nodding slightly as he read. It was a statement by Negrin.

The Spanish Government wishes to contribute not only in words but in deeds to the pacification desired by all, and resolves to dispel all doubts as to the completely national character of the cause for which the armies of the Republic are fighting. To this end the Government has decided upon the immediate and complete withdrawal of all non-Spanish combatants now participating in the struggle in Spain in the Government's ranks.

Frank passed the newspaper to Erickson, who looked at it for a long time. He said at last, "I read it three times to make sure. I've been out for two years."

"That's that," Frank said.

Gamble said, "They're already making movement plans back at Brigade, to pull us all back across the Ebro. Gee, won't it feel strange, to go back to the other side, after all this?" Neither of the others answered. "I guess the commissars are going crazy back there. They've been trying like all hell to stop the guys talking about this, and here it is." He touched the newspaper. "They're still trying to stop the news getting out. They've confiscated the whole bundle of newspapers. A fat lot of good it did them. The news went up with the mules, and the Lincolns are going wild."

"Our lads will know by now," Erickson said. "You'll see, they always know. It spreads on the wind."

Gamble went back to his truck. Frank and Erickson went to headquarters. The news had already been received there on the telephone, and an instruction to reveal nothing until direct orders had come from Division aroused only laughter. And when Frank and Erickson walked up the hill toward the company lines, men came down to meet them, shouting questions.

A crowd gathered round Erickson, growing more dense and clamorous as men came down through the trees, more and more of them. Erickson held up his arms, trying to still the noise. He shouted, "Quiet —! Be quiet, lads, will you? All right, boys, all right, keep your hair on — quiet!" The noise subsided a little. "There is something in the paper but there's nothing official. Nothing official, do you hear? I know how you feel. I know. What d'you think I'm feeling myself? But let's keep calm until something official comes through. The moment it does I'll let you know. I promise you."

Frank looked around at the men's faces. All of them were drawn, hungry with anxiety and appeal. The yelping of questions continued. Erickson gave ground. He told them about Negrin's statement and began a long explanation of the matter, trying to divert them as he intoned the familiar cadences of political instruction. For a little while Frank saw and felt only a dammed-up impatience, which might burst out and overwhelm Erickson. Then the sedative began to work. The clamour subsided. Men listened, intently but no longer keyed up, occasionally interjecting in rough voices or starting their own low conversations in small groups. They were not the sort to go wild; not this lot. In the end they dispersed, clusters of them wandering back to their lines, talking, disputing.

Frank saw Dick turning away, on his own. He hurried across to him and said, "It is official. We're only waiting for the word to pull out." Dick stopped in his tracks but said nothing. Frank said, "It's all over."

"What's going to happen?"

"The Brigade will be moved back across the Ebro."

"When?"

"Any moment."

"And what then?"

"Then we get demobbed."

Dick turned away as if he had no more interest in Frank, who said, "Dick — what are you going to do when you get back?"

Dick spoke curtly. "Why do you ask?"

"Will you still go up to Oxford?"

"I told you. Next year I shall apply for a commission in the Rifle Brigade."

"Wherever you go, I suppose we shall be able to keep in touch."

Dick gave him an odd look, a detached scrutiny. "You'll be waving the red flag again."

"You could put it that way."

"Making speeches from soap boxes."

"And platforms."

Dick smiled a little. "You'd better watch out for me then. Soap box or platform, I shall knock you off it."

"You'll give me a hearing first. Won't you? For the sake of all this." He indicated their surroundings.

"Why should I, old son?" Dick said. "You'll be on the other side." He walked away.

*

Soon after that the guns began to fire again on the other side of the hills. Frank wondered if the enemy offensive had resumed. The men that he saw as he went about the camp took no notice of it. It was none of their business any more. It was one of those days when a military camp takes on an innocent, almost a pastoral air. Men sprawl in groups, smoking, chattering, and the sound of their talk is quiet, suggestive of memories savoured and expectations aired. Some, naked as Adam, wash themselves out of petrol cans. A reedy harmonica can be heard, laughter, the clatter of utensils. The smoke of camp fires smells good and even the song of birds catches the ear.

He rounded up a party of four men to cut up logs for the cookhouse. They went off into the woods with a little cart, in great good humour, teasing him and telling him that he would soon be dipping his wick in Hackney Wick. They sawed wood all the afternoon. Life had changed. The exercise and the fresh air were enjoyable. Beyond the hills the gun barrages were going mad but they took no notice.

It was evening when Frank led his party back to the camp. Coming down through the trees he stopped, and the cart stopped and the others stood still around it. Not one of them uttered a sound. Something terrible drenched through Frank. On the road below he saw a line of trucks and the companies gathering around them, armed.

Chapter 29

Under heavy shell fire they ran into a valley between the Pandols and another sierra to the north. The men did not know where they were going except that they were heading into what sounded like an utterly demented battle. Frank heard one furious group cursing an anarchist battalion which they said had taken a vote and gone off to sleep; but when they climbed down from the trucks and he joined the headquarters group, he heard Kulich explaining that the 13th Brigade had been almost wiped out. Some of its trenches had been hammered flat. He could tell them little else about the situation. It was chaos, he said, before he tramped off across the road to join the Lincolns.

Frank heard orders shouted, saw officers beckoning. The companies began to deploy. There was confusion. No-one seemed to know what was ahead. They were on uneven ground bordering a road with higher ground at their back. A bridge on the road crossed a *barranco* which ran out to their right, where the Lincolns were taking up positions on a hill. The Canadians were on their left.

The British commander sent a strong party out to dig in and secure this flank. Fire was already coming down from the higher ground on many sides of them. At dawn a terrible barrage came down on the battalion. As it continued, they discovered that the *barranco* was occupied by enemy troops. The barrage went on all the morning. The ground around them was churned up like a No Man's Land of the Great War. Enemy troops were firing on the battalion from the hill where the Lincolns had been. Enemy 'planes filled the sky between the hilltops. All the morning the sticks of bombs fell into the fire and smoke of the barrage. Frank tried to count the 'planes. He gave up. He had never seen so many at once. He went to and fro as a messenger between the commander and the companies. He was deaf and dazed, he was in a phantasmagoria, his comrades appeared and disappeared among explosions. He was buffeted, scorched and knocked down, blackfaced, his clothing burned to tatters, but he went among the shellbursts as if incorporeal.

Enemy infantry came on behind the barrages. They swarmed on the hill across the road, three or four battalions of them there must have been, where the remnant of the Lincolns had stood. Another big infantry attack came down the road towards a flanking British company, led by five tanks. The British, little more than thirty strong, put three tanks out of action before they were overrun.

The tanks and the enemy infantry came out of the *barranco* behind the main British positions and surged on into the midst of the machine-gun company. Frank found himself in the middle of a melée. It was all a dream now. Men shouted at his ears, screamed, came furiously upon him, went down. He trod and stumbled upon bodies. He must have done things to preserve himself in this scrimmage but he had no awareness of it. Spanish voices cried out in terror, he saw hands raised, men going past him to surrender. The Spanish company and the British fought on but many of the recent recruits were seeking safety among the enemy and others were fleeing across the fields.

He saw the commander among the machine-gunners, shouting and pointing to the high ground at the rear. Frank saw a dead man in front of him doubled up over a light machine-gun. Frank pulled the weapon free, dragged a bag of magazines from the body, hung the sling over his shoulder and bolted for the high ground, the bag of magazines thumping against his hip.

He ran uphill, gulping breaths that hurt his lungs. He came up on to a ridge. Guns were already firing from the ridge. He dropped into a firing position, flipped the bipod legs forward, brought the butt tight into his shoulder, banged on a magazine, pulled back the cocking handle, steadied himself, aimed at the brown scatter of enemy soldiers coming on beyond the hand-to-hand fight, and started to fire in careful bursts of five.

He was aware of men running behind him. Parties were coming up from the Americans, the Canadians, and from shattered Spanish units. Groups of British were breaking away from the fight below and coming up on to the hill. Frank could see Fletcher and Cooney directing them. Harris was at his side, to load for him. Harris's right arm was laid open to show bone and white sinews, but he crawled to and fro to bring ammunition and with his good hand crammed bullets into empty magazines until he fainted. Frank had no feeling of human existence left. He lay, an extension to his gun, firing.

The fire from the ridge was intense now. The enemy held the battalion's old positions but was unable to come on. A last British soldier ran up to the ridge, Fletcher, the commander.

*

So they lay, until dark. The enemy did not attack again. From the ridge their dead could be seen, thick, in places heaped, surrounding the dead of the battalion and mingled with them. Shells continued to come in, and until dark the battalion was still under small-arms fire from the surrounding heights.

Until it was dark, Frank lay at his gun, with Harris's body at his side, when he saw people from his old company he shouted for news of Dick; in vain. When he went to look for Dick he did not find him, or anyone who had news of him.

Parties were stealing out into the darkness to search for the wounded. Frank went with them. He crouched by bodies, turned them over, crawled on. Twice, when he found a wounded man, he brought him back to the ridge and went down again to resume his own search. No fire came from the enemy. Searchers crouched and flitted in the darkness. Wounded were carried away in ponchos and blankets, on stretchers and on men's shoulders.

Frank found Dick lying near the *barranco*. Dick lay on his back. His eyes were wide open and he stared at the dark, clouded sky. His breathing was a harsh, slow, rise and fall of effort. He did not utter any other sound. Frank sat on the ground next to him. Dick looked as if he was thinking of things far away. Frank took Dick's hand. It was cold and flaccid. Frank pressed Dick's hand, but Dick's head did not move and he gave no sign that he knew of anyone by him. Frank watched the recurring rise and collapse of Dick's chest. Lower down, Dick's body was not to be looked at. Frank went into a reverie.

Someone shook Frank's shoulder. Erickson was kneeling by him. Erickson mouthed, only the consonants audible, "He's gone."

Dick's hand did not feel any colder but his chest did not move. Frank pulled his hand free, got up and went away with Erickson.

There was a stir of quiet movement on the ridge. Troops were coming in to relieve the battalion, Spanish troops, Campesino's men. Frank found the headquarters group and heard that, with the reliefs, the order had come to withdraw across the Ebro.

Chapter 30

The battalion had lost more than half its strength in a day. Of the British, fifty-eight remained. The next day the whole division was withdrawn across the Ebro. The British went to Marsa, near to the valley in which they had trained for the offensive. On the journey back most of them were silent, still knocked out by the day of shock and slaughter. Of the Internationals who had crossed the Ebro in July, three out of four had fallen.

The war continued. The Munich Agreement patched up a nerve-racked interval of peace for the rest of Europe. The Spanish went on with their fratricide in undiminished fury and agony.

For the British now, it was all parades, fiestas and banquets. During the next ten weeks men came back from hospitals, from the rear services and from other units. Wherever the Internationals camped they were besieged by peasants bringing gifts and thanks. The 15th Brigade paraded for the last time, with crowds watching in an amphitheatre of hills. The British were given the position of honour, the right of the line. Smartly and ceremoniously the officers fell out, to be replaced by Spanish officers, then the men fell out, the ranks at once refilled by Spanish soldiers. There was a red sunset, a band, a final bugle cell, shouts of "*Viva!*", tears. The Division held a farewell parade and fiesta. Then all the Internationals marched through the streets of Barcelona, and no-one cared about air raids. They marched ankle deep in flowers, in uniform, behind bands, between dense crowds of people who cheered and wept. Men rushed into the ranks to clasp their hands, women to kiss them. Soldiers marched with children straddling their shoulders. Pasionaria cried, "We shall not forget you." This was eighty-nine days before the enemy entered the city.

On the night of December 7 three hundred and five British volunteers marched out of Victoria Station in London. The vast barn of the station was packed to its farthest walls. Welcoming crowds filled the long street down to Westminster Abbey and Parliament Square. The soldiers marched behind three bands down Whitehall and through the old City of London to a great reception. It was the homecoming of which Frank Brendan had dreamed, but he was not there.

At Marsa, as soon as it was dark, he slipped away. No deep thought led to this action. There was little chance now that Antón's body would be found, and none that the killing would be traced to Frank; but this did not concern him. Simply, it seemed the next thing to do.

Behind the scenes, as it were, of his thinking self, experience had been at work assembling a number of props to which he had paid no attention until now, hey presto, they appeared together in a transformation scene. This inward scene did not surprise or rouse him. He took it for granted. It was the present, and just now he only lived in the present. He had no impulse to question or even examine the beliefs which had brought him to this point. Indeed, if he had been interrogated he would doggedly have reaffirmed these beliefs, but he would have done so out of a dull, uncaring mind. He went off, then, without hesitation, like an animal that is impelled only by purpose.

He was bareheaded and unshaven when he went away, his sandals broken, his clothes torn, filthy and as bloodstained as a butcher's overall. He took his pack, his tin waterbottle, his pistol and a hard loaf. He followed roads and valleys north and after a week was starving. He tried to steal a bag of food from two Spanish soldiers who were asleep next to their truck and was seized by them. They, too, were deserters. They took him to a farm where he lived and worked with the peasants, clad now in civilian clothes that had belonged to one of the three sons of the peasant family; all three killed in the war. Two months after he had left the battalion he was taken over a river by smugglers and set down dry-footed in France. From Bourg-Madame he went to Perpignan. The consul acknowledged him to be a Distressed British Person and gave him his third-class fare to London against a written promise to repay.

Frank only went as far as Paris. He had not changed his opinions during his time on the farm. He had, indeed, not reasoned at all. He had continued to live in the present. He took no interest in the occasional evidences of a continuing war. Life beyond the farm came to him only as pictures in the mind, on which he dwelt, as a spectator, sometimes with his emotions moved but never impelled by them to draw conclusions or make plans. Thus, he remembered (for instance) King's Parade in Cambridge, and the street of his childhood, and Bertram Mills' Circus, and a beach on the Isle of Wight, and his mother, and (oddly, twice) the Ivory Castle in the newspaper advertisements for Gibbs' Dentifrice. It had fascinated him when he was small. He had wanted to go there. He still, then, thought of himself as a deserter, although without regret or shame. He had no family and no friends in England except his Party comrades, whom he did not want to face. He wanted only to put off encounters, re-assessments and decisions.

In Paris an English journalist whom he knew took him on as an assistant. He lived in a slum room near the Bastille. Paris was dull and nervous, already defeated. Frank watched the miserable train of events but did not permit himself to dwell on such things. He gave all his spare time to books and to a succession of intelligent, good-natured French girls. On the first day of the following September, when the armies were all mobilized, he went back to London, and three days later in Whitehall he joined up for his next war.